Praise for Hannah Alexander's Novels

"The plot is interesting and the resolution filled with action."
—*Romantic Times BOOKreviews* on *Fair Warning*

"Reminiscent of Alice Sebold's *The Lovely Bones*,
this intelligent mystery will keep readers engrossed."
—*Library Journal* on *Last Resort*

"Alexander's latest installment in the Hideaway series is filled
with action, intrigue and fascinating medical situations."
—*Romantic Times BOOKreviews* on *Last Resort*

"Filled with intrigue, mystery and well-rounded characters,
you won't want to leave Hideaway. Hannah Alexander knows
suspense! This page-turner will keep you up at night
unable to put it down."
—Kristin Billerbeck, bestselling author of
Cool, Calm & Adjusted on *Last Resort*

"Hannah Alexander's unique ability to combine suspense
with romance and faith will have you searching for this
author's entire backlist. Grab these titles while you can and
visit this wonderful town called Hideaway—you'll never want
to leave! Each book is top-notch suspense, with just a touch
of romance. *Last Resort* is a must-buy...guaranteed to keep you
on the edge of your seat until you turn the final page!"
—*Romance Reviews Today* on *Last Resort*

"Alexander's skill at meshing spiritual truths with fascinating
suspense is captivating. Well-drawn characters help the two
separate plots move rapidly toward an exciting conclusion."
—*Romantic Times BOOKreviews* on *Safe Haven*

HANNAH ALEXANDER

Grave Risk

A Hideaway Novel

Steeple
Hill®

Published by Steeple Hill Books™

STEEPLE HILL BOOKS

Steeple
Hill®

ISBN-13: 978-0-373-78575-9
ISBN-10:   0-373-78575-5

GRAVE RISK

www.SteepleHill.com

Printed in U.S.A.

Acknowledgments

Many thanks to Lorene Cook for her constant support in every way. She keeps us going when life seems to shoot us in every direction at once.

Thanks to Vera Overall for loving and encouraging her son to persevere.

Thanks to Joan Marlow Golan, our champion, and to her excellent staff, who keep us informed, keep us straight and keep us headed in the right direction.

Thanks to our Branson brainstormers, Barbara, Brenda, Lori, Deborah, Sharon, Judy, Marty, Stephanie, Carol, Cyndy, Jill, Sandy and Jeanie, and to our support staff, Lorene and Luvena.

Chapter One

Fingers marched across Jill Cooper's cheekbones like the legs of a stalking tarantula. She stiffened, eyes shut tight.

She wanted to retreat from the intrusion or jump up from this table and escape. What horrors lay behind the other doors? What had she allowed herself to be talked into? Moral support was one thing, but this—

"Too rough?"

Jill opened her eyes and looked into the upside-down face of twenty-two-year-old Sheena Marshall. "No."

Sheena had an uncommonly bright, perky grin that matched her bright, perky voice. All the employees of this spa seemed to be infected with terminal optimism, except for Sheena's mother, Mary Marshall, who had always been on the opposite end of that spectrum, even when Jill had graduated from high school with her twenty-seven years ago.

Today, Mary's daughter was actually perkier than usual.

"It's fine." Jill wanted to ask when the sheets had last been washed on this massage table, but the question could eventually reach the ears of the owner of this establishment.

Jill was here to provide the owner—her baby sister— moral support for this venture, not to irritate her. Noelle Trask ran a tight ship, and these sheets would be pristine. She would not take kindly to having her employees verbally abused, or even questioned by a client with a few...interesting...hang-ups. Especially if that client just happened to be her bossy older sister.

Who would have thought Noelle, the wild child of Hideaway High, would have matured so well?

In fact, Noelle would be a mother before long.

That meant Jill would be an aunt. She felt her tension ease as she smiled at the thought. *Aunt Jill.* What a wonderful—

A sharp jab on her chin startled her. "Ouch!"

"It's okay. Just relax," Sheena said. "You have a few blemishes here. We can take care of that right—"

"I didn't come here to have my pimples treated." Noelle had warned Jill that the young masseuse tended to try to fix anything that wasn't just right. The young woman obviously had delusions of grandeur and saw herself becoming the makeover queen. Jill refused to be her first experiment.

"I just want a nice, painless massage," Jill said. Actually, she hadn't even wanted that.

"Jill Cooper," came a firm, commanding voice from another cubicle in the large, cedar-lined spa, "you agreed to do this. So do it."

"I agreed to a massage, not to have my face poked and prodded like a—"

"Settle down and let the girl do her job."

"Yes, ma'am," Jill replied, then muttered under her breath, "Noelle needs to get these walls soundproofed."

"What's that?" Edith Potts called again.

"Nothing. Sorry. I'll be good. I'm having a *simply magnificent* time." Could Edith hear the sarcasm?

"That's my girl."

Nope. Edith had never understood the subtleties of irony. The lady simply said what she thought.

Sheena returned to her massaging, distracted from her makeover project. "Will wonders never cease. Edith Potts must be the only person in town you can't boss around."

Jill scowled up at her, and Sheena smiled back, wagging her blond eyebrows, which had been plucked to the point that she looked permanently surprised.

The twit was right, of course. Jill would do anything for Edith. Eighty-three-year-old Edith Potts, retired principal of Hideaway High, could claim friendship with the majority of Hideaway's residents as well as a few of the flocks of tourists who escaped to this tiny lakeside village every year.

To Jill, her elderly friend epitomized courage. Since Jill often felt as if she, herself, epitomized the exact opposite, she had always been drawn to Edith's independent, nurturing spirit. It was Edith who had found a school nurse position for Jill here in Hideaway when tragedy necessitated that Jill would have to return home and stay nearby for the family business.

Once again closing her eyes, Jill tried to give herself over to the relaxation Sheena had promised. "This honey and almond cream smells heavenly."

"It's our most popular. We mix it here ourselves."

"I'd like a jar of that, if it's for sale." Still, if she came away with scars on her face from an over-eager masseuse, Jill would hold Edith and Noelle personally responsible.

In spite of her intentions to remain vigilant, her muscles seemed to liquefy of their own volition. She could feel her body merging with the soft sheets on the massage table until she wasn't sure where the padding ended and her flesh began. Moreover, she didn't care.

Jill seldom relaxed. She had been accused of being one of the most uptight, untouchable single women in Hideaway and the surrounding area. Most of the townsfolk made such comments out of her earshot—or so they thought—but Edith never hesitated to speak her mind, and neither did Noelle.

As Jill thought about it, she had recently found herself blessed—if that could be the term for it—by associates at work who never minced words with her.

They understood the term for her condition. Thanks to recent popular television shows, who didn't know what the letters OCD stood for? Yet they wouldn't let her get away with the typical behavior of someone with obsessive-compulsive disorder.

Blessed…yes. That was it. She was truly blessed by people who loved her in spite—

"Your brows could use a good plucking." Sheena's soft voice interrupted Jill's reverie.

"What?" Jill opened her eyes to see the young woman hovering over her, wielding a pair of tweezers far too close. *Now* what tortures was she expected to endure for the sake of moral support?

"I want to shape your eyebrows. I can take ten years off your face with a few good jerks."

Jill's loose muscles suddenly tightened again. "Look, Sheena Marshall," she said, keeping her voice low in deference to Edith, "I didn't come here to be plucked or jerked or tweezed, I just came for a simple massage with this green stuff you smeared all over my face. Are you finished?"

"Not yet. There are just so many things you need to have done. With your great bone structure—"

"Shouldn't someone be tending to Edith?"

"She knows how to relax, unlike you."

"Where'd your mother go? I'd be perfectly willing to let her finish this massage so you can see to Edith." At least Mary would complete the job without trying to do a total makeover in the process.

"She was only scheduled to work this morning," Sheena said, "and she wasn't too happy about having to do that."

Sheena's mom, Mary Marshall, had reluctantly agreed to come to work at the spa on an as-needed basis until Noelle could determine for sure how many full-time staff members she would require.

Not only was Mary an accomplished massage therapist who had worked for years in surrounding resorts, she was also a cosmetologist, with a good head for business.

Sheena still lived at home, at the age of twenty-two, and seemed content to stay in Hideaway the rest of her life, living with her parents and working here at the spa. Jill felt for the girl, since she, too, had stayed home out of necessity for several years after graduating from high school.

Sheena needed to get out of this place for a while and learn a little more about the world. Mary and Jed were keeping too tight a leash on her.

Jill shifted on the massage table. "I think I heard Noelle come back from her errands a few minutes ago—can't she see to Edith while you're finishing here? I hate to think of Edith waiting over there all by herself."

"I'll be…fine," Edith called to her.

With a frown, Jill glanced at Sheena. Edith sounded less peaceful and relaxed than she had moments ago.

"We won't be much longer," Sheena assured Jill. "Noelle warned me not to take too long the first time."

First time? Like this was going to happen again? What did Noelle need with moral support, anyway? Though the business was new, it was doing well.

Was that laughter she heard in the next room?

Jill gave a sigh, forcing herself to relax again. Edith had a sense of humor that had brought healing light to some of the darkest moments in Jill's life. Let her laugh.

Yet even as Jill listened to that laughter, it didn't sound quite right….

Sheena's movements slowed, as if she, too, noticed a change.

That wasn't laughter. "Edith, you okay in there?" Jill asked. It sounded as if Edith was coughing.

For several long seconds there was no answer, then came a muffled thump.

Jill lunged up from the massage bed and scrambled out, stumbling against the tray table beside her. Bottles and jars crashed to the wooden floor. She swept past Sheena and raced into the hallway, then into the next cubicle, her loose gown billowing around her.

She thrust the door open to find Edith lying on the floor, gnarled hands grasping her throat, eyes bulging with terror. Her face was still half covered with the mask of herbs, and her white hair tufted over the mask in sticky strands. The half of her face that was bare was nearly purple.

"Call for help!" Jill dropped to her knees beside her friend and wiped the green mask of goo from her face with a towel. "Edith, it's okay. We're going to take care of you."

The lady's fear-stricken gaze caught and held Jill's, begging for help. Her mouth worked silently.

"Who do I call?" Sheena cried.

"Get Noelle," Jill said, grasping Edith's hand. "I think she came back in. If not, call her on her cell. The clinic's closed today." In a more populated place, they would call 911. Here in Hideaway, that wasn't a good option.

As Sheena rushed from the room, Edith's grasp tightened in Jill's. "S…c-cool," she rasped.

"You're cool? I'll get a blanket for—"

The hand tightened further. "N-no." She closed her eyes, and her grip weakened.

"No. Edith! Stay with me. Help is on the way."

Those eyes opened again. "S…cool…" Her voice barely

reached Jill, and her mouth worked as if with great effort. "Re...cords...jet..."

"Edith, just hold on. We'll take good care of you."

Edith shook her head, obviously agitated. "Jet...bomber."

Jet bomber? "I'm sorry, I don't understand what you're trying to say. Just hold on and concentrate—"

Edith's hand relaxed from Jill's grip. Her eyes closed. She stopped breathing.

"No. Edith! Don't give up now. Edith!"

Chapter Two

Dr. Rex Fairfield seldom felt ill at ease with colleagues, whether they were strangers, friends or even antagonists. He felt perfectly comfortable presiding over large meetings, which was good, considering the requirements of his present career choice.

Today was different, however, as he sat in the tastefully decorated conference room of the Hideaway Clinic, deep in conversation with two other doctors.

His tension didn't stem from the suspicious glint in Dr. Karah Lee Fletcher's gaze or from the quiet expectancy in Dr. Cheyenne Gideon's dark eyes.

"If we can bring the clinic up to code in, say, three weeks, the timing would be perfect for an announcement at Hideaway's September festival," he said. "You've already done a lot more than I'd have expected."

"So why all the secrecy?" Dr. Fletcher asked him.

He frowned at her. "Secrecy?"

The statuesque redhead, second in command of this clinic, leaned forward, spreading her hands. "Yeah, the secrecy. The whole town supports what we're doing here. They want the clinic to become a hospital. The community's growing, we need these improvements. There's no reason to keep it a secret."

"Maybe not everyone wants it," corrected Dr. Gideon, the clinic director, "but the detractors are few in number, and they aren't adamant, they just want to have something to complain about."

"I didn't ask for complete secrecy," Rex told them, "I only asked for discretion."

"You asked us to keep your name out of our discussions with everyone, including our own staff," Dr. Fletcher reminded him.

He nodded. Aha. That was the reason for the small flicker of wariness he had detected in the demeanor of this tall woman with the commanding presence. "Please understand I'm not calling your staff's integrity into question, but there is one particular person with whom I've had… um…previous experience." He hesitated, unwilling to share all to these virtual strangers. This was intensely personal.

"I assure you, Rex, that you can trust all of our staff members," the director said. "I have found them to have the utmost integrity."

"I wouldn't dream of calling any of your staff's integrity into question, Dr. Gideon."

The dark-haired, dark-eyed woman rolled her eyes. "Please, I asked you to call me Cheyenne. We keep everything very casual around here." The woman reached up and tucked a strand of her short, shaggy black hair behind her ear. She did, indeed, appear to have some Native American blood in her lineage.

"I'm sorry—Cheyenne."

"And I'm Karah Lee," insisted the tall redhead. "Now, are you going to tell us why all the mystery?"

Rex had become acquainted with Cheyenne, the clinic's founder and director, and he felt confident in the abilities and good conscience of both the clinic's doctors. But he had never been inclined to share personal confessions with those he did not know extremely well. In fact, he had learned that even with those he thought he knew well, he must be cautious. His faith in his own judgment wasn't what it used to be. Perhaps that was a good thing, perhaps not.

"May I ask who it is you're concerned about?" The expression in Cheyenne's dark brown eyes was direct.

He hesitated, feeling foolish. His request had been impulsive, which was uncharacteristic of him. He wasn't sure how he was going to get out of this situation without looking unprofessional, even silly, to these two serious, obviously dedicated physicians. Karah Lee Fletcher's frown deepened.

He cleared his throat. "I simply wished to speak with this particular person in private before any—"

There was a clatter beyond the closed conference room door. Someone had come running into the waiting room of the clinic.

"Hello? Is anyone here?" came an urgent, feminine voice—a voice familiar to Rex, even after all these years, and even with the sharp edge of urgency that carried it down the hallway.

Cheyenne frowned at Karah Lee, who rose quickly, opened the door and stuck her head out into the hallway. "Noelle? What are you doing here? It's Saturday."

"Oh, thank goodness! I didn't expect anyone to be here, or I'd have called. Jill and Sheena are doing CPR on Edith Potts at the spa. Not sure what happened. I came to get—"

"She's unresponsive?" Cheyenne shoved away from the table and came out of her chair, yanking the door open wide.

Through the doorway, Rex caught sight of a beautiful woman with thick brown hair and small, exquisitely feminine features. She would be in her midthirties now. The only thing that marred her beauty were those blue eyes filled with dark concern. She was very obviously pregnant. Jill's younger sister.

"She stopped breathing," Noelle said. "Jill is—"

"Karah Lee," Cheyenne said over her shoulder, "grab the crash cart. Make sure there's a cric kit on it. We may have to do a cricothyroidotomy."

"There is a cric kit," Noelle said. "I checked it myself yesterday."

"Let's get it to the spa," Cheyenne said. Without a backward glance, both doctors followed Noelle from the clinic, pushing a fully loaded crash cart in front of them.

Rex rushed out behind them. It had been three years since his last official stint in an emergency department, but he would be there if he was needed.

And besides, he, too, needed to know what was wrong with dear old Edith Potts.

In frustration and despair, Jill forced her own breath into Edith's lungs through the protective pocket mask Noelle kept in each massage room, while the young massage therapist pumped rhythmically on Edith's chest. The soothing background music was a stark contrast to the sound of hard breathing. This spacious room suddenly felt far too confining.

Sheena's face was red from exertion and anxiety. Though she obviously knew the procedure, it was just as obvious she had never handled an emergency like this before.

"She isn't responding, Jill. It isn't working!" The young woman's blond hair had darkened around her neck with perspiration. "What are we going to do?"

"Stop a second."

"No, it's okay. I'm not tired, I'm just—"

"Stop, Sheena! I need to check her."

The masseuse withdrew her trembling hands from their locked position over Edith's chest.

Jill knelt close to Edith's mouth and listened for air movement. None. She pressed her fingers against the carotid artery and checked for a pulse. Nothing. *Lord, please don't take Edith!*

"Come and do rescue breathing, and I'll take over the chest compressions," she told Sheena.

"No, I can do the compressions. I'm not tired."

"I'm not asking, I'm telling you, trade places with me."

"Where's Noelle with that kit? Shouldn't she—"

"Just do it!" Jill shouted.

The sound of multiple footsteps reached them from the marble-tiled front entryway.

"Noelle?" Jill called to them. "Is that you? Did you get the intubation—"

Cheyenne burst into the room with a crash cart, followed by Noelle and Karah Lee and a bearded man she didn't recognize—

For a millisecond, Jill glanced at him again. Not a stranger. She knew that face, in spite of the short, salt-and-pepper beard she'd never seen before, and the cropped dark hair, receding hairline and slight creases of maturity around the calm, gray eyes....

Jill *knew* that man. Very, very well. Or she had known him once.

But there was no time to react, no time to think. "Chey, she's gone unresponsive—"

"We've got it." Cheyenne ripped the intubation kit open and started giving orders.

Jill gave a quiet sigh as she scrambled out of the way of the doctors and waited for her first orders. If anyone could bring Edith back, these people could do it.

Rex endured the expected sense of déjà vu, unable, for a few seconds, to drag his gaze from Jill Cooper's face, which was, at this moment, smeared with some kind of green stuff. Several strands of her hair, dark and thick as he remembered it, had fallen from the confines of a floral turban, grazing the tops of her shoulders. Her body was wrapped in a matching green-and-lavender floral gown.

After a very brief double take at the sight of him, she returned her attention to the still figure of her beloved mentor lying on the floor.

He set to work moving a lounger and a magazine rack out of the way to give the rescue team freedom of movement as they worked.

He remembered Edith Potts, even after all this time, and as he worked he said a silent prayer for her. It had been Edith to whom Jill turned for wisdom and for motherly love.

It had been the strong, wise Edith on whom Jill had depended for advice when her younger sister skipped school or decided not to return home after an evening of partying.

The older woman had also been the one to prepare special meals for Rex when he visited Hideaway on those rare weekends of freedom from the hospital. When there wasn't room at the bed and breakfast, he had stayed at her house. That was before she and Bertie Meyer purchased the bed and breakfast.

"Get a rhythm," Cheyenne barked, crouching at Edith's head.

Karah Lee grabbed the paddles from the cart and placed them on Edith's chest. "Stop CPR." She then looked at the monitor. "I've got it. Is there a pulse?"

"None," Cheyenne said, also looking at the monitor while feeling for a pulse in the neck. "It's PEA. Not shockable."

Rex slumped. Pulseless electrical activity. Bad news.

"Continue CPR," Cheyenne said. "I'm going to set up for intubation. Noelle, bag her while I get ready."

The doctor worked with quick efficiency. Karah Lee stopped compressions long enough for Cheyenne to insert the breathing tube. Simultaneously, Jill established an IV in the patient's arm, and drew blood, following normal code protocol. The breathing tube was in place in little over half a minute.

Cheyenne had been an ER doc in Columbia, Missouri, and she had obviously not gotten rusty on her skills. Rex couldn't help being impressed by this precise teamwork.

Cheyenne secured the tube and allowed Noelle to resume bagging. "Breath sounds?"

Karah Lee pressed her stethoscope over the belly first, then moved the bell to the chest. "Good. The tube is in place."

"Resume compressions. Sheena, I need you to call an airlift for us."

Sheena looked up at her. "Who do I call? What do I say?"

"I'll give you the number. Get a pad and pen and write it down."

The young woman scrambled toward the doorway.

Cheyenne's voice was calm but firm as she shot orders to the others. Rex took over the job of recording the proceedings on a sheet of notebook paper he found on a table.

He knew he should be observing this scene with professional detachment in order to best evaluate the staff's strengths and weaknesses. They would need that evaluation later as they applied for hospital designation.

He couldn't detach. He felt the desperation in this room,

could hear it in the quickened breathing of each person. He wanted to reassure Jill that everything would be okay, but she might not welcome any kind of comment from him right now. Every moment they worked over Edith with no response, he was more convinced that she was gone for good. Though he knew Jill was a woman of faith, a word from him would be an intrusion. *Lord, please help us. Guide our hands, give us wisdom.*

Why had he asked Cheyenne to keep his identity a secret from the staff? He had seldom been more sorry about a decision. His intention had been to reconnect with Jill personally before they met in a cold, professional environment. He wanted to reassure her he wasn't still the ogre she'd once thought he was.

If they lost Edith, it would break her heart. She didn't need any additional stress on top of that.

Chapter Three

Fawn Morrison sat behind the counter in the lobby of the Lakeside Bed and Breakfast, entering numbers from a ledger sheet onto the computer program Blaze Farmer had set up. She loved this part of the job. It was mindless yet engaging enough to keep her from worrying about her plans for the upcoming wedding, her adjustments to college, her preparations for the pig races at the festival.

She was racing her very own pig this year. Why had she agreed to do that, with everything else going on? She was practically the sole planner for Karah Lee's wedding, and she wasn't getting a whole lot of help from Karah Lee.

Fawn loved her foster mother, but the woman had no fashion sense, no concept of the amount of time it would take to complete their plans. Furthermore, those plans kept changing.

The front door squeaked open and the old-fashioned bell rang above it. She glanced over her shoulder to see a tall man with broad shoulders and thick, gray-streaked auburn hair step into the lobby. He looked awkward, nervous.

He wasn't bad-looking, for someone in his forties, at least. Bertie or Edith might threaten to stick him out in the garden to scare away the crows because he was a little on the skinny side. He had a turkey wattle beneath his chin and dark circles under his eyes.

Okay, so he wasn't that good-looking. He just looked like maybe he had been, once upon a time.

"Be there in a minute," Bertie called from the dining room at the far side of the lobby.

Fawn started to get up to help the man.

"Why, Bertie Meyer," the man drawled, his voice deep as the growl of a big dog, "you're just the person I was hoping to run into. What a welcome sight you are."

Fawn sat back down.

Eighty-something-year-old Bertie stopped midstride in the broad entryway between the dining room and the lobby. She held an empty waffle plate, and her white apron was stained with strawberry syrup and bacon grease. Her white hair tufted down over her forehead, and her eyes looked like those of a cat caught in headlights.

"Austin?" Bertie's voice suddenly sounded her age, which didn't happen often.

"I bet you thought I was gone for good, huh?"

Bertie set her waffle plate on a nearby table and entered

the lobby, absently wiping her hands on her apron. "I heard you and your mom had moved to California."

Fawn frowned. Austin. Where had she heard that name before?

"Mom's living with Aunt Esther down in Eureka Springs now," the man said. "I went to California for a few weeks to visit my cousin, but the traffic's a mess out there. A fella can't even make a trip to the grocery store without risking his life."

"Seems to me a real estate agent could make some good money in LA," Bertie said.

There was a short pause. "Money doesn't mean as much as I used to think it did."

Fawn realized she was partially shielded by the greenery that Edith loved to keep on the counter. And she realized she was indulging in one of her worst habits—eavesdropping.

Her best friend Blaze and her foster mother Karah Lee had nagged her so much about it that she'd almost broken the habit. Until now. Right now she couldn't leave without drawing attention to herself.

Bertie's passion for hospitality drew more customers here than to any hotel or lodge in a twenty-five-mile radius, but the tone of her voice did not sound welcoming. It sounded wary.

The man walked across the lobby to her. "I'm not here to cause trouble for anyone, Bertie." His voice softened until Fawn could barely hear what he was saying.

Austin…wasn't his last name Barlow? Was he the guy who used to be mayor of Hideaway?

"I didn't think you were," Bertie said. "I'm just curious, is all."

"Got a cottage I could rent for a couple of weeks?"

Fawn nearly snorted out loud. This place had been booked solid since early April.

She listened to the murmur of quiet voices for a moment, too low for her to hear and yet just loud enough to frustrate her when she heard a word or two now and then.

Ashamed, but unable to stop herself, Fawn finally scooted her chair back so she could hear a little better.

"Have you heard from Ramsay lately?" Bertie asked.

"Just yesterday. You might not believe this, but he's living at a boys' ranch up in northern Missouri. How's that for payback after all the griping I did about Dane Gideon's ranch for so many years?"

There was a long silence. Fawn peeked over the counter and saw Bertie's expression. Fawn knew that look. Bertie had such a tender heart.

Ramsay. Fawn remembered Blaze telling her about him. They'd been friends, or so Blaze had thought. Then it turned out Ramsay was vandalizing the town and allowing his father—Austin—to place the blame on Blaze. Finally Ramsay had flipped out completely and tried to kill Cheyenne because she had done something that made his father mad.

And what was the kid doing at a boys' ranch? Shouldn't he be in a place that took psych cases?

"Bertie, I came to apologize," Austin said in a rush, as if he couldn't be sure he'd have the nerve to get all the words out. "I thought I'd start with you. I know I have a lot to answer for, and it's time. Way past time."

Fawn couldn't make out Bertie's response, but she knew that Austin Barlow was forgiven.

Rex Fairfield shoved the heels of his hands against the yielding flesh of Edith Potts's chest, taking his turn at the grueling task of CPR. He felt the sweat of desperation on his own forehead and heard the despair in Cheyenne's voice as she continued to call orders to them.

"Where's that airlift?" Jill asked. "It should be here by now. It's been—"

"Too long," Cheyenne said, her voice brittle from the force of tight control. Grief drew lines of tension around her mouth and eyes.

It had been twenty minutes. Rex knew this would be a tough one for all of them. He also knew they had done more than was normal for a code such as this.

"Sheena," Cheyenne said, "go ahead and—" She frowned, and Rex glanced at Sheena Marshall crouched in the far corner of the room, arms wrapped tightly around herself, eyes glassy as she stared at the floor in front of her.

"Noelle," Cheyenne said, "call the airlift and cancel—"

"No!" Jill's usually mellow voice broke, ragged with pain. "Please, Chey, just a little longer."

Rex continued to pump rhythmically.

"It's been taken out of our hands." Cheyenne spoke with tender sadness.

Jill shook her head, short jerks of denial as she reached once more for the crash cart. "Atropine is next, isn't it?"

"We've already maxed out the Atropine." Karah Lee

placed a hand on Jill's shoulder and squeezed, her voice husky with sorrow.

"There's some left, though. Can't we just try one more—"

"Honey, it's time," Karah Lee said.

"Epi again, then." Jill's movements had taken on the frantic tightness of extreme anxiety. "One more dose, Chey. Please, just one…"

"Jill." Cheyenne caught Jill by the hands. "She's gone. We knew it was a reach when we saw the rhythm in the first place. We've carried this much longer than was warranted already." She nodded to Karah Lee, who had taken over the recording from Rex. "Time of death, 2:30 p.m., September third."

"Oh, Edith, no!" Jill's cry filled the room.

Chapter Four

Fawn watched Bertie return to her work in the dining room, and then saw Austin Barlow's broad shoulders slump as he reached for the handle of the front door. She suddenly felt sorry for him, though she couldn't understand why.

The guy was a bigot. He'd accused Blaze of vandalism simply because Blaze was black in a cream white town. The former mayor had complained constantly about Dane Gideon and the boys' ranch, and according to Blaze, he had even tried to cause trouble for Bertie Meyer.

Bertie didn't hold grudges, and she'd been kind to Austin after the initial awkwardness. Still, she couldn't pull a room for rent out of thin air. There was nothing to be had in town.

Fawn remembered a few more things Blaze had said about Austin Barlow. He was a real estate agent, and one time he'd rescued a starving horse from a pasture he had listed, then had taken the animal to Cheyenne's farm, since he lived in town. When Cheyenne had hired Blaze to take care of the horse, Austin had been angry. The moron had actually expected to use the starving horse as an excuse to see Cheyenne more often.

Had to give the guy credit for originality, but it was still stupid. He must not know much about women.

"I hear you used to be the mayor." The words slid from Fawn's mouth before she realized she was going to say anything at all.

Austin turned and glanced around the room, and she could tell he hadn't even known she was there. That ficus tree made a good eavesdropping blind.

She stood up.

He blinked, the heavy expression in his eyes suddenly lifting. "That's right."

"Sorry about your son."

He nodded. "Thank you. So am I."

"If you're looking to stay a couple of weeks, Grace Brennan might sublet her apartment to you. She's on tour this month."

He stepped across the hardwood floor to the counter and leaned against it, obviously to get a better look at the instigator of this conversation.

"Grace Brennan's on the road?" he asked.

"That's right. She's got a song that's a crossover hit, and she and Michael Gold are getting married."

Austin whistled softly. "When's the wedding?"

"During the festival on the twenty-fifth of this month. Karah Lee Fletcher's getting married to Taylor Jackson, too."

Austin winked at her, his eyes suddenly teasing. "How about you? When do you get married?"

Fawn scowled. Now he was flirting, not taking her seriously. "I just turned eighteen. Why would I be getting married so young?"

He shrugged. "I don't remember seeing you in Hideaway two years ago."

She decided not to tell him where she was and what she was doing two years ago. She wanted to ask why his own life had gone down the tubes so quickly. But Karah Lee and Blaze were always reminding her that those kinds of questions weren't polite.

"I came here one step ahead of some goon who wanted to kill me," she said. "Karah Lee decided to keep me."

Austin Barlow's expression didn't change, which intrigued Fawn. Usually, that announcement led the listener to ask for the whole story.

Fawn decided the winking and teasing were a cover. Austin had other things on his mind. "Why did you come back to Hideaway?" she asked.

"You should know why. You're the one who's been eavesdropping."

"So you want to make amends? For your son's actions? It's not like you're the guilty one."

Austin scowled.

"Sorry," Fawn said. "I guess a good father will always feel responsible for whatever his kid does."

The scowl faded as he studied her more closely.

"Guess I wouldn't know about that," she muttered softly.

Austin's eyes narrowed at her words, then he shook his head. "Guess I wouldn't, either. But maybe it's time to make up for a lot of things," he said, almost as if to himself.

"Are you moving back to Hideaway?" she asked. Blaze wouldn't be thrilled about that. Dane Gideon wouldn't be happy, either, though he was too much of a gentleman ever to say anything.

Austin glanced around the lobby, appraising. "I'm not sure where I'll be moving yet. I need to talk to Cheyenne Allison, Dane Gideon, make a few—"

"That's Cheyenne *Gideon*."

The guy blinked, as if startled. "Of course. I knew that."

"I heard you had a thing for her," Fawn said.

He gave a disapproving frown. "For a newcomer, you sure know a lot about me."

"While you're making apologies, are you going to apologize to Blaze Farmer?"

He leveled a long, steady look at her. "Have you suddenly decided to become my conscience?"

"I thought you said you'd come here to make amends. Seems to me you need to be making amends to Blaze for quite a few things."

Austin continued to study her thoughtfully. "Yes, it would seem that way, wouldn't it?"

His focused attention made her nervous.

Jill sat wiping the massage cream from her face with the turban that had been wrapped around her head. She couldn't stop staring at Edith's still form, listening to the soft echo of sobs coming from another room.

Sheena had run out when Cheyenne made the pronouncement, and Noelle had gone to comfort her and cancel clients for the remainder of the day. Apparently Sheena had loved Edith, too.

A quick glance told Jill that Rex Fairfield was still here. She returned her attention to Edith as Karah Lee pulled a sheet over that death mask.

Jill winced. She couldn't do this. She needed to run away screaming, needed to shake her fist at God and ask what He thought He was doing. She needed to rail at Cheyenne for giving up so easily. These weren't just impulses, they were compulsions that she had to control.

The real Jill Cooper was a rational human being, a responsible RN, an adult.

Oh, the awful terror that had been in Edith's eyes...the horrible knowledge of something—but what? What had she been trying to say? Hallucinating, no doubt, but why?

"Jill?" A deep masculine voice broke into her thoughts.

With a start, she looked up, then looked away quickly, refusing to meet Rex's gaze. Not now. It was just too much. She didn't want to deal with this—couldn't deal with it. All she wanted to do was fall to her knees at Edith's side and weep against her shoulder as she had done so often as a young teenager.

"I'm so sorry," Rex said. The gentle sympathy in his low baritone voice reawakened memories she couldn't bear right now.

She nodded. What was this man doing here? What kind of crazy, tilted nightmare was this?

"The timing is awful," Rex continued. "I would never have done this to you—"

"You haven't done a thing to me, Rex." She forced herself, then, to meet his gaze. "I don't know what you're doing in Hideaway, but I doubt either of us is hung up on something that happened twenty-two years ago."

"Some things were left in limbo then," he said. "We parted without enough explanations, which was unfortunate. I take the blame. Eventually, we'll need to clear the air. I owe you an—"

"I have other things to do right now, Rex." Without waiting for a reply, she brushed past him and knelt to help Cheyenne pick up debris.

"I need to go tell Bertie," Cheyenne said.

"No." Jill couldn't allow anyone else to do that. "That should be my job. I'll need to contact Edith's family. She has a niece who lives in Springfield, and others—"

"You need some time to recover." Cheyenne squeezed cellophane wrappers into a tight ball with more force than normal. "Bertie's—"

"Please, Chey. I need to do this." Jill touched Cheyenne's shoulder, then noticed what she should have seen earlier— the silent tears coursing down her director's face.

"How about you?" Jill asked. "Are you okay?"

Cheyenne nodded.

Jill realized this must be bringing back horrible memories for her. When Cheyenne was an ER doc in Columbia, her younger sister had been brought in via ambulance after an automobile accident. Cheyenne couldn't resuscitate her, and in the end she'd had to call her own baby sister's death.

Jill couldn't imagine how she would have felt had that happened to her with Noelle.

"I'll go with her, Cheyenne," Noelle said from the open doorway.

Jill continued to feel Rex's attention on her, and she finally looked up at him. What she saw in his expression soothed her jumbled emotions.

"I can do this," Jill repeated, striding from the room. She continued out the front door of the spa, wishing she never had to return to this place.

When would it all end? How many deaths would this tiny village have to endure?

She was halfway across the street when she heard footsteps behind her.

"You don't need to keep vigil over me," she said. "I'm fine."

"I loved her, too, you know," came a gentle female voice.

Jill softened. Noelle. At this moment she could barely focus on placing one foot in front of the other, but out of habit, she forced herself to gather her strength for her sister.

Noelle rested a hand on Jill's arm, her touch tentative, as if she half expected it to be shaken off.

Lord, wake me up! This can't be happening again, Jill prayed.

"Edith was always there for us," Noelle said as they stepped onto the grass across the street from the town square. "Especially for you."

Jill nodded. In spite of the oppressive heat, it seemed as

if a thick fog had covered the sun. She glanced up to find not a cloud in the blue sky. The sun shone brightly. It just didn't seem to be reaching her.

"She was my best friend," Jill said at last.

"I know."

Edith had taken the place of their mother when she was killed. Edith had played the role of the strong parent when the girls' father had withdrawn into a world of grief and buried himself in work.

"I went to her for guidance when I couldn't control you," Jill continued.

"I'm sorry I made it so hard for you," Noelle said.

"I'm not saying it was your fault, I'm just saying Edith was my strength."

"I was old enough to know better."

"You were acting out because you were frightened. You needed your mother, and I wasn't her. You needed a father, and he wasn't able to cope."

"Stop making excuses for me. Besides, we're talking about you for once."

Jill's steps slowed as she stared out across the surface of Table Rock Lake. As much as she wanted to reassure Noelle that she would be fine, Jill knew Noelle wouldn't believe her. And it might be a lie. In times of extreme stress, like now, an OCD crisis was always a possibility.

Her steps slowed further as they drew near the bed and breakfast that Edith Potts and Bertie Meyer had purchased and turned into a profitable business. "Oh, Noelle, what's Bertie going to do now? She still hasn't recovered from Red's death. Now Edith."

Her sister's trembling hand grasped hers. That tremor reminded Jill that Noelle, too, had just witnessed another horrible death. It brought back their past with such clarity—and they hadn't had time to recover from all the darkness.

Edith had been a constant in their lives for so many years.

"It isn't your fault," Noelle said quietly. "You can't take responsibility for this." She paused, then, still more quietly, added, "Especially not for *this*."

"That isn't what I'm doing, I'm just—" Jill frowned, then stopped and looked at her sister, studying the beautiful lines of Noelle's face. *Especially not for* this. "What do you mean?"

Noelle didn't meet her gaze, and Jill felt a tingling of alertness.

Since childhood, Noelle had been gifted with a special intuition that had frightened Jill. Now that they understood it better and realized that this intuition was pure and of God, a simple spiritual gift, it didn't frighten her as badly as it once had. Still, Jill had learned to take it seriously when Noelle experienced this special knowledge. It wasn't a conjuring. Noelle would never have sought this gift for herself, and she continued to avoid addressing it whenever possible. For her to make that remark now meant something, Jill knew.

"Are you telling me there could be something else going on—"

"Do you have any idea what Rex Fairfield is doing here?" Noelle asked abruptly.

"I don't want to talk about him right now. We need to—"

"I can't go there yet." Noelle tugged her hand away, and Jill realized she had been holding on too tightly—something she had often done to Noelle. "I'm the reason you broke up with him, aren't I?" Noelle asked.

"What makes you think I'm the one who broke it off?"

"Whoever did it, I'm the reason," Noelle said. "I overheard the two of you fighting because you insisted on coming home every weekend. And I know you did that because I kept getting into trouble. If not for me, maybe—"

"I thought you said it wasn't about you this time," Jill snapped. "The reason Rex and I didn't get married is because it wasn't meant to be, so stop wallowing in guilt."

"I'm not," Noelle snapped back. "I'm just telling it like it is."

Jill stopped and turned to Noelle then, softening her voice. "Honey, if not for you, I might have no sanity left. Because I knew I had to be responsible for you, I was willing to seek help for my compulsions."

Noelle held her gaze for a moment, then nodded. Something cleared in her expression. She looked down at her hands. "Thanks. Glad I could be of service."

Jill relaxed slightly at the gentle teasing. "Now, are you going to tell me what you know about Edith's death?"

"Not yet. I'm sorry, but you understand how it is. I just believe all is not as it seems. We need to be watchful."

Jill didn't press for more, badly as she wanted to. *What* was not as it seemed? And *who* could be hiding something?

Chapter Five

Rex designated a biohazard receptacle and a sharps container as he collected used needles and tubing from the massage-room floor around Edith's still body. He had to make do with what he had here at the spa and would place all the items in a proper receptacle later when they returned to the clinic.

The rest of the makeshift code team had dispersed to other rooms in the spa to make arrangements for Edith's funeral. The place was quiet, filled with the aura of shock and grief with which he had become familiar as an internist.

The feeling of loss after a code wasn't something he missed about his former life. He did miss other things, however. He'd loved the interaction with patients and their families and the chance to have a meaningful impact on a patient's quality of life. Internal medicine had given him opportunities for that. Still, if he had it to do over again—which he might, someday—he would have gone into family practice.

A general practice didn't pay nearly as well as internal medicine. With the diminishing returns from health insurance, the number of uninsured patients and the high cost of professional liability insurance, many of his colleagues complained that they would soon have to pay their patients for the privilege of treating them.

Cheyenne Gideon and Karah Lee Fletcher didn't seem to have that attitude, however.

When everything was collected from the floor, Rex sank onto the stool beside Edith's body. She looked almost alive. If he didn't know better, he would expect to see her chest rising and falling. There was something about her... "I'm sorry I didn't get to talk to you again," he murmured softly. "Go with God."

Footsteps echoed from the hallway, and Cheyenne stepped through the open threshold, mascara smudged around her dark eyes.

"Rex, I'm sorry you were dragged into this, but thank you so much for your willingness to help." There was a catch in her voice.

"Thank you for including me. It's been a while since I last did a code."

"Someone from the funeral home will be here soon." She reached for an empty syringe and placed it in the receptacle. "You don't have to wait."

"I'd like to, if you don't mind."

With a nod, she sank into a chair, her dark eyes shimmering with more tears.

"You must have cared a great deal about her," he said.

"Everyone did. Jill and Edith were especially close, and I hate to think what she'll be going through in the next few days."

"She'll blame herself," Rex said.

Cheyenne nodded, her eyes narrowing fractionally as she gazed at him. "Yes." There was a hesitation in the word. It wasn't quite a question, but he could almost hear her thoughts. Then her gaze returned to Edith.

"When I was practicing medicine," he said, "I made it a habit to ensure that the deceased patient was never left alone before being collected by the hearse or taken to the hospital morgue." It hadn't always been possible, of course, but he'd tried.

She nodded. "You were in internal medicine? I guess that means you did intubations."

"Quite a few."

"When I was a med student, I heard horror stories about ER docs and internists who left their intubated patients alone after a failed code in a room, where the tube was moved by a careless staff member."

"Which set the doctor up for a malpractice lawsuit when he couldn't prove he had the tube in correctly," Rex said. "I heard the same stories."

"You didn't do this intubation." Cheyenne gestured to Edith. "Obviously, you're not staying to protect your liability."

He shook his head. "Somehow, it just doesn't seem right to leave her lying here alone on the cold, hard floor. It's always been a hang-up of mine."

"A tender heart? I bet you got teased about that in med school."

"Not so much in med school as when I was a resident." He hadn't minded the teasing. His little eccentricity had actually been the first thing that had drawn Jill to him. It had taken weeks to realize why she'd been so understanding about his quirks—because she had some pretty interesting quirks of her own.

Karah Lee joined them in the room and sank onto the recliner. "Sheena's not handling this well."

"Is she going to be okay?" Rex asked.

Karah Lee nodded. "She's on the telephone with her mother now. You know Jill's got to be in agony. I'm just glad Noelle went with her."

"I need to talk to Bertie, myself," Cheyenne said.

"You'll get your chance," Karah Lee said. "And don't worry, Bertie can handle this. She's a trouper."

"Blaze and I were the ones who found her husband dead," Cheyenne said. "Red was the sweetest old man, deaf as a flowerpot, as Bertie liked to say. After his death, Edith was always there for Bertie, even willing to risk her savings to go into business with her at the bed and breakfast."

"She was a wise and kind lady," Rex said.

Karah Lee's eyes narrowed. "You knew her?"

He looked down and studied the elderly, waxen face. There seemed to be just a hint of pink still in her cheeks. If he didn't know better, he'd have thought she was wearing makeup, but anything on her skin would have been removed with all that green stuff.

"You did know Edith?" Cheyenne asked.

"I met her years ago. I take it this was not completely unexpected? Heart failure?"

Cheyenne hesitated, watching him with those dark eyes, obviously trying to decipher the implication of his having known Edith. "She's been struggling with chronic heart failure for the past year."

"Was she taking her medication faithfully?"

"Yes, and I thought we were keeping a close eye on her numbers, so this was a shock."

"You can't place the human body on a schedule," he said. "When the heart gives out, it gives out. You know that."

"Yes, but when we're especially close to the patient, we do tend to take on more responsibility for the outcome," Cheyenne said.

"You've been in Hideaway before?" Karah Lee asked Rex.

He resisted a smile at the redhead's evident curiosity. "Yes, and I actually stayed at Edith's house a few times. Edith was one of the most hospitable people I've ever known. She not only fed me and gave me a place to sleep when I visited, but she invited me to return, even after…" He caught himself and fell silent.

Karah Lee and Cheyenne waited.

"You might as well tell us," Karah Lee said. "We'll drag it out of you one way or another. What's up between you and Jill?"

He had hoped to speak with Jill before sharing this information with anyone else. Especially considering the cool reception he had received from her this afternoon, he didn't want her to feel as if he had betrayed her confidence.

However, he had never sworn to remain silent about their past together. She had done nothing to be ashamed of, though *he* had been ashamed of his words to her in the hospital cafeteria that one heartbreaking afternoon.

"Don't even try to tell us you and Jill didn't have something going on," Karah Lee said. "I saw her reaction when she realized who you were."

"We met over twenty years ago, when I was doing rotations in Springfield," he said, still reluctant to explain. "Jill was doing her clinicals at St. John's."

When he was silent for a moment, Cheyenne prompted, "And?"

He was far too conscious of Edith's still form. "Perhaps it isn't totally respectful to be talking about this—"

"Spill it, Rex," Karah Lee said. "Edith would totally approve."

He glanced at the outspoken young doctor and grimaced. "Jill and I were once engaged to be married."

Jill stood as if rooted into the grass at the side of the road. The heat of late summer blasted her face, and yet she felt cold. The graceful lines of her sister's face blurred before her.

"Are you okay?" Noelle asked.

Jill blinked to clear her vision, feeling moisture in her lashes. "Your tone implied Edith might have died from something other than heart failure."

"Yes, but—"

"Something other than natural causes."

Noelle gave a quiet sigh, then nodded almost imperceptibly.

"But we were right there in the next room. She was fine."

"I know."

"And then I thought I heard her laughing. It probably wasn't laughter, but…but she might have been clearing something from her throat, and then—"

"Jill, I can't tell you any more than that right now, because I simply don't know."

"So if it wasn't natural causes, then that means someone or something else caused her death." Suddenly self-doubt attacked Jill. "Could I have made a mistake? Could I have been wrong when I thought she'd stopped breathing, and when I initiated CPR I actually caused her heart to—"

"Stop that." Noelle seldom raised her voice at Jill, but the sudden intensity of those two words halted the painfully familiar sense of panic.

"Remember I told you that *especially this time* you aren't to blame?"

"Then someone else is?" Jill asked.

"I'm not saying that, either. Don't put words in my mouth. I just think there's something else wrong here." Noelle hesitated, her expression clouding. Jill wasn't the only one in this family who had an overwhelming amount of self-doubt. "But with Edith's heart, we knew it was probably just a matter of time."

Jill felt another twist in her gut, in spite of Noelle's reassurance. "I might have done something wrong."

"No. You did everything right."

"How can you know that for sure? You weren't there the whole time."

"Stop second-guessing yourself. You're the best—"

"Maybe I shouldn't have started CPR." Jill paced across the grass a couple of yards. "Maybe her heart was fine before I—"

"Jill!" This time Noelle did raise her voice, and she grabbed Jill by the arm. "Stop doubting yourself. That's the OCD talking."

"What if this time it isn't the OCD?"

"Even that statement suggests that it is. You know better."

"I'm handling everything appropriately."

"No you aren't! You don't need to be going to Bertie in the state you're in right now. You'll upset her in your condition, and you'll feel awful about it later."

Jill looked across the street toward the general store. "What about Cecil? He's going to be heartbroken. He and Edith have been such good friends for so many years. Someone needs to tell—"

"Cheyenne will call her husband. Dane can talk to Cecil."

Jill knew better than to try to stop the wild ideas that bounced around inside her head like poisoned arrows that confused and clouded her mind. *I've killed my friend.... I've made some kind of mistake that I can't remember.... I'm a worthless nurse.... I destroy everything I touch....*

"You could be wrong this time, Noelle," she murmured. The weight of responsibility, already heavy enough to crush her, increased yet again. "There's something you aren't telling me. I can see it in your eyes."

Noelle released her then. "Have you stopped taking your medication?"

"Don't change the subject."

"That *is* the subject!"

When they were younger—when Jill, barely past childhood herself, felt the responsibility for Noelle's welfare resting solely on her own small shoulders—she had been much worse. Caught up in the conviction that something was horribly wrong at their home in Cedar Hollow, she had feared for Noelle's life if other members of their family discovered Noelle's gift, and had slapped her to keep her quiet about it.

Something *had* been wrong then. How could Jill be sure something wasn't wrong now as well? She and Noelle were far too familiar with the specter of murder.

"Have you stopped taking your medication again?" Noelle repeated.

"I'm taking it, just not as much. I'm titrating down."

"Why?"

"I don't need as much. I can get a handle on this thing without chemicals flowing through my body all the time. You know how much I hate that stuff."

"But you hate the OCD more," Noelle said. "Look what it's doing to you right now, and this is a horrible time to reduce the meds. You need to increase the dosage, not cut back on it."

Voices reached them from the bed and breakfast, and Jill glanced in that direction, barely a block away, to see another familiar figure stepping out onto the broad front porch.

"Noelle?"

"What?"

"Please tell me I'm not hallucinating."

Noelle followed her line of vision, then caught her breath in a tiny gasp. "Depends on what you think you see," she said, voice dripping with sarcasm. "If you think that's Attila the Hun, you're hallucinating. It's just a distant descendant of his. He was in the spa earlier this morning."

"What was Austin Barlow doing in your spa?"

"Paying a friendly visit." The sarcasm didn't abate. Noelle had never liked Austin.

"We need to suggest an autopsy for Edith," Jill said, softly, so her voice wouldn't carry to Austin.

"For what? You think anyone's going to listen to us?"

"We can try."

"As you said, Cheyenne is sure it was an MI that killed Edith," Noelle said. "Myocardial infarction. Nobody's going to listen to my hunch. Remember, Cheyenne's the doctor. I'm not. So that's exactly what they'll call it—just a hunch."

"They'll listen to you before they'd listen to me," Jill said. "Remember, I've been a little jumpy since last year. I've called the sheriff a couple of times about noises around the house."

"Well, I'm the one who admitted to breaking and entering last year," Noelle said.

Jill shook her head. "You were tracking a killer. The sheriff knows that."

Noelle nudged Jill. Austin was glancing toward them.

"I'll talk to the sheriff myself," Jill said. "I'm telling you one thing now, though, sis. I'm going to run lab tests on that blood I drew from Edith."

Noelle nodded. "That's something we can take care of as soon as we've spoken with Bertie."

Chapter Six

The massage room became so silent Rex could hear the quavering voice of the traumatized masseuse out in the lobby, apparently still talking to her mother on the telephone. Cheyenne and Karah Lee stared at him, waiting.

He didn't want to say anything else.

"Jill never mentioned being engaged," Cheyenne said.

"One doesn't always like to talk about a broken relationship," he said.

"I don't know why not," Karah Lee said. "We talk about everything else around here, especially among the office staff. Who broke it?"

Cheyenne cleared her throat. "Uh, careful. We could be invading private turf."

Rex raised his eyebrows at them. *You think?*

Karah Lee spread her hands. "If we're going to be working together for the next few weeks, we'd better make sure we'll all get along."

"There will be no trouble between Jill and me," Rex assured them. How could he have forgotten that special character that had always been such a vital part of Hideaway—the…inquisitiveness?

"It sure didn't look that way to me a while ago," Karah Lee said. "Jill wouldn't even talk to you."

"She was upset about Edith. Both of us know how to behave in a professional manner."

"Does this mean you're not going to tell us what happened to your engagement?" Karah Lee asked, patently disappointed.

He glanced at Cheyenne to see if she would use her authority to curb this vein of inquisitiveness. But she appeared just as curious as Karah Lee.

Obviously, they had been well nourished in the soil of small-town know-thy-neighbor's-business. "We parted under less than ideal circumstances," he said.

Karah Lee leaned forward, as if settling in for a story.

Fawn followed Austin onto the porch, still intrigued by this man and his so-called mission. "So, did you suddenly get religion or something?"

He gave her another irritably amused glance over his broad-but-bony left shoulder. "How did you guess?"

She frowned at him. She couldn't tell if he was being sarcastic. "Well, I mean, I guess I don't know much, but I've never heard of someone going out of his way to return to his hometown and start making apologies to everybody."

"A fella does if he's smart. Especially if he wants to stay awhile."

"So you *are* moving back here?" As she asked the question, she caught sight of Jill Cooper and Noelle Trask standing at the edge of the greenway that bordered the municipal boat dock. They were staring in this direction.

Fawn glanced at Austin, and found him staring back at the sisters.

"Uh-oh," she said softly. "It must be time for another apology."

He ignored her and stepped toward the two women.

Rex decided to give his colleagues what they wanted. In fact, if he knew for sure he could trust them, he might even be willing to enlist their assistance in paving the way for a better relationship with Jill—at least a working relationship—but that was taking it too far.

"We discovered quickly that we worked well together," he said. "Jill wanted to be an intensive-care nurse. When we did shifts together, she seemed to read my mind."

"She does that with me," Cheyenne said. "She seems able to tune in to what I'm doing."

Rex shrugged. "And all this time I was under the impression there was this special bond between the two of us."

"So you got engaged?" Karah Lee asked, obviously impatient with the slow pace of the narrative.

"We were friends first. We enjoyed each other's company, often shared a meal together in the cafeteria when our shifts coincided. We found many things in common, and the relationship grew."

"That's the way it works best," Cheyenne said.

"Then we got engaged."

"And then what?" Karah Lee asked.

"Life intruded. I discovered I wasn't as patient with her as I had been when we were just friends." He had become jealous and selfish, something that continued to shame him. "Jill was forced into the role of surrogate mother at far too young an age, and she had trouble balancing her time between me and her little sister." And he'd been no help at all. *Why had he been such a pig?*

"No doubt about it," Karah Lee said, "Noelle was a handful growing up. She still gets reminded of that."

"I wasn't mature enough to handle it amid the rigors of internship and early residency. I said some things to Jill that didn't go over well. The engagement ended six months after it began."

"Ouch!" Karah Lee exclaimed.

The front door opened, and Cheyenne rose. "That's probably the hearse for Edith."

Jill watched Austin walk down the path to the circle drive in front of the bed and breakfast. He paused beside a silver Jeep Grand Cherokee as if he might get in and drive away. But, of course, she wouldn't be so lucky. Not today. She half expected to look up into the sky and see it splitting apart and Jesus calling His own home to be with Him. And she, of course, would be left behind.

That wasn't the way it was supposed to happen, of course.

She'd walked the aisle years ago, given her heart to Jesus. But the way her life had worked out—and especially the way it seemed to be working today—she could probably expect to discover a glitch in that plan, as well.

Yes, she knew better, but OCD could make a person doubt her salvation as much as it made her doubt everything else in her life.

Austin came toward her, his cowboy boots crunching loudly on the gravel.

"You know," Noelle said softly, "we could just leave right now. You don't need this. Nobody needs this. Let's just turn around and walk away, give him time to leave."

"Austin's harmless, Noelle." Jill stepped toward him. She was no longer attracted to the man, of course. A lifetime had passed since they went together in high school. Apparently God had decided to try her in a test in which her whole past was coming back to haunt her in one day. She might as well deal with it.

"I don't get it," Noelle said, falling, obviously unwilling, into step beside her. "You blew off Rex Fairfield back at the spa, so why are you going out of your way to greet Austin Barlow?"

"Because I'm not a little kid. I'm ashamed of my behavior with Rex, and I'll have to apologize as soon as I see him again." If she saw him. "I was preoccupied with Edith. Do you have any clue why Rex *and* Austin would both show up in this town on this day when I'm already losing my mind?"

Noelle looked at her. "None. But I do know there is some kind of reason for it."

"Yeah, right, God has a plan."

"He always does. You just have to wait and see it from hindsight."

"I don't like to wait for hindsight." She'd lived in this town for a lot of years, as had Austin. When he was mayor, she was school nurse. After Austin's wife died, when Ramsay was a child, there had even been talk about a resurrection of that long-ago romance between Austin and Jill.

It hadn't worked out.

In fact, the way she'd heard it through the Hideaway grapevine, Austin had developed a schoolboy crush on Cheyenne when she came to town. He apparently hadn't taken it well when Dane Gideon made the more lasting impression on her. That change in circumstances had nearly cost Cheyenne her life when Austin's son decided to act on his father's displeasure.

High-school memories seemed so much more innocent than adult ones. So much more distant, they paled in comparison to the tragedies of more recent years—though there had been tragedies even in high school.

She recalled the tragedy that had been the catalyst that ended her relationship with Austin. Another classmate, Chet Palmer, had died, and some fingers had been pointed toward Austin and his buddies.

Now, she held her hands out to Austin as graciously as Edith would have done had she encountered him on the street.

"Why, Austin Barlow, what are you doing back in town? Everything okay with Ramsay?"

The gratified relief that etched his expression made her feel sorry for him.

"Hello, Jill." His hands grasped hers with a warmth she hadn't expected. "Ramsay is still in rehabilitation. How are you doing?"

She hesitated, staring up at him quizzically. How much did he know? How much *could* he know? News about the discovery of the murder of her father and grandparents eleven years ago had made the rounds last autumn and winter. He could have heard of them from just about anyone who was still speaking to him.

Amazingly, she found strength in the touch of his hands and the concern in his voice. He sounded sincere.

She wondered again about the odds of two former boyfriends converging on Hideaway the same day Edith died.

Astronomical. Ridiculous. *Was* it possible she had made a break with reality?

No. She had a neurosis, not a psychosis. She needed to trust Noelle's faith that God was in control of this situation.

She mentally shook herself and gazed up into Austin's eyes. Familiarity and comfort seemed to lie beneath the surface of that questing gaze. How she needed comfort right now.

"We've just had a horrible shock, Austin," she said, surprised at herself for speaking about it. "Edith Potts just died. Noelle and I are on our way to tell Bertie."

Her shock seemed to transfer to him. His hands tightened on hers. His eyes widened. "What happened?"

"Cheyenne thinks it was her heart," she said, gently disengaging from his grip. Cheyenne was seldom wrong. But this time...

He released her immediately. "Cheyenne?"

She heard the sudden, lingering interest in that one spoken name. So, the rumors were true. Poor Austin must have fallen hard. "She tried everything to bring Edith back. Nothing worked." Jill knew it was the truth. She felt badly about her behavior at the spa. "You knew she was the director of the clinic, didn't you?"

"I've heard a few things, but I haven't kept up with everyone now that Mom is no longer in town. Is Cheyenne sure about the cause of death?"

"I don't know at this point."

"So she will investigate further to make sure?"

Jill hesitated and frowned at him. "Austin, is there some reason you feel it should be—"

"No, of course not. I'm sorry." He placed a hand on her shoulder. "I know you were good friends with Edith. Will you be okay?"

She nodded, thanked him, turned toward the bed and breakfast with Noelle at her side.

Amazing that she was able to behave so rationally—and politely—when her brain struggled to contain all the thoughts that tumbled through it—telling her she had killed Edith.

Noelle had been right, this was the wrong time to try to cut the meds. *I'll start back on the full dosage tonight.*

She and Noelle found Bertie in the dining room, scrambling to keep the buffet table filled with enough black walnut waffles to satisfy the Saturday-afternoon brunch crowd.

One glance, however, brought Bertie to her side, dish towel in hand.

"Jill Cooper, you look like you could use a good, filling

meal. Was that massage at the spa too much for you?" She gestured for Jill to follow her into the dining room.

"I…um…Bertie." She froze. She couldn't do this.

Bertie, diminutive, white-haired, already looked too fragile. She had suffered so many losses in her life. Her only child had died young, decades ago. Her husband, Red, had died two years ago. And now this? Her business partner and best friend?

"Uh-oh," Bertie said. "I can tell by that look on your face you saw our visitor. Wasn't Austin your old high-school sweetheart?"

"Yes, Bertie, he was, but—" She looked at Noelle.

With a nod, Noelle gently took Bertie by the arm and led her out of the dining room. "We need to tell you something."

"Well, for goodness' sake, what is it?" She looked at Jill, and her warm, friendly eyes darkened with distress. "Jill, didn't you and Edith go to the spa this…oh, no. Did that ticker of hers pitch a fit again? I keep tellin' her to remember her medicine, but half the time she goes off without it. Someday it's gonna—"

"Bertie," Jill said, "this time she didn't make it."

There was a startled pause as the words registered, then the news pressed Bertie's slender shoulders down with their weight.

"I'm sorry," Jill said, once again feeling the loss like a knife in her heart. "I'm so sorry."

Chapter Seven

❧

Hours before the funeral service at the Methodist church on Wednesday morning, Jill stepped tentatively through the front door of Noelle's Naturals and Spa.

When Jill was a horseback-riding youth, she'd been taught early to get back on the horse quickly after being tossed so she wouldn't develop an unnatural fear of horses. The concept had worked then. Would it work for her in this situation?

Of course, she'd never been a fan of spas, whereas she had always loved horses, dirty and dangerous as they could be. They still weren't as dangerous as humans.

As a nurse, she was in close contact with people every day, but *she* was the one giving the care. *She* was in control.

In a spa, she felt vulnerable. The memory of Edith's death continued to weigh heavily on her.

Soothing music emanated from hidden speakers, and an abundance of plants thrived in this roomy waiting room.

Imitating what Dane Gideon had done with his general store years earlier, Noelle had purchased two empty store buildings with a shared wall within the town square complex. She had knocked out a portion of the connecting wall and combined the space so she could easily oversee the natural herb and food shop while managing the spa. She had also dipped deeply into savings to develop a Web site and an all-out marketing campaign that reached the entire southwest area of Missouri.

"Hi, Jill. Back for another massage?"

Jill turned to find Sheena Marshall stepping out of one of the massage rooms. Her blond hair was tied back, and her pretty blue eyes had circles beneath them. She looked as if she had lost weight since Saturday. Gone was that characteristic perky smile.

"Not today, thanks."

"Didn't think so." Sheena went into Noelle's office and sat at her desk. She pulled open the top drawer and took out a pad of sticky note paper.

"Are you with a client right now?" Jill asked.

"Nope. It's been slow, so I'm making a supply list." She closed the drawer and stood up. "I guess no one wants to come to a place where a nice old lady died. Like maybe she was contagious or something." Sheena shook her head sadly. "You know how superstitious people can be."

Jill nodded as she glanced toward the broad entryway to

the herb and food shop. "I'm sure it'll pick back up. It's just a time of mourning."

"You're looking for your sister, I guess." Sheena stepped back out into the hallway with a pen and the notepad.

Actually, Noelle wasn't who Jill was looking for. They'd had another long talk last night.

"She's gone to Springfield to pick up some supplies," Sheena explained. "Nathan decided to go with her. Those two are so sweet to each other, Mom says sometimes she just wants to gag." Sheena smiled, and it was a sad smile. Ordinarily, she was the giggling type, but since Edith's death, the young woman had lost her usual effervescence.

Jill hesitated, feeling intrusive. "Since you mentioned the day Edith died, do you remember much about that morning?"

Sheena blinked at her, then glanced again toward the connecting entryway between the spa and the shop, as if concerned someone might overhear them. "Sure I do. I don't think I'll ever forget it. I'm sorry I was such a brainless idiot that day."

"You were understandably upset. It was a horrible thing for you to see."

"It's just that…well…Miss Edith was always so good to everyone. And I know everyone has their time to die, but I didn't think her time would be on my watch, you know?" She gave a shudder for emphasis. "I don't like death."

"Nobody does."

"I know. I guess death has to come, and it's best if it comes for someone who's lived a good, long life and is ready, you know? But still, I hate that it had to be like that."

"Did the shop get a lot of visitors that morning?" Jill asked. "I mean, not clients, but drop-in visitors."

Sheena's gaze sharpened then. "Why? Are you checking something out?"

"To be honest, I'm not sure what I'm doing, unless it's just a search for closure. You know how much I cared about Edith."

Sheena nodded sympathetically.

"She was the one who convinced me to have a massage in the first place," Jill said. "She was already in a robe Saturday afternoon when I got here. Do you know how long she'd been here when I arrived?"

Sheena's eyes narrowed in concentration. "Couldn't have been more than ten minutes, but I might be wrong. You know how these old folks who know everybody can talk for hours about nothing in particular."

"Who else do you remember being here that day?"

"You'd probably get a better answer from Noelle. She was the one who opened up that morning."

"She was on the computer in her office most of the time, working on August month-end things. She didn't see many people."

"Well, then Mom would have seen them, I guess. She'd left just a little before you got here."

"Austin Barlow was here, I understand," Jill said.

"Sure, you know how he always liked to check out the new businesses in town. He thought it was his civic duty to do that when he was mayor."

"Did he have anything to say? Do you remember if he spoke with Edith?"

"I didn't hear if he said anything to her. Remember when he got into an argument with her during that church business meeting, then somebody up and killed her cat? Some said Austin might've done it, but now we know it wasn't him, don't we?"

Jill shook her head. Austin's son had killed Edith's cat. What agonies Austin must have gone through when all of this painful information about Ramsay was revealed at last. "Did anyone else drop by that day?"

"Well, Dad came by to pick up Mom. They were going to a show in Branson that afternoon." Sheena lowered her voice. "Before they left, Junior Short came by to talk to Dad."

Junior Short. Another bad memory—possibly another connection? Austin had been buddies with Junior Short and Sheena's father, Jed, when they were in high school. Edith had been the high-school principal at the time.

A vague unease stirred in Jill's mind, but she dismissed it. Those three had been deeply involved in a high-school scandal, but that was far in the past. "Your dad and Junior are still friends after all these years?"

Sheena's face scrunched up in a good imitation of her mother's look of distaste. "I guess. I see them drinking coffee together sometimes at the bakery. He never comes around the house because Mom can't stand the man."

Jill nodded. Junior could be obnoxious. It was a trait he'd carried with him into adulthood and passed on to the next generation—a tendency to pick fights easily, and just generally irritate everyone around him. Possibly Jed felt sorry for him. Junior didn't have many friends.

"I don't suppose Cecil Martin came by for any reason?" Jill asked. "I thought I saw him walking from the direction of the spa when I passed him on the sidewalk on my way here that day."

"Now that you mention it, he probably did come by to see Miss Edith." Sheena grinned. "You know, I think those two might have been sweet on each other."

"Sheena," came a warning call from one of the doors near the end of the short hallway of massage rooms. Mary Marshall, Sheena's mother, stepped into the hallway, wiping her hands with a paper towel. "Don't start any rumors."

"They'd been spending a lot of time together lately, Mom."

"They were friends." Mary strolled down the hallway and tossed her towels into the trash can beside the reception desk. Her gray-blond hair was pulled back in a tight knot, as if to draw taut the wrinkles that now marked her once-pretty face. Her makeup made her look washed-out, and her clothes did nothing to enhance barely existent curves on her slim frame.

Jill decided that if Sheena wanted to do a makeover, she could begin with her own flesh and blood.

Mary nodded at Jill; no smile of welcome touched her face.

Jill knew better than to take it personally. When Mary was in a mood, no one was spared her sharp words or brooding silences.

"Why do young people always have to make up some silly storybook romance for everything?" Mary complained to her daughter. "Like such a thing even exists."

Jill studied Mary's drawn expression in silence. Sheena's mother was talking like a bitter old woman, not the wife of a man who seemed to still love her, and with whom she had a beautiful grown daughter.

Do I sound like that sometimes? Will I be a bitter old woman someday? Though Jill hadn't been blessed with a long-lasting relationship, she did enjoy seeing evidence of love in the eyes of others. Cheyenne and Dane, for example. Or Karah Lee and Taylor. Noelle and Nathan.

"Like you always say," Sheena murmured, "friendship is the best foundation for a marriage."

"Can't a man and a woman just be good friends without everyone in town making a big thing out of it?" Mary grumbled.

Jill found herself wondering the same thing. In spite of herself, a thought of Rex intruded. Jill and Rex had become friends soon after they started working together. The romance had developed some time afterward, hadn't it? Or had she actually felt an attraction to him immediately?

Man, oh, man, how wonderfully the romance had developed. She dismissed a memory of his kisses with some difficulty. The worst part of their broken engagement wasn't only the failed romance. Could be the very worst part was losing someone who had become one of her best friends. Maybe even *the* best of her friends. She'd certainly felt as if she had become the most important person in his life.

"So what's with the twenty questions to Sheena?" Mary asked Jill. "We all know what happened to Edith. I saw her here late Saturday morning, and she was happy and chattering a blue streak to Noelle. If you're trying to say someone upset her enough to cause her to have that heart attack—"

"I'm not," Jill said.

"Then why are you grilling Sheena?"

"Mom, it's okay. She's not—"

"The only other person I remember coming in that morning besides clients was Fawn Morrison," Mary said. "No one caused any problems. Don't go stirring things up or pointing fingers where they shouldn't be pointed."

Jill pressed her tongue to her teeth for a few seconds to keep from snapping back. "I'm not pointing fingers. Fawn was here?"

"She came to talk to me," Sheena said. "She and I hang out sometimes. You know, when you're single in a town like this, you won't find a lot of single girlfriends your age. All my high-school friends moved on."

"At least you have the good sense to stay where you belong," Mary said.

Sheena grimaced. "Fawn's smart for a kid, and I'm trying to talk her into going to cosmetology school like I did. Then she can learn massage while she works as a hair stylist. She's already really good at it."

"So unless you think Fawn might have had something to do with Edith's *heart attack*," Mary said with emphasis, "you're probably wasting your time here. I know you loved Edith. We all did. But the only closure you're going to find is at the funeral this afternoon, just like the rest of us."

"Has your husband said anything about why Austin Barlow's back in town?" Jill asked Mary.

The woman frowned. "Not a word. I put an end to their good-old-boy carousing years ago, Jill. They don't come around the house, and Jed knows how I feel about them.

He wouldn't tell me if he did know." She gave a quiet sigh, glancing at her daughter.

With that glance, Jill was touched by the wealth of tenderness she saw pass between mother and daughter.

Disappointed, she thanked Sheena and Mary and left the spa. If Mary did know something, she wouldn't give it away.

Jill thought about the visitors who had been at the spa the day of Edith's death.

What was it Edith had said? S...cool. And something about a jet bomber—what on earth could she have been talking about?

By that time, of course, considering the difficulty Edith was having, she might simply have been hallucinating due to lack of oxygen in the brain.

However, she did mention records. And possibly instead of saying *cool,* she might have been talking about *school.* Interestingly enough, almost all the visitors Sheena had mentioned were somehow connected to school, and had known Edith there. Maybe that was why she'd mentioned school to begin with. Could be she was simply reminiscing.

She might have seen Austin and Junior, and the sight of them had brought back memories. Just as the sight of Rex and Austin on Saturday had brought back memories for Jill.

She hadn't expected to search out Edith's nemesis in one little interview, but she'd hoped to find some kind of evidence that pointed to what had really happened to Edith the day she died.

So far, no such evidence. Would Austin, Jed or Junior be

more forthcoming? Or would she just make herself look like more of a fool if she approached them with questions?

The lab tests she'd had run on Edith's blood had turned up nothing. Grilling Sheena had turned up nothing. And yet, Jill knew she couldn't just leave things as they were. Her instincts—and Noelle's—compelled her to keep searching for an answer.

Chapter Eight

❧

After Edith's funeral on Wednesday, Fawn Morrison practically ran from the cemetery, desperate to escape the heavy shadow of grieving that seemed to loom over the whole town. This past year, sharing a cottage on Lakeside Bed and Breakfast property with Karah Lee, she'd come to love both Edith and Bertie as if they were her own grandmothers.

She missed Edith already. She knew Bertie did, too. And yet, wasn't Bertie the one who always reminded everybody that it did no good to linger on the sad memories?

Fawn had a plan forming in her mind by the time she reached the boat dock. It was crazy, she knew. But still she couldn't stop thinking....

"Hijacking my boat?" came Blaze Farmer's familiar voice from behind her.

She had one foot in the canoe and one on the dock in what Bertie would call an unladylike pose, considering the dress she wore. If she lost her grip on the post, she would tip the canoe and hit the water.

"I wouldn't say *hijacking,* exactly. I figured you'd show up sooner or later, and I needed to talk to you."

She settled carefully into the front and glanced up at Blaze. He, too, was dressed for the funeral, and he really cleaned up good—a term Bertie liked to use. He wore a gray suit that set off his black skin and those pretty, dark eyes…which looked as if he'd been crying.

She gestured to the other seat. "Come on. Let's get out of here for a while. I'll even let you steer."

He glanced back toward the town square, then to the church where they had just said goodbye to Edith's body for the last time. "I've got things to do at the ranch."

"You've always got things to do." She picked up a paddle. "Just a few minutes, okay? Come on, Blaze. You never get a break, and we both need one. I promise not to keep you long. I need somebody to talk to, and I don't want to bug Karah Lee right now. She's freaking about all this."

"You think I ain't?"

"Watch your language. Nobody's going to believe you've got the top scores in your class if you talk like that."

He sank to the narrow seat of the canoe and unwrapped the rope from the post on the dock.

Fawn knew everyone dealt with grief a different way. She stuffed everything deep down, as if she could hide it from herself for good if she could ignore it long enough. Blaze was one of those people who immersed themselves in the moment and got it all out of their systems.

But then, Blaze had grown up with a dad who loved him. His mom had her own problems and hadn't ever been there for Blaze, but he and his dad had had a good relationship when his dad was alive. His dad had tried hard to be both father and mother to his only child.

Fawn had never experienced that. Instead, she'd had a father who'd run out on the family, a mother who'd married a lecher—Bertie's word for him—then blamed her own daughter for being raped. Stuffing emotions away was the only way to survive where Fawn came from. She'd stuffed a lot since Great-Grandma June had died.

Fawn paddled slowly as Blaze guided them across the lake toward the far shore. There, five newly built houses with Victorian gingerbread trim nestled into the side of the cliff, surrounded by gold, bronze and yellow mums and hundred-year-old oaks and cedars. Blaze, Fawn knew, loved to paddle past those houses and dream about having a house like that himself, someday.

In Fawn's opinion, Blaze deserved a mansion five times larger than any of those houses.

"Did you see Austin Barlow at the funeral?" she asked.

Blaze stopped paddling. "You know him?"

"I met him Saturday. He came into the bed and breakfast to apologize to Bertie just before Jill and Noelle came with the news about Edith."

"You talked to him?"

"He was looking for a place to stay for a couple of weeks.

He said he came to apologize to Bertie for things he did. I asked him if he was going to apologize to you."

She could tell by the sudden, alarming shift in the canoe that Blaze had leaned forward, and she wished she'd been facing him in the boat so she could see his expression.

"You didn't."

"Sure I did." She placed her paddle across the sides of the canoe and carefully raised a leg to turn around, glad her skirt was full. "He treated you like trash—you told me so yourself. And all the time his own son was doing the things he blamed you for."

"I figure he's paying enough already, having his only kid locked away. If you aren't careful, you're going to dump us both in the lake."

"Ramsay's not locked away. He's in a boys' ranch up in northern Missouri." She swung the other leg around and managed to do it gracefully enough that Blaze's eyes didn't pop out of his head, and she didn't plunge them both into the water.

Blaze frowned at her, his thick black eyebrows nearly meeting in the middle over dark eyes. "You eavesdropping again?"

"Not completely. I talked to Austin Barlow myself." She picked up her paddle.

"Not completely?"

"I was stuck, Blaze. He started talking to Bertie before he knew I was behind the counter, and when he started telling her all the juicy stuff, I couldn't bring myself to—"

"Yeah, I know. You eavesdropped. That's not—"

"*Anyway,*" she said with a hard glare at him, "he said he

came back to town to make up for some of the things he did and said when he was here."

"Could be he's had a change of heart in the past couple of years. It happens, you know. People change." There was a catch in his voice as he stared back across the lake toward the bed and breakfast.

Fawn knew he was still grieving over Edith. He'd be this way for days, maybe even weeks. He was just like this when Pearl Cooper was killed in that sawmill accident last year, and he hadn't even known her well.

Aside from that flaw, though, she didn't know a better man. At eighteen years of age—a few months older than she—Blaze wasn't a kid anymore; he was as mature as most adults she knew.

He kept so busy, she didn't know how he even found time to breathe. She was busy, too, but as Bertie would say, a body had to take some time to just sit every once in a while, or what was the use of living?

"Maybe he's come back here to live," Blaze said. "He owns a house in town, and he's been renting it out. Maybe he's decided to pick up where he left off before the mess with Ramsay."

"But why come back here?" Fawn asked. "Everybody knows about Ramsay here. Why not go where no one knows his past?"

Blaze shrugged. "It's home. Austin was born and raised here. Maybe he's just decided to come back home."

"How do you feel about that?"

"It's not for me to say what he does."

"I didn't ask you to say, I asked how you *felt*."

He picked up his paddle and started to steer the canoe again. "Stop 'shrinking' and stick to wedding plans, or Karah Lee's going to send you back where you came from."

"Where are you taking us?" she asked.

"I've got chores at the ranch. I'm taking you back to the dock."

She sighed and stuck her paddle in the water again. "I can help with chores."

"You told Bertie you'd help feed the family. Don't let her down."

"I know I told her that, but all the ladies from the church are coming over. There won't be room for me."

"She'll want you there," Blaze said. "She's hurtin' enough right now."

Fawn sighed. Good old Blaze, always thinking of his own responsibilities…and hers. "Okay, fine. Dump me at the dock." She gave him a dark stare. "I guess when you're a man in demand, you don't have a lot of time to spend with old friends."

He chuckled. "You don't, either. You're as bad as I am, what with the wedding to plan, and you'll probably be needed more at the bed and breakfast now that Edith's not there to help Bertie. And you know, you do still have school work to keep up with."

"And after the wedding, I might be looking for a new place to stay."

"Why would that be?"

"No newlywed couple wants to start their married life with a teenaged kid in the house."

"That what you needed to talk about?"

"Part of it." She just wasn't sure she wanted to talk about anything more right now. Blaze was in too much of a rush.

His movements slowed. "You really worried about what's going to happen to you after the wedding?"

"I guess so."

"Well, don't. You know Karah Lee and Taylor better than that. They're good folks. They're not going to dump you out in the cold."

She gave a one-shoulder shrug. She'd been dumped out in the cold before.

"Karah Lee's nothing like your mother," Blaze said, reading her mind. "And Taylor'd be mortified if he knew you were comparing him to your wicked stepfather."

"Eeww."

"Sorry. You just don't have anything to worry about. I thought you and Karah Lee were both all set to move into that house Taylor bought up on the hill near Jill's place."

She paddled in silence as they drew near to the dock once more. "Yeah, well, I've been doing some thinking, too, and I just don't think it'll work. I may have other options, though."

"What other options?" He maneuvered the canoe against the dock and reached out to steady her.

She took his hand and climbed out, managing to retain some dignity as she did so. "I'm still thinking on it. Better get to your chores."

Chapter Nine

Rex stood at the edge of the cemetery as the crowd slowly dispersed. Funerals had high attendance here in the rural areas, and folks lingered after the interment, as if their lingering might set the memories of their loved one more completely in their hearts.

There was going to be a special evening meal back at the bed and breakfast, hosted by the women from Edith's church. Half the town would probably be there, maybe more. Last night, during the visitation at the funeral home, the line of people paying their respects had filled the building and spilled out onto the front lawn.

It had been a beautiful testament to the love this town held for the former high-school principal.

Now, watching the crowd mingle in conversation groups among the tombstones, Rex saw one lone figure separate from the rest. Jill.

During the funeral, she had remained detached from Edith's family, sitting with her sister and brother-in-law, Noelle and Nathan Trask. Edith's extended family had filled the front half of the small church, and other mourners had overflowed the little sanctuary.

Surprising himself, Rex strolled toward that lonely looking figure in the dark gray dress. Her brown hair had been pulled back into a knot at the nape of her neck, though some strands had refused to behave and fell in tendrils to her shoulders. Her eyes, devoid of makeup, were red-rimmed, her nose pinched.

He hadn't seen her since the afternoon of Edith's death; the tragedy had thrown the clinic—indeed, the whole town—into turmoil, and Jill wasn't working at the clinic this week.

As he studied that grieving face, he remembered how beautiful Jill had always been to him. She had a mouth that was slightly wide for a classic beauty, but could spill into a smile that could dazzle the sun. Her blue eyes, often sober and serious, could suddenly soften with warmth.

She had walked to within ten feet of him before she looked up and saw him. He could see the conflict in her expression. She was too close to turn away and avoid him without being obvious about it, but she just as clearly didn't want to talk to him right now. He could tell her emotions were too close to the surface.

"Jill," he said quietly, "I'm not going to bite, and I don't want to make things difficult for you."

Her eyes darted up in a quick glance at him, then away again. "I'm just embarrassed, is all. I was rude to you the other day, and I apologize."

"You've done nothing wrong, and I wasn't offended. It was a horrible time for you."

"Thank you, but I'm still sorry. You must have thought I was still upset with you after all this time, which would be childish."

"Edith's death struck you a nasty blow. It was a blow for everyone, but I know how much she meant to you."

Another glance shot his way, this time a little longer. She was feeling awkward, he could tell.

"Did Cheyenne tell you why I came to Hideaway?" he asked.

She nodded, glancing back toward the crowd around the grave. "After I jumped her about it. Karah Lee said you didn't want me to know you were here until you had a chance to talk to me."

"That's right."

"Well? I didn't get a call from you, and you didn't come to my house."

"I'd intended to speak with you over the weekend."

She spread her hands. "Well, now you've spoken to me. I don't see why you're trying to make such a big deal out of it. We had a broken engagement half a lifetime ago. We're adults. We can behave like it, right?"

"I never completely forgave myself for my behavior at that time. I was a jerk."

She rolled her eyes. "Okay, so we were both jerks back

then. Now can we get to work on the hospital designations and stop rehashing ancient history?"

He felt the sting of her words. He felt foolish again. "An excellent idea."

She stepped past him toward the far edge of the cemetery.

He caught up and fell into step beside her. "I hear you never got married."

She frowned. "And I hear you got a divorce. We're still rehashing, here."

Obviously, she wasn't quite as ill at ease around him as he'd imagined her to be. "I don't recall relaying the information to anyone here about my divorce."

"Since when do you have to tell anyone? We have a deputy in town who makes it his business to check people out online. Tom's never mastered the skill of keeping a secret. I guess that's why you decided to come to Hideaway?"

He blinked at her, not quite sure what she meant. Jill had apparently retained that special ability to throw a conversation off center with a simple statement or question. "Excuse me?"

"You know, *Hideaway?* As in, people come here to hide away, either from past tragedy or from danger."

"Aren't you being a little melodramatic?"

She slanted a glance at him. "You were the one making a big production out of coming here, and *you're* calling *me* melodramatic?"

"You're absolutely right." He would lose this argument if he continued it. "So this place really is a hideaway. I never knew that before. Tell me about it."

She watched him for a moment, as if trying to determine

if he was patronizing her, then she relented. "For instance, Cheyenne came here initially because of the tragedy of pronouncing her sister dead after an automobile accident. Karah Lee came here to escape her father's political manipulation—he was a state senator before his murder this spring. Willow Traynor—who will someday become Mrs. Graham Vaughn, even though she doesn't seem to realize it yet—came to escape a killer who stalked her from Kansas City. You don't know them yet, but you'll probably meet them."

"What about you?" he asked.

"This is my hometown."

"Last I heard, you were living and working in Springfield."

Her steps slowed as they drew near the city square—a cluster of old brick buildings that faced outward to an encircling street. He had always thought this was one of the most beautiful little towns in Missouri.

That could be a simple reflection of the beauty of Table Rock Lake, which surrounded Hideaway peninsula, on which the town had been built. Or it could be that he'd always felt this way because of the company he'd kept.

Far too long ago, he'd forgotten how to appreciate true beauty. He glanced at Jill. Inner beauty.

"That was a long time ago," Jill said. "I was needed here at home."

"Noelle needed you?"

Jill shook her head. "The sawmill needed me."

"The sawmill? But you have scads of extended family members to run that."

"Had. Past tense. My father, grandparents and others ran

it until…" She swallowed and glanced back toward the cemetery briefly. "There was a horrible…incident in which my father and grandparents were crushed to death by a load of logs eleven years ago."

He felt a chill at her words. He could see how the memory affected her even after all these years. "I'm sorry. I didn't know."

"Why would you? It isn't as if we kept up with each other's lives. Anyway, my cousin and I had to take over."

"So once again you gave up your own dream in deference to your family?"

She glanced up at him. "You make it sound as if that's a bad thing."

"Giving up your dream for someone else's?"

"I was needed. Having loved ones who need you isn't such a bad thing. Besides, I got a job here in town as the school nurse."

"And how about Noelle? Did she ever have to give up her dreams and career and join the family business?"

He heard the censure in his own voice a fraction of a second before annoyance registered in Jill's expression.

Suddenly, this was not boding well for a comfortable reunion. Maybe they did need to rehash ancient history. Or maybe that history wasn't so ancient.

Jill felt the prickle of antagonism make a flying leap up her scalp. "You already apologized for being a jerk, Rex. Why do I get the feeling you didn't really mean it?"

"Sorry. I didn't realize I was going to say that."

"You didn't *realize* it? My little sister lost her mom before she was old enough to understand the meaning of death."

"You lost your mother, too."

"I was eight years older than Noelle. She got stuck with me—a bully of an older sister and a very poor substitute for a set of parents—because, in truth, our father pretty much abandoned us emotionally from that point on."

"You never told me that."

"I was ashamed to admit it even to myself at the time."

"I'm sorry, I shouldn't have—"

"No, you shouldn't have, but you did." She paused beneath a willow tree, arms crossed. "I've got a good rant going and I want to finish it for once. I realize you always resented Noelle because her need for love interfered in our relationship—"

"You're right, and I was very wrong—"

"But in truth, for her sake, I should never have gone away."

"I'm sorry, I can't agree with that. You're saying you should never have become a nurse?"

Jill hesitated. "I left home too soon. She wasn't ready to be abandoned by the person she needed the most. I could have put nursing school on hold for a couple of more years."

"And yet, you'd already put your life on hold for three years after graduating from high school, watching all your friends go away to college."

"I went to college." She could hear the defensiveness in her own voice.

"You drove to School of the Ozarks at Point Lookout for classes, then back home at night to be with Noelle."

"I got the preliminaries out of the way." He was still itching for a fight, was he? She could give him one. Strangely, though, she didn't really want one. Not with him. "Not everyone has to leave home as soon as they graduate high school."

"You're trying to tell me you were the only person who could take care of Noelle? At that time you did have extended family."

Jill wasn't prepared to explain to him about the concern she'd had for Noelle's safety at that time in their lives. *Would Noelle still even be alive if I hadn't been so obsessed for her welfare? That was a time when my OCD came in handy, hard as it's always been.*

"You made that sacrifice because of your unique ability to love," Rex said, as if he'd read something of her thoughts in her expression—much as he used to do. "Few people I know have that ability."

The sudden gentleness in his tone undercut her momentum. She paused and looked at him, and felt an unwanted pang of regret.

What if they hadn't broken the engagement?

Chapter Ten

Fawn was halfway between the dock and the street when she saw a familiar head of blond hair poking up over the railing of the pastel-blue gazebo. The tiny structure was surrounded by a riot of red and yellow flowers held in place by a bricked flower bed. It was Fawn's favorite gazebo.

She stepped to the small, round picnic shelter and paused. "Sheena?"

The woman raised her head and peered over the railing.

"How're you doing?" Fawn asked. Sheena looked as if she hadn't slept much. She had such a sensitive nature, and events like Edith's death and the awful experience Saturday would have left her upset for days. Kind of like Blaze, Fawn guessed.

Sheena shook her head. "I couldn't go, you know."

"To the funeral? I know. I didn't see you there. Your parents were there, though, and it was a packed house."

Sheena nodded, her gaze returning to the surface of the lake, where a flock of wild geese came in for a noisy landing.

Fawn stepped up into the gazebo and sat down next to her friend on the wooden bench. "Hey, are you okay?"

Sheena hugged herself, still staring out across the lake, the water now momentarily gray under the shadow of a passing thunderhead. A fitting day for a funeral, Fawn thought.

"How'd you do it?" Sheena asked, still staring at the lake. "You seem to…I don't know…handle things so well. I mean, I know what you went through." She didn't look at Fawn, but shuddered. "Your mom disowned you, and yet you're happy."

"Sure I am." Fawn gestured around them. "Look at this great town we live in. And Karah Lee and Bertie practically smother me with love. Even Taylor treats me like a favorite niece." Though she wondered how long that would last after the wedding. Sure, Taylor was a good guy and all that, but still…

"You're not bitter." Sheena did look at her then, lowering her voice, though no one could hear them. "I heard you were…that your stepfather…"

Fawn sighed. Even though she was making peace with her past, she still had trouble talking about it sometimes. "Raped me?"

"Yes. That's just so horrible."

"But it isn't something that's happening now. You can live with a lot of things when you can convince yourself it's over. It isn't like I'm going to crumble."

"But your own stepfather," Sheena said, her voice barely above a whisper.

"My mother could really pick 'em."

"And then when you ran away to Las Vegas, you had to…you know…support yourself by…" Sheena's face flushed.

"Man, oh, man, a girl can't keep anything a secret around here," Fawn said.

"You mean you really did that?"

"I was a hooker. Yeah." Fawn ignored the shocked expression on her friend's face. People freaked way too easily about some stuff. "It isn't like I'm one now, you know."

"Uh, no. Of course not."

"I was starving on the street, and I didn't have anywhere to go, so I figured if somebody was going to take advantage of my body, I might as well make a living with it."

"What was it like?"

"You don't want to know. It was like the worst nightmare a person could have."

Sheena stared at the lake in silence for another moment, then glanced toward Fawn again. "Do you still think about it?"

"Sometimes."

"Is it still horrible?"

"Once in a while I wake up screaming at night. When that happens, Karah Lee sets up a cot in my room and sleeps near me."

Sheena stared at her, eyes filled with sympathy. "How do you stand it?"

"I've got help. I know I'm loved, and I make sure to fill my mind with things in the present and the future, not things from the past. If I focus on the good things and re-member the Bible verse Bertie likes to quote to me, then I can do okay."

"What verse?"

"It's from Philippians. The part that talks about how we should focus on whatever things are true, honest, pure, lovely and of good report. That means if you try *not* to think about ugly stuff, it doesn't work. So I have to keep my mind filled with good things, and there'll be no room to think about the bad."

Sheena nodded gravely. "That's sensible. I like that. So you can change the direction of your life if you just focus on the right things and forget about the rest?"

Fawn frowned. "Well, yeah. I guess. Except, I can't do it on my own. If I didn't have Someone to pray to, then I couldn't escape my past. I had to get to the point where I felt so badly about my past that I was ready to give it all to Jesus. He took it, and now when I try to take a dip back into the cesspool of my past, I just give it back to Jesus. He al-ways takes it."

"You make it sound so easy," Sheena said.

"It isn't. Not always. But the Bible's full of good common-sense directions about cutting through the bad stuff. Of course, it's also full of other stuff that I can't even begin to understand."

"The Bible's always been so confusing when I tried to read it," Sheena said.

"I think it takes time to learn everything. Especially for someone like me. I've got so many things going on at once that I can't always focus like I should."

Again, Sheena transferred her attention to the lake, as if it were a refuge for her mind.

"Sheena, have you ever been...you know...taken advantage of?"

The question obviously startled Sheena, and she looked back at Fawn. "No, not me. I don't know what I'd do if that happened to me. My parents are kind of overprotective."

Fawn didn't bother to comment about that understatement. She didn't feel they'd done Sheena any favors.

"I know someone who was raped once, though," Sheena said softly.

"Somebody from here? Right here in Hideaway?"

Sheena nodded. "She never got over it. That one incident changed her whole life."

"It doesn't have to. If you want, I could talk to her about it. Let her know there's more to life than brooding about something she can't do anything about."

Sheena thought about it for a minute. "She wouldn't talk to you about it, but maybe if I could tell her that verse you quoted? Would you write it down for me?"

"If you have a Bible, I'll write down where to find it and you can look it up."

Sheena's expression went blank, and Fawn realized that Sheena probably wouldn't know where to find Philippians. If not for Bertie and Karah Lee harping at Fawn to read her Bible this past year, she wouldn't know, either.

Fawn pulled out her small scratch pad, in which she

kept her lists for the wedding plans and computer pro-
grams for the bed and breakfast. She wrote the words she
had quoted. It was a rough draft, but the message was there.

What did people do who didn't know about the love
Jesus had for them? What would *she* have done last year—
what would she be doing now—if someone hadn't taken her
in and told her about the comfort and love and goodness
that could fill her life?

She would probably still be filled with anger and resentment—even hatred for those people who had hurt her. And
that hatred could have cut her off from the very God who
now gave her peace.

What a horrible way some people lived. If only they
knew what she knew.

Jill walked in silence beside Rex for about half a block.
The warmth of the day was eased, somewhat, by the thunderhead that seemed to hover overhead. Blue sky surrounded the clouds, but for the moment the sun's light was
shielded from them. She was glad. Summer's oppressive
heat could often creep deeply into September, and sometimes even October.

She glanced again at Rex's profile. Her initial attraction
over two decades ago had not been to Rex Fairfield's appearance, but to his intensity, his passion for treating patients
as human beings and not ailing body parts.

He had also been kind to nurses, aides, janitors, secre-
taries, clerks. He'd been kind to her. In a world where Jill
had seen a few residents and attendings behave as if they
were divinities, Rex had been a refreshing exception.

Now she really looked at him. His forehead was a smidgen higher than it had been when she knew him, his dark hair now salted with gray. His short, trim beard and mustache—a new feature since she'd last seen him—were salted a little more liberally than his hair. He still had those kind gray eyes, with quite a few more lines around them to add character.

Okay, so he was good-looking. But the most prominent characteristic that had attracted her to him then had been patience. He'd always taken the time for explanations to patients, to families and caretakers. He'd been patient with Jill's mistakes when she was the newest student nurse in the hospital.

Rex had always been the embodiment of patience when their friendship was first deepening into something more. That hadn't changed until after their engagement. When they were first engaged, she'd loved being the object of his adoration. Later, it became too confining, especially after their conflicts about her obligations at home.

"My sister was who she was, Rex," she said at last, this time more softly, realizing that she still found herself very attracted to this man who had suddenly reappeared in her life. "She made wrong decisions about her life because she didn't have someone wiser to help her with those decisions. Had I been more available, maybe she would have made better choices."

"You can't blame yourself—"

"You don't know what I can and cannot do." She was sharper now. He still had the ability to disturb her thoughts.

"You're right," he muttered. "What I meant to say was that

if you have a brain in your head, you'll know better than to blame yourself for the circumstances in your life at that time."

She blinked at him in surprise. "This is something new with you. When we were engaged, you weren't good about saying what you thought until everything built up and exploded." She remembered a couple of heated arguments. "If only we had known how to fight without being destructive."

"You're right, of course. I've found that counseling really does change things," he said. "That, and the motivation I felt to prevent a family from splattering against the rocks."

She heard the desolation in his voice. Obviously, that family had splattered. "I didn't know you had children."

"Two stepsons. I don't think I could love them any more if they were my own flesh and blood."

"Do you see them?"

He was silent for a moment, and she realized she had invaded a painful space. "Right now we're talking about your family situation," he said.

"Oh, so it's okay to expose my failings to the light of day, but not yours?"

His eyes crinkled at the corners when he smiled, more deeply than they used to. "Did I say you had failings? If I even implied that, I'm sorry. That wasn't what I was trying to do. Of course, you're perfect."

"Thank you. I'm glad we agree about that."

His smile widened into a grin. Jill had always loved that grin.

But he sobered all too soon. "I don't get to see my stepsons as much as I would like, and I think they would like to see me more, as well. But since I'm only the stepfather, I don't have much choice about it."

"That's got to be painful."

"It is."

"Was the divorce bitter?" she asked.

"I tried to make sure it was as amicable as possible for the sake of the boys."

"What's your ex-wife's name?"

"Margret. Spelled the way Ann Margret spells her name."

"Did she try to be amicable?"

He walked for a few seconds in silence, and she remembered his motto about speaking gently about someone, or not speaking at all.

"I see. I'm sorry," she said.

"Thank you." This time she could tell the smile was forced. "Now it's your turn. We were talking about your family situation."

She narrowed her eyes at him. "Is this a trade-off?"

"It most certainly is." He grinned and spread his hands. "See? I did learn something from the counseling sessions."

The lane grew steeper, and her steps slowed. "Our family has had a lot of tragedies in the past years. We're still reeling from some of the aftershock."

"Noelle seems like a well-adjusted adult."

"She's happily married, stable and mature, but I will always be there for her. That will never change, and I'll never apologize for it."

"I don't think you should ever apologize for caring for someone. Too many people lack the capability to care for anyone but themselves."

"You say that as if you're talking about someone in particular," she said.

It was his turn to scowl at her.

"If our mother had lived, she would have been there for Noelle," Jill said. "But she wasn't. I had no choice, and wouldn't have done it differently had I been given the choice."

He shoved his hands into his pockets and kicked at a pebble in front of his right foot. "What I've been trying to say, and doing a very poor job of it, is that I'm sorry I resented Noelle. It's become obvious, since my divorce, that I don't have the ability I once thought I did to communicate my thoughts clearly." He sounded irritable, as if a sore spot had been jabbed too deeply.

"It sounds as if you still resent your ex-wife."

"I think *resent* is too strong a word. I'm still frustrated by her. I'm trying not to blame her for our breakup. A divorce is almost always the result of the actions of two imperfect people, not just one."

"Just like us," Jill said. "Both of us were at fault."

"In that situation I do blame myself more, because I didn't communicate my thoughts as well as I should have. I have no excuse except that I was so involved in pursuing my career that I allowed my interpersonal relationship skills to slide."

"You sound like you've been reading too many books about relationships."

"I know, but it's better than never trying to figure out what went wrong," he said.

"You weren't the only one who made the decision."

"So, we were both immature."

She knew he was right.

"I've worked hard to break some old habits, Jill. All of us have ingrained ways of dealing with situations that could probably be improved. You included."

"You're saying I need counseling?"

Back came the smile, tentative this time, as if concerned about her response. "I'm concerned that you will, out of a desire to help your family, lose out on the opportunities for happiness in your own life. That's all I'm saying."

"And I'm saying you still don't understand. I think perhaps we did the best thing when we broke the engagement. You obviously still don't grasp the concept of—"

"You're wrong." He said it softly. "Had we worked through our problems then, I believe we could have had an amazing marriage."

Jill stopped breathing for a few seconds. How could she respond to a statement like that? Was he saying he wished they had gotten married?

It would be too easy to dwell on twenty-two years of might-have-beens. That would just be painful. How would her life have been different had he been by her side? Or, if they had married, would her decision to return to Hideaway and protect Noelle have destroyed their marriage, as well?

She glanced at him as they walked, and couldn't help feeling he would have understood. Had he known everything that was going on in their lives, he would have been beside her, helping her with Noelle, with all the loss in her life.

He still had those shoulders that had once seemed to her to be able to carry the world, though now she had the impression that he had attempted that very thing and discovered he couldn't do it.

"I grasp it so much better than I ever did before," he said. "Your example of sacrifice kept me hopeful through some of the roughest times of my marriage." This time he stopped and turned to her. His gaze was direct, and there wasn't even a hint of a smile in his eyes now. "It helped to know that there was at least one person out there who knew how to give of herself with no expectation of reward."

She was touched. "You really mean that?"

"I wouldn't say it if I—"

"I know. You always meant what you said."

"But now, as you've pointed out, Noelle is happy and settled. The tragedies will always be horrible memories for you, but they are in the past. You no longer need to make those same sacrifices over and over."

She shrugged and started walking again.

"I'm concerned," he went on, "that you will lose out on opportunities in your life because you give more of yourself than is necessary."

"Who's to say what's necessary?" she retorted. "I once sacrificed more than I felt was necessary, and in the end, it saved my sister's life."

His eyes widened. "Are you going to tell me about that?"

"It's a very long story. She was in danger, and I was there."

"Is that danger past?"

"Yes." She looked at him, then frowned. "I think." But she wasn't sure if it truly was past, or if it had just come disguised in a different set of circumstances this time.

He leaned toward her. "Jill, is something wrong? Is there some kind of trouble?"

She hesitated, sorry she'd said anything. He was, after all, working with her employer. She had already relied too much on the sheriff and Tom. "No. Edith's death has just shaken my sense of security. I have a tendency to be paranoid about safety. It's a habit I developed years ago, and I'm not likely to change."

She knew he wouldn't betray any of her confidences, but too many people already questioned her veracity.

He reached out and touched her shoulder, urging her to stop again. "What if you have a compulsion to sacrifice for others? That isn't healthy for you or your loved ones."

Jill caught her breath at those words. "I can't believe you just said that."

He closed his eyes for a second. "Neither can I, but I've said it before."

"You were wrong before." Disappointment seeped through her. He was no different from the rest. He thought she was nuts.

His hand tightened on her shoulder. "Jill, I wasn't completely wrong. You don't have to lose your whole self in the lives of others to the point that you have no life of your own."

She pulled away. "You don't know anything about the situation."

"Then maybe we could talk about it. What about that long story? What danger are you talking about? Is there something still going on?"

She hesitated again, fighting the temptation to confide.

But what would she say? That she suspected a problem with Edith's death? That Noelle, who had also suspected a problem, might place herself in trouble once she thought about it a little longer?

Besides, he would think it was her OCD talking. "How can you believe you still know me after all these years?" she asked.

"I know OCD doesn't just disappear. I'm not going to ignore the facts for the sake of politeness."

"*Politeness?* Well, far be it from me to accuse you of being polite. How can you come dashing into town and accuse me of—"

"Jill—"

"It's a rhetorical question. You've said enough, I think. If you were waiting at the cemetery just to harass me, then your job is done."

"Jill, I'm sorry. I'm not trying to—"

She raised a hand to silence him, then turned and stalked up the hill in the direction of her house, two blocks away. She knew there had been talk about her and Rex. She knew Blaze and Fawn and probably others had been hopeful about matchmaking.

The next person who tried to set her up with a man was going to get socked in the mouth.

Chapter Eleven

❦

Rex stood watching Jill's retreating figure, and felt a sharp stab of regret. Why had he forced the issue? It was the same subject about which they had argued so many times when they were engaged. Had he suddenly decided he might just win the argument after all this time? What a moron he had been!

There had been a few times that he'd wondered what his reaction would be if he ever came face-to-face with the woman he had once loved more than anyone else in the world. Well, he didn't have to wonder any longer. Some things didn't change, even after this much time. He still behaved like an idiot in her presence.

Yes, he'd loved Margret, and had made sure he would

have a good relationship with Jason and Tyler before he asked Margret to marry him. And he hadn't allowed himself to fantasize about any "might-have-beens" with Jill. He'd put his whole heart into the marriage.

But once that marriage was over, it had been so easy to make a comparison between Jill and Margret. Not fair, he knew. Still, the facts stood. Jill had sacrificed her life for others. Margret had always expected others to sacrifice for her.

He understood why. She had been a forgotten child from a broken family. Now, for her, love meant the object of her affection must dance completely to her tune. She'd needed that kind of love from him, and she apparently also needed it from her sons.

With a sigh of self-reproach, he turned and walked slowly back down the hill toward the Lakeside Bed and Breakfast. Maybe the church ladies would allow him to help serve in the kitchen. He knew he had things he needed to do at the clinic—checks and double-checks to make, reports to file—but he had the keys, and could go in anytime. Yes, it was better to work there when it was quiet, and today it would be, with most folks attending the memorial dinner for Edith. Still, he wasn't in the mood to work. There wasn't as much to do as he'd initially expected.

This day had a pall over it that far surpassed the cloud that was beginning to allow sunlight through once more. Possibly just seeing Jill again, being shot back in time, had given him this feeling of heaviness. He was still haunted by Edith's death. That dear lady. Everything had suddenly gone so wrong since he'd come here.

He stepped past a thickly flowered rose arbor and caught

a breathtaking view of the town square surrounded by the street, and a broad lawn on three sides that served as a border between the lake and the civic center. Dotted across that lawn, between the street and the community boat dock, were numerous gazebos in assorted pastel colors. The dock, the lawn and the gazebos were all new since he'd been here last.

He saw two blond women with their heads together in the shade of a blue gazebo. The woman with short hair had her arm around the woman with long hair, as if to comfort her. If he wasn't mistaken, the short-haired young woman was Karah Lee's foster daughter, Fawn. He'd seen her around the bed and breakfast, where he'd learned that Karah Lee was living for the time being.

The other woman looked like Sheena Marshall, from the spa. Both were most likely grieving Edith's death, like the rest of the town.

What a presence Edith Potts had been in Hideaway.

The September afternoon sun suddenly burst through the cloud cover and struck Jill like shots from a laser gun seeking its target through the thick overhang of trees on the street to her house. She wanted to hide herself in the protective shadows and hibernate for the rest of the year. Or for a lifetime.

Strains of the final solo that had been sung in Edith's honor continued to echo through her mind. "If You Could See Me Now." It had reminded her that Edith was now walking streets of gold. This melody would continue to haunt her until another one replaced it. She'd lived with music in her head for years, which grew louder when she was stressed.

Right now there was a complete brass band clanging around between her ears as she trudged up the incline of the hillside road.

Too many things...she couldn't deal with them all.

At Noelle's urging, Jill had returned to the full dose of her medication on Saturday night. Unfortunately, it took several days, and often weeks, for the effects of the drugs to become noticeable.

So she waited. And she grieved more profoundly than anyone around her could ever imagine. The grief itself became an obsession. Any distraction was welcome.

Rex's arrival was definitely a distraction. Even Austin's, though much less intrusive. After all, she and Austin had seen each other around town for years, especially during class reunions at the Hideaway festivals in September.

With that thought, she remembered the one coming up later this month. The one she was supposed to help plan. In fact, she had promised to take part in a pajama party in a cabin at Big Cedar with three women who had been her closest friends in high school. They were in charge of activities for their reunion.

She was already dreading it.

Jill had never been a great one for small talk, particularly when it became personal. Though she had kept in touch with Doris, Peggy and Sherry over the years—or rather, they had done a great job of keeping in touch with her—she couldn't help worrying that she would quickly run out of things to talk about with them Saturday night.

She hadn't exactly been a joiner in high school. Trying to be a full-time mom for Noelle had taken up most of her free hours. Her girlfriends had done their best to give her a social life. Apparently, the role they assumed in helping Jill had never changed.

She glanced back along the street. Rex was already out of sight around the curve with the rose arbor. She was methodically destroying any hope of a social life before it could even begin—and that wasn't her intention.

Not only had she asked Cheyenne about the possibility of an autopsy on Edith, but she had approached the sheriff about it, as well. Greg had been willing enough to suggest to the family that they could request an autopsy if they wished.

The family did not wish, In fact, they were adamantly opposed to the idea. Most likely half the town already knew that eccentric Jill Cooper was suggesting there might have been more nefarious deeds in Hideaway—another murder to add to Hideaway's growing list. She was bound to hear about it for months to come.

She was still trying to find a good excuse to miss the all-nighter Saturday when she pushed open the gate to her front yard.

She stopped at the edge of the flagstone walk that led to the porch of the sky-blue Victorian two-story with rose and navy trim. Something was wrong.

For a moment, she couldn't figure out what it was, but then she noticed that the sitting-room curtains had a gap between the panels.

She never left the curtains gapped. That was one compulsion she had never quite overcome, even with drugs and behavior modification. Maybe that particular quirk had nothing to do with a mental disorder and everything to do with a woman living alone.

She looked around the neighborhood. Many of her neighbors had been at the funeral, and she saw no one on the street.

She couldn't go inside. What if someone was still in there? Instead, she detoured around the side of the house and down the grassy embankment to the back. This old residential section of town was built into a hill, which offered a forever changing view of the lake that surrounded this peninsula.

She loved it here. Until this past year, she'd had no reason to feel concerned about living in this house—which she had inherited from her grandparents. Now even this sanctuary seemed to be a source of concern.

Everything looked okay, but then she checked the back storm door. It wasn't latched.

She always made sure the door was latched. Another entrenched habit. Someone had gone inside this morning. Family, maybe? Noelle had a key to the front door, but she would never have reason to leave this back door unlatched. Neither would their cousins, who understood her concerns from personal experience.

Nervous tension crawled up her arms. Someone had broken into her house.

She pulled her cell phone from her purse. It had been… what, two days since she'd called Greg about the autopsy?

She could imagine his reaction this time.

And yet, *she* wasn't the one doing it. She wasn't the one who intuitively knew there was something wrong about Edith's death. Noelle simply wasn't confident enough in her gift to make waves. But Jill knew Noelle was right. Not that anyone was willing to listen to either of them.

And *she* wasn't the one who left those curtains parted. This time she had good reason to call Greg. He would have to understand.

Chapter Twelve

The lobby and dining room of the Lakeside Bed and Breakfast was already filled with Edith's mourners when Fawn stepped through the door. She saw Bertie sitting alone in an alcove across the lobby from the curved front desk.

"You okay, Bertie?" she asked, stepping across the creaky wooden floor to join her.

For once, Bertie Meyer looked and acted her age. "I'm fine. But it seems like I've been going to a lot of funerals this past year. First Pearl Cooper, then Karah Lee's dad. Now…Edith." Her voice cracked. "Before that, my husband. Sometimes things just change too much for a gal to stay on her feet."

Fawn sank into the ornate Victorian love seat beside Bertie and wrapped an arm around her stooped shoulders.

"I don't know how many times I've heard somebody say she's better off in heaven now." Bertie sniffed and patted Fawn on the back, as if to comfort her. "And I know it's true, but what about the rest of us? What'll we do without her?"

"I don't know." But Fawn was thinking about an idea she'd had a couple of days ago. Would this be the right time to mention it?

Bertie disengaged the hug and looked up when another group of mourners came in through the front doors and crossed the lobby to the dining room, where the church ladies were gathered.

This alcove where Fawn and Bertie sat was a great place for a quiet conversation. Fawn loved to come here and sit with a book, or to do her homework. She could see everyone who came in, but she wasn't in the middle of everything, and the greenery with which Edith had decorated the entryway tended to redirect the attention of those just stepping into the lobby away from the alcove.

As she and Bertie sat in companionable silence, Austin Barlow came in through the front door, then hesitated, as if he were having second thoughts. Or perhaps he was unsure of his welcome. The door behind him opened again, and he was forced to cross the lobby with the incoming crowd. The dining room looked packed.

"It was worse when Red died, of course." Bertie blotted her face with a handkerchief, then blew her nose.

"Wish I'd known him."

"I wish you had, too." Bertie leaned back and folded her hands, a faint smile crossing her face. "That goat dairy of ours was a lot of work, but Red never complained."

"You did all the work yourselves?" Fawn knew the answer, but she knew Bertie loved to talk about the past, and about Red.

"Sure did. At least, until the ranch boys started helping out. We raised vegetables and served this community for more than sixty years."

Fawn tried not to be obvious about watching Austin at the entry to the dining area, but she couldn't help herself. He was, as Karah Lee would say, quite the schmoozer. As he shook hands and greeted people who were apparently old friends, his gaze darted around the room as though he were looking for someone in particular, someone he hadn't spotted yet.

"That Red was the most superstitious old cuss," Bertie said, distracting Fawn from her study of that strange man.

"Superstitious?"

"One time he cut down a cedar tree in Cheyenne's yard because he believed some old tale about it being bad luck."

Fawn chuckled obligingly. She'd heard that story before, too. "He was like a grandfather to the ranch boys."

Bertie nodded, glancing toward the dining room when talk and laughter swelled.

"You'd think they were at a party," Fawn grumbled.

"They are. A remembrance party. I've noticed, over the years, that it seems the more loved a body was by the community, the louder the party gets."

"Then I bet they had a wild party after Red's funeral." The front door opened again, and Jed and Mary Marshall stepped inside. Mary carried a casserole dish covered with a towel.

Fawn found it hard to believe that Jill and Mary were the same age. Though Mary had the same wide-set blue eyes and blond hair as her daughter Sheena, Mary's eyes looked too old, not enhanced by the typical laugh lines that usually added to an older woman's beauty and warmth.

Mary's mouth was set in a permanent frown. Any time Fawn saw her, she was frowning. She seemed to disapprove of everything and everyone. Poor Sheena. How had she learned to be so cheerful? Her father, Jed, never seemed to be that happy, either.

"I know Blaze loved him like a grandfather," Bertie said after a moment, and Fawn knew that Bertie was still in the past.

"Blaze still talks about him all the time."

"Guess I do, too, don't I?" Bertie patted Fawn's hand, then slapped her knees and started to get up. "Guess I should see to my guests."

"Oh, no, you don't." Fawn grabbed her by the arm. "You let the rest of us handle the dining room today. You aren't on duty. Tell me more about Red and Blaze. I heard Red was the one who taught Blaze how to train pigs to race."

Bertie chuckled, hesitated, then settled back. "That's a fact. I know Dane likes to think he taught Blaze everything he knows, but Blaze was always hanging around our house, helping Red with the milkin', picking his brain about things. I remember hearing Red tell Blaze one day, 'Kiddo, pigs is just like folks. They want what they want, and what they want is Oreo cookies. Long as they know they'll get what they want, they'll run for you.'"

Fawn rolled her eyes. "Blaze told me that a dozen times. I thought he was kidding."

"Worked for the pigs." Bertie sighed as the laughter quickly died from her eyes. She looked tired.

"You haven't eaten yet," Fawn said. "Why don't I fix you a plate?"

"The tables are all full in the dining room, I s'pose."

"We can sit right here. It won't hurt us to have food in here this once. I'll get us a tray."

Jill followed the sheriff's large bulk up the back steps of her house, her neck and shoulders screaming with tension. She'd endured this particular scene a couple of times within the past year.

Okay, three times.

Normally, she was not a timid person. Even though she lived alone, she didn't cry wolf unless she saw a long gray snout with fangs. She had never wanted to appear to be a needy single woman always asking for help.

However, it had been less than a year since the tragedy that had finally exposed the root cause of all the deaths in the Cooper clan. She was understandably on edge. It was unfortunate that Greg and Tom—the sheriff and his deputy—had encountered this edginess far too often.

Though they appeared to have listened with concern as she'd described her fears, she fully expected them to write her off as an hysteric, overreacting again. Chicken Little. Especially after the autopsy request.

She still wasn't sorry she'd asked. She trusted Noelle's instincts. Had the authorities conducted an autopsy on Edith, Jill had no doubt they'd have found something.

Too late now, however. The lab test had revealed nothing helpful.

She would probably have done the same thing, herself, if she was in Greg's place. Probably.

Still, in spite of her suspicions about the big man's opinion of her, she was grateful for his bulk in front of her as she followed him through the back door and up the stairs into the kitchen-dining area.

Tom, the deputy, had entered through the front door with her spare key, and met them in the kitchen-dining area, stalking in from the sitting room, gun drawn.

"Tom, would you put that thing away," Greg groused. "You're liable to shoot somebody with it, and I don't want that somebody to be you or me or the lady in distress."

Jill's teeth clenched at his words. Did he realize how patronizing he was being? Yes, she did have a few hang-ups, but did he think she was too dense to pick up on his doubts?

"Nothing and no one in the house now, boss," Tom said, holstering his shooter. "I've been upstairs and into every room. Definitely no signs of forced entry."

"That fast?" Jill asked. The officers had barely been here five minutes.

Tom nodded. "Done my share of searches. Whoever was here, they've already gone."

"Did you check the attic?" she asked.

"Sure did. Not a single sign of dust bunnies or cobwebs. Jill, you keep a clean house."

"Why don't we look around and see if you notice if anything's missing?" Greg suggested.

She went slowly through the house, flanked by the two men; Greg behind her, Tom in front. If she didn't know better, she'd have thought they were taking her seriously.

She stopped at the closet beneath the stairwell. "That door's ajar. It wasn't that way when I left today."

"Sorry," Tom said. "I'm bad about not closing doors behind me."

"Was it closed when you first saw it?" she asked.

He hesitated. "I'm sure it was."

"How sure?"

The two men made eye contact and said nothing.

Suppressing a sigh, she glanced inside the closet, turning on the light to reveal her filing cabinet, which held financial records for the past seven years. Most people around here knew she was one of the owners of Cooper Enterprises, which consisted of a busy sawmill operation and a cattle ranch of two thousand acres. Most people should also know she wasn't naive enough to leave valuables around the house.

Still, she went through the files to see if anything had been taken, feeling uncomfortable as the sheriff and deputy watched her every move. Did they feel she was wasting their time? She'd never been a people pleaser, but she didn't want to be considered an alarmist.

After completing a search of the files, she walked with the men back into the sitting room. "Nothing is missing as far as I can tell."

"Any idea who might have come in?" Tom asked.

She could hear the doubt in his voice. "If I'd known, I'd have told you." She also heard the irritation in her tone.

Stop it, Jill. It won't do to tick off the town's protection. Still, she couldn't dismiss the knowing glance she'd caught them sharing over her head.

"What about Noelle?" Tom asked. "Think she might've paid you a visit? That's been known to happen."

She cringed at his condescending tone. Yes, Noelle had used her key to come inside one day last spring to pick up some records for the bank and had neglected to tell Jill. Calling the sheriff about it hadn't exactly endeared her to Tom and Greg.

"I know, but Noelle hasn't had an opportunity today to come to the house since I left this morning. She's been at the funeral. Besides, she's learned her lesson. She always tells me when she's coming to get something."

"We'll look around the yard and ask the neighbors if they saw any suspicious cars around the area," Greg said.

"Most of them were at the funeral. Look, Greg, I know it isn't that obvious to you, but I remember exactly how this house looked when I left this morning to help set up for the funeral dinner. I never leave my curtains that way." She pointed to the heavy drapes in the sitting room window— thick enough that no light spilled out onto the porch at night when she read by the fireplace.

Greg removed his hat. "Now, Jill, do you think it's possible you could be just a little overwrought with all that's happened lately? I know I've been on edge, just waiting for something else to come down on us."

"I'm not being paranoid about this."

He lowered his brows and gave her an entreating look.

"Okay," she said, unable to keep herself from glancing behind the kitchen door, and studying the shadows beside the sitting-room sofa. "I could be a little jumpy, but you know how…particular I can be about some things. The way the drapes hang is one of them."

Again, a knowing look passed between the men. *Fine.* What made her think she could expect anything else?

Greg turned to her then, his manner fatherly and gentle, although he was four years younger than she. And there was a slight hint of reproach in his expression.

"Look, I know Edith's death has you upset. You two were always close."

"I'm still not convinced her death was from natural causes."

"So you're upset because we didn't ask for an autopsy?" Tom asked.

"I'm not upset," she snapped. Since they didn't share her opinion that an autopsy was indicated, they obviously thought she was pressing the point. Did they think she was making all this up just to convince them there was danger afoot?

Greg held her gaze for a few seconds, then glanced away.

"I see. You think this is all in my head." Often in her life, Jill had felt isolated from the rest of the world. Why wasn't she accustomed to that feeling by now?

"It's going to be okay, Jill," Greg said, still placating her. He placed a beefy hand on her shoulder. For him, it wasn't an intrusive or intimate gesture, just typically friendly and kind. "Give yourself some time to recover, okay? Tom and I aren't so busy most days that we won't come if you need us to."

Even as she wanted to be comforted by the kindness of his voice, she felt as if she were being cut adrift. He wasn't taking her seriously. Nothing worse than she had expected, but still, it stung. She silently prayed she wouldn't need to depend on Greg and Tom for anything else.

Chapter Thirteen

❧

The noise level had increased in the dining room of the bed and breakfast, if that were possible. Fawn saw Edith's nieces and nephews and great-nieces and great-nephews clustered around the tables out on the deck that overlooked the lake. One of the men, a chubby guy with black hair, who had spoken at the funeral about his aunt, departed from the lodge alone.

The rest of the family stayed on the deck. Fawn didn't blame them. The shady deck on a pretty day was a lot better than sitting in a crowded dining room with a bunch of noisy strangers. Edith's relatives weren't from around Hideaway.

Back when Fawn was a newcomer, she'd tried to avoid

the strangers, as well. Bertie and Edith had put an end to that in a hurry. With their help and Karah Lee's encouragement, Fawn had quickly made friends. She'd discovered that quite a few of the church people—and most of the people in this town were church people—welcomed her. They wouldn't let her get away with much, but most of them eventually accepted her as one of them.

Nothing like she'd expected church people to behave. She'd gone to church once, in Vegas, just to please a guy she was seeing. Apparently, she hadn't worn the right clothes. How was she supposed to know how to dress? When she'd walked into the sanctuary of the church in a short skirt and camisole, an older, well-dressed woman looked as if she were about to lose her eyeballs. The guy Fawn attended with never asked her out again. The poor guy might have fainted if he'd known her profession at the time.

When Fawn was growing up, she'd only attended church when her Great-Grandma June took her, and that wasn't often, because Mom complained about Granny June "filling Fawn's head with all that Jesus garbage."

So Fawn had decided long ago that she didn't belong inside a church building.

Now, thanks to the Hideaway grapevine, most everybody in town knew her background. Sometimes she felt as if she had twenty mothers and ten grandmothers—*interfering mothers and grandmothers*. She suspected Bertie and Edith had used their influence with the locals to get her accepted. They'd certainly used all their influence with Karah Lee to get Fawn to their church for the first time.

She grinned at the ladies standing around the buffet table,

just waiting to refill a pan if food got low. She picked up a tray and set two plates on it. She wasn't really hungry, but Bertie probably wouldn't want to eat alone.

She knew how those ladies felt, standing back there, looking out for the needs of everyone here. She loved doing that. It was something she'd discovered last year, when she started working for Bertie for some extra money.

She loved this part of the business most of all. Blaze said it was because she craved acceptance, and that was the best kind of acceptance she could get. Sometimes Blaze thought he was some kind of shrink.

As she selected some green beans and roast beef so tender it could practically be eaten with a spoon, she decided she did have an appetite, after all. Then she saw Austin Barlow, with no food in his hands, leaning over the table where Mr. and Mrs. Marshall sat.

Mary Marshall's face looked as if she smelled something bad—not much of a change from her usual expression. Jed shook his head, glowering. Austin leaned closer, face reddening. Some people from other tables looked in their direction.

Hmm. This could be interesting....

"How about some of this dessert?" came a voice from behind Fawn.

She turned to see one of the church ladies—Melva Cooper—holding out a serving spoon of cherry dump cake. Melva was married to Jill's cousin. She was fluffy and comfortable, like the food she cooked. She had a kind smile, and her stepchildren adored her.

"Sure, Melva. I'll take some for Bertie, too. She loves this stuff."

By the time Fawn turned back to glance across the dining room toward the interesting conversation taking place, Jed and Mary Marshall were leaving, and Austin stood watching them go.

He looked frustrated. Once again, Fawn felt sorry for the man. It didn't look as if the whole town was accepting his return with open arms, as he seemed to hope.

Settled back in the lobby alcove with Bertie, Fawn stuck a fork into the roast beef. "Bertie, what do you know about the Marshalls?"

The older lady looked up from her plate. "I know Mary's an artist with desserts." She raised a spoonful of cherries and cake. "See this here stuff? Melva Cooper can do a dump cake. All she has to do is dump cake mix, cherries and butter into a greased cake pan, stir it a tiny bit, then bake it. When people rave about it, Melva just glows. It makes her whole day. It doesn't take much for Melva."

"She's nice."

"Now, our Mary, on the other hand, will spend hours and hours on her desserts, fancy cakes and pies and pastries. She can cook like some famous chef. Oughta be on television. You know, one of those cookin' shows. But when anyone tries to compliment her on one of her cakes or pies, she gets all grim and points out exactly why she thinks they're wrong."

"Has she always been so grumpy?"

The white brows drew together. "Grumpy? That's how you see her?"

"She never smiles, never says boo to me."

Bertie shook her head sadly. "When I look at Mary Marshall, I see someone who's always trying hard to do the right thing, and is never satisfied with the results. She wants so badly to please, and she's constantly frustrated because she doesn't think she measures up."

"Who's she trying to please?" Fawn asked. "I'd think she'd smile and be nice if she were trying to please somebody."

"It ain't us. It seems to me it's God she's hoping to satisfy, but I think she's tryin' to do it under her own steam. She hasn't realized yet that nobody's perfect."

"So I guess nobody else measures up to her standards, either," Fawn said.

Bertie shook her head sadly. "Only person she's ever shown open approval of was Sheena, and I think that's one reason that girl hasn't moved out on her own yet. She can't bear to disappoint her mother." Bertie took a bite of the scalloped potatoes.

"I still say Mary's a grump."

Bertie gave her a look over the rim of her glasses. "Can't all people be cheery and bright all the time. It ain't in their nature. Some people are just cursed with the blues." Bertie spooned a bite of the dessert into her mouth and closed her eyes as if to savor it.

Fawn felt sorry for Mary.

"I met Mary when her folks sent her to Sunday school," Bertie said. "Quite a few years ago. I was a Sunday-school teacher in those days. Mary was a sweet little child. It wasn't until she was all grown up that I met her on the street one day, and wondered what happened to the real Mary."

Fawn finished her meal listening to the racket in the dining room. She wondered how Edith's family must feel, sitting out on the deck, listening to the chatter getting louder. Laughter squeezed through the talk like butter melting into freshly toasted bread.

"Bertie, what are you going to do about this place now?" Fawn asked when the noise level dropped enough that she could actually hear herself.

Bertie sat back with a tired sigh and glanced around the room, plushly furnished with elaborate Victorian pieces that were surprisingly comfortable. "Don't rightly know. There's a lot of work that goes into this place, and while I can keep parts of it going, I depended on Edith for a lot."

"Will her family be taking over her part of it?"

"Nope. They told me this morning that the business is all mine now. She left her part to me."

"Can she do that?"

"She could do anything she wanted with her own money. Besides, most of her nieces and nephews are very well off. They don't want for much. They're nice people, and offered to help me with the transition."

Fawn couldn't miss the way Bertie's gaze roved along the walls and fixtures, the doors and windows, lingering on a portrait of herself and Edith standing on the porch the day the deal closed on this bed and breakfast.

"You still love this place, don't you, Bertie?"

"'Course I do. We ain't had it long enough to get disenchanted with it. Edith and I fixed this place up the way we liked. I've always loved Victorian, and Edith had a way with colors and decorating."

"What if you still had someone to help you with it?" Fawn asked.

"I've got help, and I could hire more, if it came to that. But you know what? I'm a tired old woman, working far past her prime. Shoot, Edith and I were too old when we bought this business. Now I'm the one responsible for the whole shebang. I don't want all that responsibility."

Fawn picked up Bertie's discarded, half-empty plate and set it on top of her own. "So what are you saying?"

"I'm saying the spirit might be willing, but the body ain't goin' along with it much longer. Austin mentioned I might want to sell."

"What?" Fawn stiffened. Even though she felt sorry for that man, Blaze didn't trust him, and she shouldn't, either. "Is he trying to get you to list with him?"

Bertie shook her head. "He didn't say a thing about that. He just said I might want to check with him if I was thinkin' about sellin', because he'd make sure I got a good deal."

Sure he would. "And you trust him?"

Bertie gave her a sharp glance. "Didn't say that, but I can't deny there seems to've been a change take place in that man since he left town two years ago."

"Blaze says it takes more than a few days to take the measure of a man's worth. Or maybe that's word. Anyway, I think he's saying let Austin prove himself for a while."

"You think I don't know that?"

Fawn shrugged. "What if you didn't sell the place right away?"

"Doubt there'd be a problem sellin'. This here's a goin' business, and there've been plenty of investors lookin' to make a deal with us just this past summer."

"Ever heard of sweat equity?"

Bertie gave Fawn a pointed look. "Sure have. It's the only way I know how to run a business. I've sweated enough in my lifetime, don't you think?"

"Well, what if you were to find someone else to do the sweating so you wouldn't have to? You keep receiving plenty of income from the business, and you could retire anywhere you wanted to, or you could stay right here on the property in your own cottage and talk to the lodgers when they come in."

"Why would I want to do that?"

Fawn fingered the edge of the heavy paper plate, suddenly unwilling to meet Bertie's gaze. "Because you love this place and you don't want to leave it. You're always saying that the reason you love it so much is because of the people."

"I'd end up working. Besides, who'd be crazy enough to let me stay here without doin' the work?"

"Someone who loves this place, and loves you, and doesn't have any money to buy it." She looked up then.

Bertie's eyes narrowed. "You know anybody like that?"

"Well, now that you mention it, I might just know someone who'd be crazy enough to do it."

Bertie leaned forward. "Someone who'd love this place enough to work themselves to death keepin' it goin'?"

"Someone like that. Yes."

"Mind tellin' me who this crazy person might be?"

"That would be me."

For a moment, Bertie's sharp eyes brightened with something like joy. Even pride. Or maybe just amusement.

"What do you think, Bertie? You wouldn't have to draw up any legal papers or anything."

"Oh, honey." Bertie slumped and shook her head. "Honey, it's just not gonna happen that way."

"But it could work—"

"I'm not saying it couldn't work. You'd do a good job. I've never seen a harder worker, unless maybe it was Blaze. But Fawn Morrison, you've got your whole life ahead of you, with schoolin' and—"

"I can do that, too. Blaze is. He works at the ranch, and at the clinic, just to get what he calls practical experience. Jill Cooper went all the way through college, living right here in Hideaway. I'm going to the same school she did. Same school Blaze is going to. It can be done."

A burst of laughter suddenly rang out from the dining room as Bertie hesitated. For an agonizing few seconds, Fawn held her breath.

Bertie's eyes narrowed. "This got something to do with Karah Lee's upcoming wedding?"

"What's the wedding got to do with anything? This is what I want to do. I want to settle here, be a part of Hideaway. I love this place, and I love this business."

"And you want to make a place for yourself in case the same thing happens to you again that happened to you before. Haven't you learned, yet, that Karah Lee ain't like that? She's not going to kick you out of your home."

"Of course she's not. I know that."

Bertie shook her head. "I'm not sure you do. Besides, you need to set your sights higher than this place. It may be a good retirement investment for two old ladies, but I'm not gonna let it tie down a young girl like you, not when you've got the whole world out there waiting for you."

"I don't want the world out there," Fawn said quietly. "I want the world right here."

"You've seen the wrong part of the world, so that's all you know. But there's better things out there." Bertie slapped her knees and stood. "Now, where'd that Karah Lee get to? Didn't I hear you tell her you were going to give her a new hairstyle for the wedding? Don't you think she oughta try it on for size first, in case she needs time to get a wig or something?"

Fawn slumped. Just like that, her idea had been shot down.

Chapter Fourteen

Jill reconnoitered her house like a trapped cat, unable to sit down and relax. She was not imagining all this! Someone had been in her house. She should have purchased an alarm system years ago, but years ago she never would have thought she would need it here in Hideaway.

As Tom had noted, she kept a clean house, and so dust would not reveal strange prints or scuff marks. Though she did have a tendency to like her house in order, her OCD did not extend to being obsessive about having every single thing in place.

However, she'd found a few more things that seemed out of place since the men left—a stack of papers on her desk in her office upstairs had been searched, she felt sure. She had a tendency to make sure all the edges were straight.

A closet door on the second-floor landing, which she kept shut at all times, wasn't latched. Of course, that could be the result of Tom's sloppy search methods. The hanging file folders in her filing boxes in the attic were all pushed to the front of each box, whereas she always left them evenly spaced—another compulsion.

She'd tried to call Noelle, who wasn't home, and wasn't answering her cell, which meant it was turned off, as usual. She was at the memorial dinner, Jill felt sure. It had been tempting to call there and ask to speak to her, maybe even give in to temptation to break her rule about asking if Noelle had any "impression" about who might have been in the house.

But Noelle would have contacted Jill if she'd had any intuitive uneasiness.

There was something Jill didn't understand about this gift of Noelle's. Last year, and many times in the past, God had used this gift to warn of danger. When Jill and Noelle's twelve-year-old cousin, Carissa, had been abducted, Noelle's intuition had saved the young girl's life. And yet they'd had to find the culprit the hard way.

Why did the Holy Spirit touch Noelle with this discernment at some times and not others?

But then, why did God do any of the things He did? He was God. One didn't question Him.

Okay, Jill had found herself questioning Him quite often lately, but in reality, she had no right. Did the pot question its maker why it was a pot?

Jill's phone rang, startling her for the third time since Greg and Tom had left ten minutes ago.

She picked up, recognizing a neighbor's number on caller ID. "Hi, Nancy."

"Jill Cooper, are you okay? What's going on over there? Didn't I see—"

"Yes, the sheriff was here. No, he didn't find anything or anybody. I don't suppose you saw anyone you didn't know hanging around here the past day or so, did you?"

"I sure didn't. Nobody I didn't know."

Jill caught the inflection in her neighbor's voice. "You mean you saw someone you did know?"

"Well, I saw our old mayor knocking at your door, but he left when no one answered."

"When was that?"

"About two o'clock yesterday afternoon. He had his hat in his hand and everything. You two sweet on each other again?"

"Nancy!"

"Sorry. Did someone break in or something?"

"We're not sure right now." She didn't want to say more. The buzz was most likely all over town by now, anyway, because another neighbor, Cynthia Ratcliff, who couldn't keep her mouth shut about anything, had stopped Greg and Tom as they were leaving. Jill had watched them hold a long conversation at the front corner of her lawn.

Cynthia, of course, held a casserole dish in her hand, which she was surely taking to the funeral dinner at the bed and breakfast. If she didn't spread the word to every person in that dining room this afternoon, Jill would eat that whole okra-and-cheese casserole herself—no doubt that was what she'd made. It was her signature casserole. Cynthia didn't cook often, because she spent so much of her time nosing into everyone else's business.

Finally saying goodbye to Nancy—after repeated insistences that she and Austin were *not* going to be a hot item—Jill settled into her recliner in the sitting room, then opened a book on her lap. She read the first paragraph about five times before she gave up.

This wasn't working. She needed to get out of this house for a while. Every time she heard the rattle of the air conditioner kicking on or the sound of a car cruising by on the street outside, she tensed. It felt as if something in this house was hovering…waiting.

Foolish imagination, of course, but she felt vulnerable.

A car door slammed outside. The book went flying. Jill was at the door before the doorbell rang, and she opened the door quickly, startling the familiar, dark-haired, chubby man on the porch.

"Jonathan, hi." It was Edith's nephew, Jonathan Etheridge. He and his aunt had been very close when he was growing up. In later years, Jonathan had visited her often, including her in his family activities much more than other family members. Some of Edith's friends had hinted in the past that Jonathan was scouting for a sweet inheritance, since Edith was purported to have some hefty bank accounts. Her husband, a banker, had invested heavily in Jack Henry stock before that company had taken off.

Jill wondered if Edith's friends realized what an insult their suspicions had been to Edith. Were they implying that Edith didn't merit love and devotion from a nephew?

"Hi, Jill." The sad-eyed man in his sixties looked tired.

"I didn't see you down at the dinner, so I thought I'd check to see if you're okay."

"Well, thank you, but I'm fine." Had news of Greg and Tom's visit already made the rounds, even to the out-of-towners? She glanced out toward the car, a late model, dusky-gray sedan. He had apparently come alone. "Did you want to talk to me about something?"

He gestured toward the car. "I have some boxes for you."

"Boxes?"

"From Aunt Edith's house. She left you a few things in her will, including some jewelry, some novel collections, her study Bible, some cookbooks."

"For me? I had no idea she'd mentioned me in her will."

His expression softened. "Of course she did. She was always talking about you, Jill. You were more like a daughter to her than just a friend. That study Bible of hers was one of her most precious possessions, and I know she wanted you to have it." His voice thickened, and he looked away for a moment.

"She took the place of my mother when my own mother was killed," Jill said. "I never knew anyone with a bigger heart."

He nodded. "I guess that ol' heart just gave out on her."

Jill didn't argue. The family, including Jonathan, had already made it clear that they were convinced Edith's death was from a heart attack. Jill didn't want to get into a discussion with him about it now.

"I also brought a box of old files and papers," he said. "I think they're mementoes from the years she was high-school principal. Guess she was going through them. I figured, since you were the school nurse, you'd be most likely to know what to do with them. My wife Gloria and I and my cousins have been delivering things to people all morning."

"Were the school files medical records of some kind?"

"Student records, mostly. I'm not sure why she had them in her home office, but we don't want to leave anything in the house when we go home tomorrow, especially after last night."

"What happened last night?"

"When we arrived in Hideaway and pulled into Aunt Edith's driveway, Gloria thought she saw somebody running across the backyard."

Oh, no. "Was there any sign of a break-in?"

"None, but we decided to go through as many of Aunt Edith's things as we could while we're here, make sure everything gets safely into the hands of her friends." He paused, cleared his throat. "She kept her house in such good order, everything marked and dated. She made it easy for us. I know she'll be glad I took the time to bring these things over." He turned and stepped off the porch. "If you'll hold the door for me, I'll carry the boxes in."

Jill watched from the porch as he opened the trunk of his car, revealing six large storage boxes. She went to help him.

By the time they had everything unloaded, Jonathan was perspiring heavily, but he declined to come inside for a glass of iced tea. In spite of his thoughtfulness, Jill felt slightly relieved. She had a heightened sense of suspicion right now about practically everybody.

"I overheard someone asking about you down at the bed

and breakfast, Jill," he said. "It looks like most of the people who came to the funeral showed up for the dinner. I know my family would love to have a chance to share memories with you. I'd be glad to give you a lift down."

"Thanks," she said, glancing at the boxes in her sitting room. "How long will you be there?"

He shrugged. "Knowing Gloria, she'll stay until the last dishwasher goes home. She's shy around strangers at first. She was still keeping herself isolated with the rest of the family out on the deck when I left, but I have a feeling that once she gets to talking, she'll be inside chatting with every-body."

"If you're staying at Edith's again tonight, I might stop by there later. I don't think I'll go to the dinner just yet."

The telephone rang just as she thanked him and stepped back inside. Again, she felt her nerves tense. Would this ringing stop at all today?

She snatched up the receiver without glancing at caller ID. "What!"

There was a moment of silence, then, "Uh, Jill?"

She slumped. Great, she'd just snapped at Karah Lee Fletcher. "Yeah, that's me. I realize you've probably heard about all the excitement, and—"

"What excitement?"

"About the sheriff coming to the house. You didn't hear?"

"Nope. I was just going to ask if you were coming down to the funeral dinner."

"You, too? What, are they placing bets on whether or not I'll show?" *Stop the sarcasm, Jill.*

"Is everything okay?"

"Sure, no problem. Greg and Tom did their thing and left, assuring me that no one was in the house." The wimps. They didn't even stick around for a more thorough check. The more she thought about it, the more she resented their attitude, even though she knew it would do no good to resent them. They'd only done their job. Usually, they were good at it.

"Well, good," Karah Lee said. "Look, Bertie and Fawn have their heads together, and Fawn's decided to give me a new look for the wedding."

"At a *funeral dinner?*"

"The church ladies are swarming all over the place, keeping people fed and cleaning everything up. They have things well in hand. Cynthia Ratcliff is passing around a scrapbook for everyone to write down a special memory about Edith. She's going to present it to the family before they leave. I know you'll want to contribute to that."

"Well, yes, but—"

"And after you've done that, I need someone on my side in case Fawn and Bertie decide to get carried away. I mean, I could end up bald, here."

"I can't believe they're doing this *today.*"

"We're distracting Bertie. Look, if it gets her mind off losing Edith, then I'm all for it. Old Cecil Martin took it hard, too, but most of his fishing cronies are gathered around him, keeping him occupied. Bertie's not her usual, gregarious self today. Come down and run interference for me?"

"Isn't this a little irregular, even for Hideaway?"

"Yes, well, it all started when Cecil drew Fawn aside a few minutes ago and gave her a good talking-to about how

Edith's promotion to glory should be a celebration, and that they should spend this day reminiscing about the good things Edith did in her life, and going on with life. Fawn was closer to tears than I've ever seen her by the time he finished. I figured we could all use a little break from the grief."

Jill sighed. She lived in a strange town among strange people. Why didn't she feel as if she fitted in? She couldn't be any weirder than others in Hideaway.

"Please, Jill? Bertie's asking about you, and so is Fawn. You loved Edith as much as anyone else. You know she'd want you down here, even if it is to watch me get scalped."

Jill shook her head. It would be better than hanging around here, waiting for someone to jump out at her from some dark corner of the house. She glanced at the boxes Jonathan had just brought, tempted to stay and go through them—and guard the house.

Still, she didn't want to appear any more antisocial. And her neighbors—if there were any who hadn't gone to the funeral dinner—would probably keep watch over the house.

She had a suspicion that Karah Lee might have indeed heard about the suspected break-in, and was doing what she could to get Jill out and among people.

Jill already had her shoes on and the boxes stuffed into the closet beneath the stairwell when she realized she was going.

Chapter Fifteen

❦

Rex hefted a tray of dirty dishes through the dining room, taking care to dodge toddlers and crawling babies—what were these people thinking, allowing their children to crawl through the germs tracked in by a hundred different sets of feet from possibly a hundred different contaminants?

And yet, the feeling of community in this room was thick with rich tales of Edith's life, seasoned with some tears and laughter. It soothed something inside him, and he was sure it comforted the people who had known and loved Edith all these years.

In the past, his medical education had put a negative spin on his opinion of community...community-acquired pneumonia…community-illnesses of all kinds. What he saw today was restoring the true meaning of the word for him.

He was making his final turn past the buffet table toward the kitchen when he spotted Jill Cooper entering the lobby. She was no longer wearing the gray dress, but a pair of silky-looking burgundy slacks and a pink, dressy T-shirt. Her thick, luxurious brown hair hung loosely around her neck, nearly touching her shoulders. In Rex's opinion, the years had enhanced her beauty.

Her blue eyes widened when she saw him, and then he thought he saw a brief flicker of amusement. He realized how he must look.

She glanced at the stack of dishes he held in his arms, destined for the kitchen crew, and the disposable apron he had tied around his waist, now with various stains on it.

When her gaze returned to his face, he winked at her. She scowled, but it wasn't an ugly, threatening scowl. Jill Cooper had a respectable temper when the moment warranted, but she also knew the meaning of forgiveness.

"I can take those, doc," said Richard Cook from behind him.

Rex turned and handed his stack of dishes to Cook—the fiftyish man whose sole ambition in life seemed to be house-keeping and cooking for the residents of the boys' ranch.

"Well, would you look at her," Cook said, nodding toward Jill, who had stepped over to the front desk to talk to Willy, one of the ranch boys who worked part-time at the bed and breakfast. "Wouldn't've expected to see her here. Heard tell the sheriff was at her place just a little bit ago."

"The sheriff? Why?" Rex asked.

Cook shrugged as he hefted his load off toward the

swinging kitchen door. "Suspected intruder. Third or fourth time this year, from what I hear. Woman alone like that, she's bound to feel afraid from time to time, 'specially after all she's been through."

When Rex glanced back at Jill, he saw her leaning into the alcove where Bertie and Fawn had been huddled since he arrived.

Rex untied the dirty apron, tossed it into a nearby trash can and crossed through the lobby.

Karah Lee Fletcher had joined Fawn and Bertie in the Victorian alcove, and Bertie was smiling at something Fawn had said.

Jill turned to Rex when he stepped up beside her. "Don't you have a hospital to plan?"

"It'll keep for a couple of hours. Do you have a few minutes?"

Jill glanced back at Bertie, hesitating.

"We're going to our cottage," Karah Lee said, getting up to leave the room.

"I didn't mean to run anyone off," Rex said.

"You're not," Karah Lee assured him. "Bertie and Fawn have this crazy idea that I need a new look before the big day. As if I haven't already had my appearance changed so drastically in the past few months that my own sister won't know me when she comes to the wedding."

"Don't start without me," Jill called after them, then turned back to Rex. "What's up?"

Rex watched Bertie, Karah Lee and Fawn file from the alcove, talking about hairstyles and makeup as they walked across the lobby and out the front door.

"Hello?" Jill waved a hand in front of his face. "Is everything okay? What did you want to talk to me about?"

How could he have forgotten her trademark impatience? Once, in the middle of winter, he had taken her to a mountainside down at Roaring River, on the far end of Barry County, where bald eagles were known to roost during January and February. They'd hiked for thirty minutes up the mountainside.

When they arrived, breathless and perspiring, she'd glanced at her watch. "You said they'd be here at five-thirty. It's five-thirty-three. Where are they?"

He smiled at the memory, then realized she was watching him with that same, familiar impatience.

"What would happen if I apologized again for being a jerk?"

"I'd tell you that actions speak louder than words. Prove it."

He gestured for her to have a seat on the sofa in the alcove. She hesitated, watching him.

"I mean it, Jill. I did not intend to start an argument with you today of all days. You've been through enough."

"What you said to me wouldn't have gone down easy, no matter what day it was."

"Of course not. Jerks don't usually take that kind of thing into consideration."

"You're right, they don't."

"But some jerks mean well."

"So they say." At last, she relented and sat down on an ornate, overstuffed chair.

He sat across from her on the sofa. "I heard some interesting news a few moments ago. Did the sheriff visit your house today?"

She rolled her eyes.

"I take that as an affirmative."

"It isn't my favorite topic of conversation right now."

"Mine, either, especially if it means you could be in trouble. Is everything okay?"

"The sheriff and deputy didn't see signs of forced entry, and no one was in the house." Her hesitation spoke volumes. "I'm sure it's just my overactive imagination. Again."

He frowned. There was obviously a lot more to know. "I'd like to hear the whole story, Jill. Especially if it's about your safety."

Her blue eyes searched his for a long few seconds. "Since my aunt Pearl died last year, I've earned the reputation of being afraid of my own shadow," she said at last.

"That's interesting, since I've never known you to be afraid of anything."

"Maybe you don't know me anymore."

"Or maybe something has given you a reason to be afraid now?"

She looked down at her hands, as if giving herself time to decide how much to tell him. "There have been a few incidents this past year when I felt the need to call the sheriff. Once I panicked when Noelle came to my house when I was gone, and she didn't tell me. I saw signs that someone had been there, and thought the worst. Another time, I believed someone had broken into the clinic, but it turned out that Blaze had come back, looking for a file, after I had closed up for the day."

"Have you been expecting a break-in now?"

She paused, as if trying to decide how much to tell him. "Last summer, a killer broke into the clinic searching for Fawn, and nearly killed her and Karah Lee before he could be stopped. We've all been on especially high alert since then, but I guess I've been worse than the rest."

Rex leaned forward, elbows on knees. "You told me about the tragedies with your father and grandparents, but you haven't told me much about last year."

Jill glanced toward the lobby, where Richard Cook and Willy consulted about tables and chairs. "Fawn witnessed a murder in Branson and was followed here after disguising herself as a boy. She's good at disguises."

"I do remember reading about that incident with the Beaufont Corporation when their condo building collapsed in the middle of town due to faulty surveying. I'm not always good about keeping up with the news," he said, "but I paid attention because it was about Hideaway, and I've always had a soft spot when it comes to this place. You weren't mentioned in the news reports. I watched for your name."

She blinked, startled, but didn't pursue the subject. "I wasn't interested in speaking to the news media then. That was a bad time for our town."

"What else happened last year?" he asked.

"You remember my cousin Cecil?"

"Sure. Big guy, doesn't smile much. Didn't Edith tell me your cousin was named after old Cecil Martin?"

"Yes. Old Cecil's a good friend of the family." She smiled. "Used to be, it was Big Cecil and Little Cecil. Now it's Old Cecil and just plain Cecil. Anyway, my cousin doesn't smile much because he, too, was forced to come back to Hideaway to take care of business. And he's been under the Cooper curse as much as the rest of us."

"Cooper curse?"

She glanced at her watch. "I'll spare you too many details, but I'm sure you know that OCD runs in families. It's quite prevalent in ours. Last year, our great-aunt Pearl abducted Cecil's daughter, Carissa, to try to cover up the fact that Pearl also had OCD."

"Why would that be such a concern?" he asked. "It isn't a psychosis, it's a neurosis. Not usually life-threatening."

"It was to our family. There was a codicil in our great-grandfather's will stating that no one with obsessive-compulsive disorder would inherit Cooper holdings."

"Why would he do that?"

"Because we had a family member whose compulsion was to hoard papers and magazines of all kinds. She filled her house with them. They caught fire and burned the house to the ground, killing her. There were other incidents involving other family members. My great-grandfather called OCD a curse—that was before obsessive-compulsive disorder became a common topic of discussion. Nowadays, it seems nearly half the population in this country is affected by some degree of mental illness, and OCD is usually easier to live with than many other neuroses, such as depression or bipolar disorder."

"So he chose to leave the property only to those family members who weren't affected by the disorder," Rex said.

Jill nodded. "Unfortunately, everyone is affected, whether or not they have the illness. Anyway, long story short, Aunt

Pearl reacted badly. Over the years, she was the one who killed my mother, and then later my father and grandparents."

Rex swallowed hard, struggling with the shock.

"We don't know for sure if she had a compulsion to kill," Jill said, "or if the compulsion actually prevented her from killing even more people, but she was determined not to allow anyone to discover that she had 'the curse.'"

"No wonder you've been afraid. Why do you stay here? Have you considered leaving this place, and the memories?"

Jill slowly stood up. "The memories will always be with me, and I'd rather face them here, with the people I love, than go somewhere else and start all over again."

He stood with her. "Why doesn't that surprise me?"

She smiled at him, a sad smile. "You're probably going to ask about my sister now, and warn me not to overcompensate for—"

"That isn't true."

"She doesn't have that family curse." Jill glanced toward the lobby, where some people were leaving, and she lowered her voice. "But she is uniquely equipped with God-given discernment in some situations. For instance, she found Carissa when no one else could. She was aware of danger when no one else was." She paused, then stepped closer to him. "She believes there's more to Edith's death than a simple heart attack. I know her too well to doubt her, because she is never wrong. Never."

"How can you be sure? Does she know what happened to Edith?"

Jill shook her head. "If a word of knowledge is truly from God, it is never wrong. When Noelle was a little girl, she had a very pure and powerful faith in God. Even as a child, she had that special gift. It frightened me then, and after our mother died, I did everything I could to prevent Noelle from speaking about it to anyone else."

"Why did it frighten you?"

"I thought she was conjuring spirits or something. I didn't get that it was something completely different, even though she never did anything to encourage the gift, never did anything unbiblical. During her teens and early adulthood, she strayed from the faith and…well, you know about that rebellion. I never saw any evidence of her gift during that time. But when Carissa was abducted, Noelle's gift returned in force."

Rex felt the tiny hairs stir along his neck and shoulders. "You never told me."

"I was afraid to talk about it. But now I believe her. If she says Edith's death is suspicious, then I'm suspicious about it. Simple as that. I want to do all I can to find out what really happened."

Another group of people came through the lobby.

Jill leaned forward, lowering her voice. "Edith's nephew, Jonathan, thought he saw someone running from the back of her property when he and his wife arrived last night. Could have been just some curious neighbor kids, but after what Noelle said, I don't think that's all it was." She straightened and drew back. "I'm going to Karah Lee's. They'll be wondering why I'm taking so long, and I'm not in the mood for a lot of silly teasing today."

"But what about—"
She turned away, tossing a wave of hair over her shoulder.
He had been dismissed.

Chapter Sixteen

Fawn deftly tweezed Karah Lee's thick, golden eyebrows, then filled them in with just a hint of deeper color. She loved working in front of an audience. Jill and Bertie were good for the ego, and Fawn appreciated it every time Bertie said, "Girl, you've got a gift," or Jill studied a technique, as if memorizing each movement.

Last year, Fawn had transformed Karah Lee from an outspoken, larger-than-life, fun-loving woman to a beautiful, fun-loving, outspoken woman with a fiancée—a man who adored her beyond belief.

Not that Fawn's makeover of Karah Lee actually had anything to do with Taylor's attraction to her. Those two had made a heart connection before Fawn performed her magic.

With a quick glance in the mirror, Jill gave her own reflection a brief study. It didn't look to Fawn as if that reflection pleased Jill at all. Which was silly. Jill was a pretty woman, especially for her age. So many women gave up on their appearance and just let gravity take its course. Jill kept active, and had recently lost weight. She didn't even have much of a double chin, as some women of her age had.

Jill caught Bertie watching her from Karah Lee's lounger, and grimaced.

She eyed the set of scissors on the dresser. "Fawn."

"Yeah?"

Jill fingered the over-long bangs that fell into her eyes. "How did you get so good with hair and makeup when you've never been to cosmetology school?"

Fawn grinned at her. "You think I'm good?"

"Stop fishing for compliments," Karah Lee teased.

"You worked a miracle with Karah Lee," Jill said.

Fawn felt a flush warm her cheeks.

The miracle lady shot Jill a glare. "She simply enhanced what I already had."

Bertie chuckled. "She did a good job of it, though."

"I had a roommate who was a cosmetologist." Fawn brushed powder onto Karah Lee's face in circular motions to create a flawless foundation. "She taught me how to do hair. I hung around the drama club at school, and I learned how to do makeup. Want me to fix yours, Jill?"

"What do you mean 'fix'?"

Fawn glanced at Karah Lee and nearly laughed. *Okay, someday my mouth will get me into trouble.*

Jill frowned into the mirror. "You think you could make my face look more…dignified?"

"What's so great about looking dignified?" Bertie asked.

"I mean, a little less…um…unsophisticated."

Fawn knew what Jill meant. She wanted to look less like a wild woman with OCD. That was what Jill thought about herself. She had such a hang-up about her…hang-up.

Noelle had told Fawn that she'd nagged Jill for years to change her hairstyle from a short, sprayed-on helmet of brown to something more feminine and appealing. And so Jill had allowed her hair to grow. But the lion's mane the poor woman sported now couldn't be described as appealing, either.

Fawn couldn't help teasing a little. "How about attractive? You know, like, you want to look good for…someone?"

"I want to look good for me," Jill said. "Is that so strange?"

"How old are you?" Fawn asked.

"What does age have to do with this?"

"What I mean is, you've lived with the way you look for what, thirty-five years?"

"Don't patronize me, kid. You know I'm older than that."

"So why are you suddenly wanting to change?" Again, she couldn't stop the grin. She winked over her shoulder at Bertie. "There's nothing wrong with wanting to look good for a guy. Dr. Fairfield isn't bad-looking."

"That's *not* what this is," Jill said.

Fawn shrugged. "Suit yourself." She reached out and fingered Jill's hair. "I could take a machete to this mess and change your world."

"Fawn," Karah Lee warned, "don't make promises you can't keep."

"How much of my world can you change in fifteen minutes?" Jill asked.

Karah Lee rose from her chair. "We can work on my haircut later. Jill, grant me a reprieve and have a seat."

Ordinarily, Fawn wouldn't allow Karah Lee up until she was finished, but she'd wanted to get her hands on Jill for a year now. Jill was like a blank canvas to an artist.

"Come and be amazed," she invited.

Jill glanced at the chair, then at Karah Lee. "You're in quite a hurry to move on out, aren't you?"

"You're the one who said I worked a miracle on Karah Lee," Fawn reminded her.

"As Karah Lee said, there was already quality under the girding," Jill reminded Fawn.

"You make me sound like a condominium," Karah Lee complained. "Just let her do your hair, Jill, and see what you think."

Jill frowned at the scissors Fawn held in her hand, then backed toward the door. "Amaze me later. First, I need to talk with Edith's family before they leave, and I want to write some memories down in that book Cynthia's passing around. Then I have some things I need to do at home."

Fawn and Karah Lee exchanged glances in the mirror. Karah Lee nodded.

"What?" Jill asked, stopping in the doorway between the bedroom and living room of the small cottage.

"And Rex is probably still out there," Fawn said.

Jill didn't grace them with a reaction as she pivoted away.

"When will you be back?" Fawn called after her.

"You have school for the rest of the week," Jill called back.

"I'm out early tomorrow afternoon. I could do it after you get out of the clinic."

"Fine, I'll check with you then," Jill said as she stepped out the front door. "Unless I come to my senses and change my mind."

Bertie chuckled. "Guess you'll have to be content with that."

Fawn shrugged. Diverting Bertie's mind from the grief of this day had been their main goal.

Rex was nowhere to be seen when Jill returned to the lobby of the bed and breakfast—not that she was looking for him. She did see Junior Short in the dining room.

True to his name, Junior was barely five foot six, with muscle turning to fat these days, and a thick bull neck. Junior never missed a free meal. His son, Danny, sat beside him, chowing down on a plate of spareribs, barbecue sauce on his chin and the front of his T-shirt.

She was about to join him at the table and ask him a few questions about last Saturday when good ol' Cynthia Ratcliff stuck her circulating journal under Jill's nose, accompanied by a pen.

"Jill, you knew Edith as well as anyone in town, except maybe for old Cecil. Got any memories you want to share with her family?" Cynthia had hazel eyes, bright with curiosity. She would be pretty if not for her personality. Even in a town like Hideaway, where everyone knew everyone's business, Cynthia took the prize for being the nosiest, most annoying gossip.

Jill accepted the journal with a nod, searching the dining room for Jed and Mary Marshall, or Austin Barlow. They weren't around.

"So, you going to tell me what that hullabaloo was all about at your house this afternoon?" Cynthia asked, following Jill toward the alcove in the lobby.

"Hullabaloo?" Jill opened the journal and found a blank page near the back of the book. It occurred to her that she might want to see what memories others had of Edith in these pages.

"The sheriff. Really, Jill, he and Tom are busy men. If you're just looking for attention, give me a call and we can go to lunch or something."

Jill smiled to cover her annoyance. "Why, thank you for the offer, Cindy, especially since I know what a sacrifice that would be for you." Cynthia hated to be called Cindy. "Next time someone breaks into my house, I'll gladly call you before I call the law. I'm sure you'd be better protection."

Cynthia's fake smile died. "With that sharp tongue of yours, you could slice any intruder to ribbons without even having to think about it."

Jill didn't reply. Good thing Cynthia wasn't called on to think very often. She seldom had two intelligent thoughts in a row.

Cynthia fixed her with a pointed look and a raised eyebrow. "You thought someone broke in before."

"Of course. What could I have been thinking? My imagination must be working overtime again." Jill didn't attempt to conceal her sarcasm. "Listen, I'd love to share some memories," Jill said, holding up the journal. "Mind giving me a few moments to write them down?"

"Go right ahead," Cynthia said. "I tried to get Jed and Mary to write something, but they had some kind of little tiff. Last I saw of them, Mary was storming out the front door with Jed right behind her, grim as the reaper. Then I saw Austin and Junior with their heads together a few minutes ago. Any idea what's up with that?" Again, that lively, curious gaze. Sharp words never slowed her down for long.

"Why would I?"

"Well, you used to know all those guys in school, half a century ago." Cynthia liked to serve hyperbole with her sarcasm, especially when she was emphasizing their age difference. She had graduated from Hideaway High three years after Jill.

"I knew them then," Jill said. "People change." She held up the journal. "I could use some time alone to do some writing. Do you mind?"

The woman left with obvious reluctance.

Settling at the secretary desk in the far corner of the alcove, partially concealed behind a ficus tree, Jill opened the journal and paged through it.

She was immediately touched by what she read, and her eyes filled.

So many lives had been affected by that wonderful woman. "She checked on me every day in study hall, to make sure I was doing my homework"... "She's the reason I graduated"... "Mrs. Potts was there for me when no one else was" … "Miss Edith had a forgiving heart. I wonder, did she forgive too much?"

The last entry was from Cecil Martin. Jill read it again. Was she just imagining some deeper meaning? She hadn't had an opportunity to speak with Cecil since Edith's death, and questioning him about that day would only deepen his grief. Still, maybe he would be able to give her a better explanation of his entry. Maybe she would stop by the general store in the next couple of days and talk to him, since he'd already gone home today.

She continued to page through more entries. Some were sappy, some barely legible and some were humorous.

She found nothing from Junior Short or Mary or Jed Marshall. Granted, not everyone would have written in the book. Austin had. His entry was short, and he hadn't signed it, but she recognized his handwriting by the deep slant and over-indulgent swirls. His entry simply said, "She kept three innocent kids out of jail."

She reread the words, then sat back, closing her eyes. Had they been innocent? From time to time, that question had resurfaced in her mind.

That high-school incident was one of the only times when Jill and Edith Potts had disagreed. Edith had been adamant that Austin, Jed and Junior were innocent of Chet Palmer's death, in spite of the evidence revealing their presence in the school the night before the awful explosion. Shoe tracks in the mud outside the science lab had matched Austin's tread. But Austin couldn't have set the trap alone, and there were three sets of tracks in that mud. Austin had been stupid enough to wear those shoes again the next day.

None of the boys had an alibi for the night before the tragedy. Jill was pretty sure they had at least been playing a practical joke that went bad. But their lives had been impacted by his death forever.

Austin Barlow had become quieter, brooding often. Jed Marshall, who had been class president at the time, had stepped down from his role and had not become involved in school politics again. Junior Short had chosen that opportunity to start his drinking career.

Had one of them intended something more sinister than a mere practical joke?

The sheriff at the time had backed Edith up, and since the former sheriff was buddies with Jed Marshall's parents, and wasn't interested in justice so much as popularity, the boys had been reprimanded and gone free without ever admitting to the crime.

Now Jill's suspicions once more haunted her. What had happened that night? She needed to talk to Cecil Martin, who had been the science teacher then.

Maybe tomorrow.

Chapter Seventeen

The plan was going to work.

Rex Fairfield leaned back in his chair in the clinic conference room late Thursday morning as he stared at his laptop. Cheyenne Gideon sat beside him, beaming at the numbers on the spreadsheet he had designed.

"I think we're almost there," she said. "We'll be up to code in no time."

"Exceeding code in many areas." He couldn't keep the pleasure from his voice if he'd wanted to. He was more than impressed by the amount of work these doctors and their staff had done before he'd even arrived at the clinic.

"So you think a critical-access designation is the way to go?" Cheyenne asked. "We're limited to the number of patients we can take."

"But it will be a perfect size for the needs of this community, and that designation will bring in excellent reimbursement. Technically, you can have up to twenty-five beds in a critical-access hospital, and you're unlikely to have that many patients here at one time."

Cheyenne nodded, apparently satisfied. "As Hideaway grows—and it's definitely growing—we can see about expansion."

"From what I've heard from others this week, I think there's even enough interest to look into funding a new building," Rex said. "Until then, this clinic has the room you're going to need. You mentioned you wanted to add a surgical suite."

"Eventually. Dr. Graham Vaughn has already expressed an interest in joining us on a part-time basis for surgery, and Willow Traynor is an ICU nurse. She's eager to get to work."

"Are you looking forward to announcing it at the festival?" Rex placed his paperwork in a neat stack in front of him on the polished conference room/break room table. "That's coming up in two weeks."

"As are the weddings, the pig races, the class reunion." Cheyenne chuckled, twirling her pen with her fingers. "We've got a full schedule this year."

"Do you always schedule a wedding or two for the festival?"

Cheyenne gave him a mischievous grin. "I don't know about always. Dane and I were married last year in the park during the festival. I know it's been done before, but I don't think it's necessarily an annual event."

Cheyenne Gideon had a serious nature. Still, her dark

eyes could light with a teasing glint from time to time. This was one of those times.

"You have any ideas for a couple for next year's event?" she asked.

He laughed. He'd heard a couple of veiled insinuations that he and Jill might be interested in picking up where they had left off twenty-two years ago.

But those who teased didn't know about all the complications. Granted, much of the town knew more about the situation than he would have liked, but Jill could be stubborn about some things. She was obviously not interested in reviving the friendship. Or at least she hadn't given him much encouragement.

Today, she had avoided eye contact with him when they'd passed in the corridor or ended up in the same room for something. He couldn't understand why. When they'd spoken yesterday, she'd been open with him about some very private matters. Did she now regret that she'd spoken to him about those things?

"I saw you and Jill talking after the funeral yesterday," Cheyenne said. "Don't get me wrong, I'm not prying for information. Karah Lee does enough of that for both of us."

"So you did notice."

"I warned her not to push too hard, or she could mess up a good thing. She said she wasn't going to push *too* hard, just hard enough."

Rex grinned and shook his head.

Cheyenne's smile died, and her dark eyes turned serious. "I don't suppose Jill mentioned anything to you about the day of Edith's death, did she?"

"Yes. We talked about a lot of things."

"Knowing Jill, she's blaming herself, at least partially, for what happened. I wish I could convince her otherwise, but she's still haunted by it, I can tell."

"She didn't say anything about that." He was careful to guard Jill's confidences. "I do know she's always had a tendency to take too much responsibility on her own shoulders."

"Yes, and we let her do that far too much around here. She handles it so well."

He glanced at Cheyenne. She knew Jill as well as anyone in this town, and she obviously had a great deal of respect for her. The two of them had worked together since Cheyenne had established the clinic two years ago. No doubt she knew Jill better than he did now.

"I'm afraid I got off on the wrong foot with her again yesterday," he confided. "I made the remark that she tends to take too much on herself."

Cheyenne rolled her eyes, shaking her head. "Wrong thing to say, you know. Especially since she's far too aware of her compulsion to do that very thing. To her, it probably felt as though you were nagging her—"

"Like I'm trying to rub it in her face that she has that compulsion." Of course. Why hadn't he realized that? He'd never understood, even when they were engaged, that his concern for her emotional health had been misconstrued. She might even have believed he was taunting her, or pointing out why their relationship wouldn't work.

Her perception of his behavior couldn't have been further from the truth. Obviously, they needed to try harder to understand each other so these misperceptions didn't crop up.

"Jill is far too cognizant of the difference between herself and the rest of us so-called 'sane' people," Cheyenne said. "I've tried to point out how badly she's mistaken about that."

"As have I, except I haven't done a very good job of it."

"You've probably seen how much I depend on her here," Cheyenne said. "She can work circles around me, and she keeps every patient in line, knows their foibles and weaknesses and knows how to guilt them into taking care of themselves and exercising. She's nursed quite a few of our patients since they were children, and I think she's the reason many of them come here to the clinic. They trust her. I say if a person has that much influence over that many people, there's nothing wrong with her."

He slumped in his seat. He just needed to learn how to accept Jill as she was, celebrate their differences and let her know how much he appreciated her.

Shouldn't be hard. He was already beginning to realize that he was in love with her. In fact, it was quite possible that his love for her had never ended.

The aroma of homemade Mexican casserole lingered in Jill's house as she washed up her dishes, glad she'd paged through Edith's personal, handwritten cookbook last night. Since Jill was a child spending time at Edith's house, she'd loved that old cookbook. Putting together this casserole had been a labor of love before going to bed last night. She'd fixed one for herself, and one for Cecil, knowing he'd always loved Mexican food.

At the thought of Cecil, she checked the clock. She still had thirty minutes before she had to be back at the clinic. Time to look through the rest of those boxes Jonathan had brought her yesterday, and give Cecil a call while she searched.

The one box she had gone through last night had offered up other great treasures besides the cookbook. Edith's old Bible held years of wisdom and insight penned neatly into the margins of practically every page. Jill planned to read through it in the next few months, and savor every single morsel of strength she could mine from between those pages.

Edith Potts had taught a women's Sunday-school class for years in their small church, revealing nuggets of truth from Scripture that Jill never would have found in her own hit-and-miss searches.

How she wished she still had Edith here to answer the questions she had about so many things. She knew what Edith would say to that, however. She would pat the cover of her worn Bible and say, "My dear, it's all in this book. All the struggle you're going through now, others have gone through before. There's nothing happening now that hasn't happened to someone else."

And she'd be right, of course.

What would Edith have said about Rex's sudden reappearance in my life?

She would probably say, "If at any time you have doubts, if forgiveness is involved, just swallow your pride and do the forgiving. It's what makes the world go 'round."

Oh, Edith…

Jill had no trouble forgiving Rex. In fact, she'd discovered that she had forgiven him years ago for whatever things he had said that had hurt her. Obviously, she'd been a bit on the prickly side, herself.

But now she was discovering that, even though she had forgiven him, the slate had not been wiped clean. There was a lingering attachment—a feeling of such rightness when she was with him, as if they spoke the same language.

She knew that when two people loved each other, they could often become so attuned to each other that one could begin a sentence and the other could finish it. She had experienced that with Rex.

Yesterday, it had seemed as if they'd easily fallen back into that pattern again. Was she imagining something that wasn't real? It frightened her. After all the pain of their breakup twenty-two years ago, she had vowed she would never suffer that heartache again. With Rex she felt vulnerable. She didn't want to go there. And yet, something continued to draw her.

She shoved aside the box that held Edith's costume jewelry and good pearls. That dear lady could have started an antique jewelry store with her stash of favorite pieces, most of which had come from her mother and grandmother.

Before opening another box, Jill picked up the cordless telephone and dialed the general store. Old Cecil usually allowed Richard Cook or Dane Gideon from the boys' ranch to come into the store and spell him for lunch. He would be at the table in the storeroom in back, munching on his meatloaf sandwich and apple.

He answered on the third ring.

"Cecil, it's Jill. I was hoping I'd get to talk to you at the funeral dinner yesterday."

For a moment, he didn't answer, and she frowned. "Cecil? Are you okay?"

"I'm fine, Jill. How are you holding up?" Weariness made his voice reedy.

"I'm okay. I've been going through some of Edith's things."

Another pause. "What things?"

"Some boxes of mementoes her nephew, Jonathan, wanted me to have."

"How many boxes?" Was there a sharpness in his tone?

"Six."

"What mementoes?" Again, that hint of an edge.

"Oh, cookbooks, her Bible, some other odds and ends I haven't been through yet."

"You haven't opened them all?"

"Not every one of them." Even as she said it, she lifted the lid of another box, and found a manila envelope with some student files. Surprised that Edith had taken any of them home with her, she checked the names.

A chill stiffened her fingers. "Cecil, did you talk to Edith last Saturday?"

"Sure did. She was trying to get me to have one of those massages. I told her I'd had every one of those massage therapists in school at some point or other, and it just wouldn't feel right to have their hands all over my body."

"And she let you get away with that?" Jill asked, looking at the records one by one. "She made me go. Said it would give Noelle moral support." Austin Barlow. Junior Short. Jed

Marshall. Again. These were copies, not originals. Why were those names suddenly turning up together so often? Why had Edith been interested in their records?

"And you fell for that?" Cecil asked.

"Guess I did. Cecil, do you have any idea why Austin Barlow's back in town?"

Another long pause.

"Cecil?"

"Funny you should ask that."

"Why?"

"Edith asked me the same thing Saturday."

"And?"

"Don't have any idea."

Again, she thought she sensed a hesitation in his voice. "You're sure about that?"

There was a long sigh, then, "I could jump to a lot of conclusions, Jill Cooper, but I know better than to do that. Edith knew better, too. You're upset about Edith, and I understand. Believe me, I sure do. I don't guess her death's hit anybody harder than it has you and me. But trying to place blame won't help anybody."

"Who said I'm trying to place blame?"

"It's been hinted around. That request for an autopsy might've had something to do with it."

"Well. Okay. What if there's blame to be placed? What if you did jump to a conclusion, just this once? What would it be?"

"Nothing worth repeating."

"Cecil, you remember when that practical joke went bad and killed that high-school kid?"

A long, soft sigh. "Chet Palmer," he said softly. "I'm not

likely to forget that. It was one of the worst disasters in our school history."

Chet Palmer…Chet Palmer. The way he said the name stirred some sense of recognition.

Palmer…palmer…pommer…bommer…

Jill caught her breath. Bomber? "Cecil, did Edith say something to you about him on Saturday?"

A long pause. He didn't reply.

"Because," she continued, "the way you said his name just now, it reminded me of one of the last things she said to me. She was having trouble talking, and it sounded to me as if she was saying *jet bomber*. It didn't make any sense. But what if she was trying to say Chet's name?"

"Nope. I'm not going there."

"Why not?"

"Because all that happened nearly three decades ago."

"Twenty-seven years."

"Why bring up that whole tragedy all over again? What's done is done. It can't be undone, and placing blame now will only destroy more lives. That's what I told Edith. That's what I'm telling you."

"Is that what Edith was doing?" Jill asked. "If she was, do you think it's possible she might have placed herself in danger?"

"No. Jill Cooper, you can't talk crazy like this. Just stop it. You hear me?" His voice cracked, and she thought she heard fear clearly, trembling to the point of panic.

"We need to get together and talk," she said. "Something's going on, and—"

"I'm not talking about anything, not with you or anybody

else. And don't you stir things up now, after all that's happened."

"But Cecil—"

The line went dead.

He'd hung up on her.

What was up with that?

Disappointed, she replaced the receiver in its cradle and read through the copies of records for Austin, Junior and Jed. There was nothing particularly noteworthy in any of the papers, as far as she could tell. Austin Barlow had been a star student in speech and debate, and his teachers had felt he was likely to get into politics. He'd been mayor of Hideaway for a few years, and that had ended in tragedy.

Junior Short was a below-average student in most subjects, but he was a popular football player, brawny and unafraid of any opponent. His IQ was, interesting enough, quite above average. There was no reason for his low grades. He just never tried.

Jed Marshall had had the highest grades, and he especially excelled in math and science classes. He, too, seemed interested in politics, and was class president their senior year in high school. Sad that now, he had attained no higher status than that of Hideaway's city clerk.

She upturned the envelope, and a small button clattered out onto the coffee table. It was the color and shape of a bluebird.

What on earth could this be?

Jill checked her clock and found she just had time to get to the clinic if she left now.

She'd have to continue this search later. She picked up the button and slipped it into her pocket. For some reason, it intrigued her.

Chapter Eighteen

Fawn turned off Highway 76 onto Y toward Hideaway, tired of being quiet while Blaze sat in the passenger seat, doing his homework. She wanted to talk. He'd been preoccupied on his cell phone throughout the whole forty-five-minute drive to school this morning, talking to a worried farmer with a colicky newborn calf.

Okay, so Karah Lee always pointed out that for Fawn it was a thirty-five-minute drive. But they'd been running late this morning, thanks to a sick piglet at the ranch.

Blaze was a man in demand, and word had spread about his special ability with animals. Some of the other students at College of the Ozarks were calling him Dr. Dolittle, because one day during a break at school, he'd been sitting on a bench overlooking Lake Taneycomo, and a squirrel had jumped right up on his lap.

Of course, as soon as the poor animal realized it was sitting on a human lap, it went flying off, tail twitching in every direction at once. It nearly hurtled off the cliff into the water before it came to its senses and scrambled up a nearby tree, its outraged chatter echoing across the lake.

Fawn and Blaze shared rides to school when their classes and work shifts coincided, like today. He'd long ago learned to keep his mouth shut about her driving, unlike Karah Lee.

"Aren't you done with that assignment yet?" she asked, slowing to take a curve.

"Just about. It'd be easier if the ride was smoother, you know."

She grimaced. Okay, so he didn't always keep his mouth shut. "Did you know Jill called the sheriff to her house yesterday?"

Blaze looked up from his sheet of paper at last, his espresso-dark eyes suddenly filled with alarm. "Why?"

"She thinks somebody was in the house while she was at the funeral."

"Poor Jill. She's been so shook about Edith."

"And about…men," Fawn said.

"How do you know that?"

Fawn shrugged, picking up speed as she reached one of the few straightaways on this road. "A woman knows these things. You men just don't always get it."

She could feel, rather than see, the grin spread across his face. He loved to argue. "We men know some things. Who was the one that brought Dane and Cheyenne together?"

"Dane and Cheyenne brought themselves together. Don't flatter yourself that you had anything to do with it."

"Oh, yeah?"

She glanced sideways at him. His thick, dark brows were drawn together in a feigned glare. "Yeah."

"A lot you know," he said. "I had everything to do with it."

"The way I heard the story from Bertie, you nearly ruined the relationship before it began," Fawn said.

"I wasn't the one who sprayed Dane in the face with Mace. Cheyenne did that her own self. And they aren't the only ones the great Dr. Blaze brought together. Who else could have convinced Taylor and Karah Lee even to speak to each other?"

Fawn slowed the car to keep the tires from squealing around a curve. "Well. I'll have to admit you helped me with that one."

He laughed out loud. "Helped! I'm telling you, all the primping and haircuts and dresses in the world wouldn't've done any good if I hadn't dragged Taylor to her side at Cheyenne and Dane's wedding." He returned his attention to his school work.

"Okay, so that one was a team effort," Fawn said, unwilling to allow silence to settle in the car again. "You could help me make sure that relationship keeps going in the right direction."

He looked up again, obviously intrigued. "How's that? Are they fighting?"

"No, but they're going to need all the help they can get after the wedding vows are said. You know how bullheaded they can both be. Help me convince Bertie that I'd be a great help to her at the bed and breakfast."

Blaze frowned. "You're already working part-time for her. And what does your working for Bertie have to do with Taylor and Karah Lee?"

"I'm looking to earn myself a partnership and help Bertie shoulder the load of that place. In return, I'll ask for room and board."

"What! Fawn Morrison, you've done lost your mind."

She should have known he'd argue about that, too. "What's so hard to believe about that? I could help run things now," she said. "Learn everything I'd need to know about the business, then when Bertie decides she doesn't want to fight it anymore, I could maybe take it over for her, buy it from her as I get the money."

"You don't have time for that. How're you going to finish college and work the place at the same time?"

"I don't have to take as many hours a semester. I can do this. I know I can." She glanced over to find him glaring at her.

"You're willing to stay in school for six years or more, and expect Bertie to work that much longer, just so you can take over her business?"

Stung, Fawn returned the glare. "You act like you think I'm trying to get a free ride from Bertie."

"That's not what I'm saying. Besides, no way Karah Lee's going to let you do that."

"Karah Lee shouldn't have to support me for years while I piddle away my time in classrooms, learning stuff I don't even need to know."

For a few seconds, they exchanged glare for glare, until Blaze returned his attention to the road. "Watch where you're going!"

She swerved to miss an oncoming car and returned to her own lane.

For a few seconds there was silence in the car, then Blaze said softly, "That's what this is all about, isn't it?"

"What are you talking about?"

He leaned toward her. "You don't think you deserve the time and money Karah Lee's spending on your support."

"I got used to supporting myself, I guess."

"Not the right way, you didn't."

Her hands tightened on the steering wheel so she wouldn't reach across and smack him.

"You never had much chance to be a teenager, except for this past year," he said. "Why don't you give yourself more time to do that?"

"Like I told Bertie, Karah Lee and Taylor aren't going to want me hanging around after they get married. Newlyweds need time alone. I'm a big girl, and I don't need a mommy to wipe my nose and pay my way."

"How do you think that's going to make Karah Lee feel, after all the time she's spent loving you and supporting you?" Blaze asked. "It'll be like you're spitting in her face."

"She knows I wouldn't do that."

"And you should know she wouldn't want you to throw away all the time and effort she's put into getting you into school."

"But it's a work study. She doesn't have to pay my tuition. And I'm good at these kinds of things, Blaze. I'm planning a wedding, aren't I? All by myself. And I'm doing a good job, even after they decided to change the date."

"They decided to change the date because they knew you weren't going to have it ready in time for the original plan."

Fawn gasped and glared at him.

He stomped his own imaginary brake, eyes widening at the road. "Look out!"

She recovered from the blow of his revelation in time to slam on the brakes and squeal around the tight curve in the road. "You're lying to me!"

"I'm not a liar."

She couldn't believe how much that hurt. She felt as if she'd been kicked in the gut. For the whole year she'd been here, she'd felt like a useless kid who'd messed up her whole life and had to have strangers rescue her. With the wedding, she'd felt as if she was finally giving something back to the one who had supported and helped her the most. And now? Had she ruined Karah Lee's plans?

"Cheyenne just convinced Karah Lee and Taylor to have the wedding at the festival, the way Cheyenne and Dane did last year," she told Blaze.

"I'm not saying it was a bad idea, but I heard Karah Lee telling Cheyenne she was going to have to postpone the wedding because she didn't want you stressed out over everything. You know she wants you to be able to concentrate in college. Don't go disappointing her. And don't get Bertie's hopes up."

"I've already talked to Bertie about it."

"What'd she say?"

Fawn pressed the accelerator down a fraction of an inch.

"Slow this car down or I'm not ridin' with you again," Blaze said. "Bertie thinks you're crazy, too, right?"

Fawn glowered at the road. "Blaze Farmer, you're a jerk. She does not think I'm crazy, she thinks I'm too young. But I'm not. I could stay right here and earn my room and board. I don't want to end up like Sheena, living with her mother and father for what looks like might be the rest of her life. I mean, there comes a time when a woman needs to be independent, stand on her own feet and stop letting others coddle her."

"Yeah, a woman, not a kid."

She felt the heat rise up her neck and spread across her face. "You think I'm a kid."

He groaned. "Fawn, you're barely eighteen. Girls your age shouldn't have to take on the whole world to make a living. Don't rush into a decision that could affect your life and Bertie's, too."

"You are *such* a jerk. You're hardly older than me."

"If I'm a jerk, at least I'm an honest jerk, and I'm too good a friend to let you rush into something you can't handle."

"You don't know what I can handle." Jerk.

"You think Sheena needs to move out?"

Sure, change the subject when it got too hard. "I'm saying I wouldn't want her life. And I sure wouldn't want her parents." And right now, she wasn't sure she wanted to keep Blaze for a friend.

Fawn covered the final three miles to Hideaway in irritable silence.

On Thursday evening after work, Jill sat on one of the two wooden chairs on the deck of Karah Lee's cabin on the grounds of the Lakeside Bed and Breakfast. Droplets from her wet hair drenched the shoulders of her scrub top, a comforting coolness that gave her a break from the lingering heat of the day.

A company of ducks paddled across the lake to the opposite shore, chattering amongst themselves as if they knew something she didn't. The stretch of Table Rock Lake that surrounded Hideaway peninsula on three sides had been a meandering river until the dam had been built. This peninsula had once been a hilly ridge.

The glass door slid open, and Fawn Morrison stepped onto the wooden deck, carrying a wire basket of beauty supplies, a plastic cape and a pair of beautician's scissors. Her usual smile was nowhere to be seen. In fact, she looked downright broody, her cheeks a little too pink, her pale-blond eyebrows lowered in a near glare.

"Looks like you brought out the whole arsenal." And those weapons in the hands of an irritable young woman tended to make Jill nervous. "I only agreed to a simple haircut."

"I'll take what I can get," Fawn muttered.

"And you're sure you know how to cut my hair? Mine is different from Karah Lee's. The texture and curl and—"

"Trust me." Gone was the normal, teasing lilt that typified Fawn's speech. "I've done Bertie's hair and Edith's, and one time I even trimmed Sheena's."

"But my hair is more difficult to—"

"And I taught Karah Lee how to do her makeup and pluck her eyebrows and—"

"Don't want to go there."

Fawn dropped her things with a clunk onto the round, glass-topped table beside Jill's chair. "Fine. I guess you feel the same way everyone else in this town feels about me. I'm just an incompetent kid who can't do anything right."

"Whoa. Hold it." Jill pulled the other chair out and indicated that Fawn should sit down beside her. "Did somebody else suddenly inhabit Fawn Morrison's body? Where'd this attitude come from?" She had never seen this kind of behavior in the fourteen or so months Fawn had lived in Hideaway.

Fawn slumped down, arms crossed over her chest, obviously unhappy. "Did Karah Lee tell you I messed up her wedding date because I couldn't get it planned in time?"

Uh-oh. Nerves were stretching thin as the wedding date drew nearer. "Is that what you heard?"

Fawn's eyes narrowed. "Don't stall on me. I asked you what she said."

And then she burst into tears.

Chapter Nineteen

Rex stepped out of the clinic into warm sunshine, and nearly collided with Cecil Martin, who looked wide-eyed and worried. The elderly man quickstepped along the sidewalk, gray hair—what there was of it—flying in the breeze, as he cast an occasional glance over his shoulder.

"Everything okay, Cecil?" Rex called out to the already retreating figure.

The old man glanced back at him without slowing down. "Yep, got to keep a move on, get back to the store, you know. Can't keep the customers waiting."

"How long will you be open tonight?" Rex called after him.

"At least until seven," Cecil called back. "Maybe later, depending on when I find time to do more stocking." He gave a wave over his shoulder.

Austin Barlow sauntered along in Cecil's wake, cowboy hat perched at an angle on his head to best thwart the still-bright sun, hands stuffed into the pockets of his jeans. For some reason, at least three people had seen fit to point Austin out to Rex this week, and explain that Austin and Jill had once been an "item."

Austin nodded at Rex, then glanced toward Cecil with the expression of a serious fisherman who had let a big one get away. He shrugged, slowed his steps. "Say, aren't you that fella who came to turn our clinic into a hospital?"

"That's right." Obviously, people had also been as eager to point Rex out to Austin.

Austin stopped and held his hand out to Rex. "Barlow's the name. Austin Barlow."

"Rex Fairfield." Rex shook. The man had an overfirm grip, as if he had spent a lot of years attempting to establish his boundaries, and had never quite overcome the need to intimidate.

"I hear there's a title attached to that name. You're a doctor, right?"

"You can call me Rex."

"You planning to establish hours of your own once you get settled?"

"Hadn't considered it."

Austin tilted his hat back a little, as if to get a better look at Rex—or maybe to give Rex a better look at him. "I heard you've had some experience with Hideaway in the past."

"I've visited here before, many years ago."

"That's what I heard. Visited quite a few times, from the sound of it." His lips tilted in a smile that didn't reach his eyes.

"That's right."

Austin held his gaze longer than was necessary. Rex had never been fond of playing the macho games of domination, but he could hold his own. Austin looked away first.

The clinic door opened, and Cheyenne stepped out. "Well, there you are, Austin Barlow. I saw you at the funeral yesterday, but didn't get a chance to speak with you."

Austin removed his hat and nodded to her, suddenly all warmth and welcome. "You're looking better than ever, Cheyenne."

Was that a blush Rex saw on the man's face? And did he hear a sudden strain of shyness in Austin's voice?

"I'd like to come by and talk with you and Dane sometime when you have a few minutes to spare," Austin said.

"Just give us a call." Cheyenne studied him for a brief moment. "Austin, are you…is everything okay with you?"

The man looked away, then back, and his smile suddenly seemed forced. "Right as rain today. No need to worry about me." He excused himself, nodded to them both again, and headed toward the general store.

It seemed his prey had not eluded him permanently—if, indeed, he was pursuing Cecil Martin.

"Austin's sick," Cheyenne said.

"Did he tell you that?"

"No, he would never do that. He's one of the biggest chauvinists I've ever known. Even though he was very friendly to me when I first came to Hideaway, I don't think he ever took me seriously as a physician until he thought I was going to leave. I can't see him ever willingly admitting to a weakness to a female physician."

"How can you tell he's sick?"

"He's lost at least forty pounds," she said. "And you can't possibly have missed those circles beneath his eyes."

"From what I've heard, he's had a difficult couple of years. That could cause weight loss and baggy eyes."

She watched until Austin disappeared through the front door of the general store. "He's trying to convince people around here that he's a changed man. I'm beginning to think he's actually telling the truth." She shook her head and turned to walk across the street in the direction of the municipal boat dock, where her boat awaited to take her across the lake to the ranch.

Rex walked with her. "Because you think he's sick?"

"I don't know. There's something disturbing him. He's anxious about something."

"Could it be bad news about his son?"

"I hope not." Her steps slowed when she reached the other side of the street. "I'd just like to know what it is."

Jill glanced around the perimeter of the cottage and toward the lakeshore to make sure there was no one near enough to overhear her from the cottage deck. "I don't know what's going on with you right now, Fawn, but you're jumping to some faulty conclusions."

"Not according to Blaze." Fawn's pretty blue eyes filmed with more tears, but this time they didn't fall. Jill had seldom seen the girl cry.

"Is Blaze being mean to you? If he is, I'll beat him up for you."

Jill was rewarded by a bare hint of a smile in those eyes.

"He said Karah Lee had to postpone her wedding because she didn't think I could pull it off in time," Fawn said. "He makes it sound like I mess everything up."

"Are you sure about that?" Jill asked. "Because it looks to me like you're a pretty capable young woman." And Fawn had always prided herself on that capability. She was more fiercely independent than anyone Jill had ever known. Except maybe for herself.

"Then why did Karah Lee postpone?" Fawn asked.

"I wasn't privy to all the scuttlebutt."

Fawn frowned at her. "Huh?"

"I obviously didn't hear what Blaze heard, but my impression was that she just wanted to have more quality time with you before adding Taylor to the mix."

"Why would she do a dumb thing like that?"

"Because she's a wise lady. Because she takes her foster-mother role seriously. Because she loves you."

Some of the lines of resentment slowly eased from Fawn's face. "Did she tell you that?"

"She doesn't have to," Jill said. "It shows in everything she does. Karah Lee isn't very good about verbal expression, but she doesn't have to be. She lives what she believes, and she loves you."

Fawn swallowed. "Okay."

"I doubt she's told you that very often," Jill said.

"No."

"Sometimes, when a person's lived in a dysfunctional family, the L-word is hard to say."

"Yes."

Jill fingered some droplets from the side of her face, amazed by her sudden ability to spurt wise words to a teenager, and just as amazed by the certainty she felt in those words. "I guess I can speak from some experience, being a single woman myself, but if I had a fantastic kid like you under my protection and was getting ready to marry a man I loved to distraction, I'd do all I could to make sure all three of us would make a good match."

"You mean you wouldn't secretly want the fantastic kid to move out on her own and give you time alone with the love of your life?"

"Why would I want that? Life is about relationships—not just one, but many. I have a lot of people I love, and one man isn't going to meet all my relationship needs. A woman who has her head on straight isn't going to destroy one relationship in order to build another one. She's going to do just what Karah Lee's doing. She wants to make sure you and she and Taylor have time to bond before you all start living together."

Fawn sat staring at Jill for a long moment, as if she were trying to decipher a different language. "You really think that?"

"Why don't you ask her? For that matter, you could ask Taylor the same thing. But first, I want you to cut my hair, and I want you to do a good job."

The gamine grin gradually resurrected itself across Fawn's features. "You don't think I'll ruin your chances with Dr. Rex?"

Jill's eyes narrowed. "Excuse me?"

The grin peeked out further, and she continued to tease, sliding her gaze over Jill's face. "Karah Lee didn't want her eyebrows tweezed at first, until I showed her what a good eyebrow shape could do for the rest of her face."

"Karah Lee is better with pain than I am."

Fawn appeared to settle for the haircut, but Jill didn't trust her.

Jill winced as the young woman snipped the first few strands, bending over to look at the long, dark locks that drifted to the wooden floor of the deck. "Not too short."

"It'll be okay. Trust me, I said. I'm thinking something cute and perky." Fawn snipped more from the top.

Jill watched in alarm as a few more longer strands of hair fell in front of her. "I've never thought of myself as perky."

"Sure you are. It's a kind of in-your-face perky, but it's do-able."

"I want people to recognize me on the street."

"Maybe Dr. Rex will learn to appreciate you a little more if—"

"I don't even want to go there."

"Why not? And I know I saw you with him yesterday after the funeral."

"Maybe, but—"

"So he, like, walked you home."

"No. We didn't make it all the way there."

"Why not?"

"Because we ran out of things to talk about." It wasn't a lie, exactly.

"Well, you obviously had more to say later, at the dinner."

"You're pushing it, Fawn."

"You know, you're a babe, and Rex isn't bad for one of those stuffy doctor types. He's single. You're single."

"Don't even talk about it, Fawn. It isn't happening."

"Sure it isn't." Snip-snip. "How about a perm? Or, hey, we could maybe even go blond for—"

"Hold it right there, young lady." Jill suddenly doubted her sanity for allowing this child, who was barely eighteen, to make such drastic changes in her appearance.

"Okay, no perm. You're right. Curls wouldn't look good with your features. Still, a few streaks of blond and a bouncy, short—"

"Fawn Morrison, I'm a forty-five-year-old woman, not a cute, perky teenager." Jill grabbed the armrests of the chair, prepared to escape if she had to. "I have more important things to do with my life than fake a good haircut and face to encourage a man."

"It's not fake when you've already got the goods, Jill." Fawn pressed Jill back into the chair, all the old self-assurance back in place. "Let me finish. You'd look like a freak if you paraded down the street with your hair like that, and excuse me, but you don't need the extra publicity, if you know what I mean."

Jill glared at her. "No, I don't know—"

"When I'm done with this hair, I want to pluck, and don't argue. If you don't like it, the hair will always grow back. But when it comes to this kind of stuff, I'm an artist. Just be my sculpture a little longer."

Jill relented, reluctantly. What*ever.*

"Why wouldn't you let Sheena do this when she wanted to last week?" Fawn asked.

"You may not have noticed, but Sheena Marshall is a bit of a space cadet. There's no telling what she might decide to do once she got her hands on me."

"Space cadets need love, too. And she's not as much of a cadet as you think. She's just...had a strange life. She doesn't see things the way others do, because of her poor mother. I mean, that woman has issues."

For the first time since the haircut began, Jill's attention focused on Fawn instead of what Fawn was doing. "Yes? Issues?"

"Well, you know I always thought she was just a grouch. I've known a lot of grouches, and she's queen of 'em all, no matter what Bertie says about her. I mean, Bertie's been walking with God so long she just automatically thinks the best of everyone. She says the reason Mrs. Marshall is never happy is because she's always trying to please God on her own, and failing. Or something like that." Fawn put down her scissors and picked up tweezers.

"Hold it," Jill said. "Sheena's eyebrows make her look surprised all the time."

"Sure they do. That's because I'm not the one who does them. She overplucks, but we had a talk about that the other day, and she's letting them grow back."

"You and Sheena are really buddies?" Jill asked.

"Sure. She's nice, and she doesn't treat me like a kid." Fawn reluctantly put the tweezers down and picked up her scissors again. "She said you stopped by the spa and asked a few questions about the day Edith died."

"A few."

"Did her mother chase you off?"

"No, but she wasn't exactly welcoming."

"Didn't you two go to school together?"

"Yes, but Mary's behavior is a mystery to all of us. She just suddenly changed, and she never changed back."

Fawn's movements slowed, then stopped. "Why did you ask Sheena about who was in the spa that morning? You think something in the clinic killed Edith? Like, maybe she was allergic to something?"

"I don't know. I'm just not sold on the theory that she died of a heart attack."

"But Cheyenne and Karah Lee—"

"I realize there were three doctors in attendance at the time of Edith's death, but it's this…gut feeling." That wasn't a lie, either. It was her own gut feeling, combined with her sister's gifted knowledge, which only intensified her concerns.

"Sheena's a sad case," Fawn said, snipping again, this time shaping instead of removing length. "I think she's still at home because she feels so connected to her mother. I'm so glad I never had to worry about that kind of thing."

Jill's attention suddenly riveted on Fawn's voice. So much bravado, and yet, beneath that there was a hurt child, still wondering why her own mother didn't love her.

"You may have to worry about it with Karah Lee," Jill said. Yesterday evening, just before she left for home, Bertie had stopped her and told her about Fawn's sudden idea about working at the bed and breakfast. It wouldn't fly, and Fawn would learn that very quickly if she would just speak to Karah Lee. Unfortunately, she was going about this whole thing the wrong way.

Fawn placed the scissors down and reached once more for the tweezers. "Come on, Jill, let me at 'em. You'll love the way it makes you look when I do it. It'll open your eyes."

"My eyes are already open."

"It'll make you look younger."

"I don't want to look younger. I'm proud of my age. I'm forty-five, and I want everyone to know it."

Fawn gave a quick, impatient sigh. "Are you just afraid to let men see how attractive you can be? You're built like Karah Lee, with all the goods in all the right places. With a good wardrobe, you'd be—"

"I like my wardrobe, and I don't want to be on display. In fact, the only reason I'm letting you do this is so you can practice."

"Oh, really? You mean practice handling cranky customers?"

Jill glared, then winced. "Ouch! You snuck up on me!"

"Just a few. Let me do a few."

What have I done? She sighed and braced herself. "What do you call a few?"

"Enough to give you an arch, but not enough to make you look like a freak. Don't worry, Dr. Rex won't have any trouble recognizing you next time you see him."

"If you continue to take that tone with me, young lady—"

Fawn chuckled. "Sorry. You'll thank me later. Just let me make you beautiful this once."

"Ouch!"

"You're tough. You can take it."

Jill closed her watering eyes. "What sadist decided thin brows were beautiful?"

"It's the eyes. You need to open up the eyes."

"Ouch!" A tear from pain reflex trickled down Jill's cheek. "This isn't opening my eyes, it's closing them!"

Had she lost her mind? Yes, obviously she had. How did Karah Lee do it?

For a moment, there was no more pain, though Jill couldn't open her eyes. Then she felt stinging cold on her eyebrows.

"Ice," Fawn said. "It'll reduce the swelling."

"Swelling? What swelling? Fawn Morrison, if I walk out of this place looking like Frankenstein's monster, I'll—"

"Would you calm down? I never realized your face mottled red like that when you were mad."

Okay, Jill knew she could do this. And as she'd said, the hair would always grow back. But was she going to have to walk home with a paper sack over her head?

It should be relaxing to close her eyes and listen to the chatter of the ducks down on the lake, and—

"Ouch!"

"Just a couple more, then I'll start on the other brow." Fawn giggled. "You're gonna love this!"

It wasn't relaxing. It was stressful. Even worse, it was uncomfortable to have someone interested in her love life to the extent that they wanted to give her a makeover. Not that she had a love life.

Still, the fact that someone believed she *could* have one made her wonder what it would be like to become a part of the human race. Normal.

What was normal?

"Ouch!" This was definitely not normal. Or at least it shouldn't be.

"Done!" Fawn fluffed Jill's quickly drying hair, then held up a hand mirror. "Now, aren't you glad you let me do it? Just think what you'll look like with the right clothes and makeup. You're one hot chick."

Chapter Twenty

Edith had been gone a week.

Jill checked her bedside clock. Actually, it would be a week in six hours, seventeen minutes.

The sun wove an exquisite tapestry against the bedroom ceiling, casting elaborate shadows of dark and light through the branches of a spruce outside Jill's window. All she wanted to do was cover her head and sleep the day away.

But it was time to get a grip on her emotions. Maybe it was a good thing she had the slumber party tonight, as silly as it sounded to have four grown women in their midforties trade insults and recipes at a bunking party.

But there was still the whole day to endure until she drove to Big Cedar. What else could she do to kill time?

She had already gone through the things Edith had left her. The study Bible was the best item, especially since Edith had made her own notes in the wide margins of the script. Her words had been a calming influence these past few days, when every crack between door and jamb sent Jill rushing to see if someone could be watching her from the other side of that door. Every odd sound in the house made her tense with fear.

She thought about the boxes she had shoved beneath the stairwell. If there was any kind of clue about Edith's death among those things, she certainly hadn't found it. She remembered the bluebird button, which she had placed in her medicine cabinet for safekeeping. The button looked handmade, and it still intrigued her.

She had found a sheet from Mary Marshall's, then Mary Larson's school record, though it was incomplete. The record contained notes of Mary's grades—which had spiked during the first semester of their junior year, then dropped sharply at the end of that year.

Jill had found a handwritten list of dates for conferences with Miss Marilyn Sheave, but no record of those conferences. Maybe Mary had picked them up.

Jill couldn't place Miss Sheave. Maybe she would ask the others about it tonight.

She'd done a cursory inspection of the files Jonathan seemed to think Edith would want her to have. Why he thought that was anybody's guess. There were some other student records besides those of the three boys. The file folders had looked much like her own, which she had picked up in August when the school placed an announcement in the paper that they would be destroying all old student records that weren't picked up before the next school year began.

Her own records were pitifully inadequate, with half the information wrong. Obviously, Edith hadn't been in charge of forms and student records back when Jill was in school, or they'd have been done properly and completely.

Anyway, there was nothing more there through which she might dig and kill some time. Maybe she could show up at the clinic this morning. Ginger Carpenter was covering it with Karah Lee and Blaze. The clinic was open only two Saturday mornings a month now, since it also provided later hours on Tuesdays and Fridays for the convenience of those who worked weekdays.

Jill usually loved her days off. Today, however, she'd rather be cooped up in the clinic with a rush of patients. It was better than being cooped up in this house with the darkness of her memories pressing at her from every side, and a silence from God that implied, in her opinion, that she wasn't worthy of a reply to her prayers.

This week she'd been in a tug-of-war argument with God about the OCD. God wasn't budging.

Shouldn't an obedient, dedicated Christian be able to work up enough faith to overcome these tormenting compulsions?

And yet Cheyenne, Karah Lee, Ginger and every other medical professional reminded her that what she struggled with daily was no less a disease than diabetes or multiple sclerosis. She could tell that most people, however, certainly behaved differently around her than they would around, say, someone with heart disease. Someone like Edith.

Maybe Ginger wouldn't mind a break from the clinic this morning. All these thoughts were getting far too heavy.

A quick glance at the clock told Jill she'd slept two hours later than usual. The clinic had already opened for business. She was just about to pick up her bedside phone when a muffled thump outside her window startled her.

Her bedroom, on the second floor of her Victorian house, overlooked the street, and was, unfortunately, above the roof of the porch. She couldn't see who might be on the porch—if anyone.

The muted tones of the doorbell echoed through the house, reaching her even through her locked bedroom door.

Taking slow, deep breaths to calm the unreasonably fast beat of her heart, she slid from bed and pulled on her red silk robe while checking the street for an unfamiliar automobile. She saw it immediately. The silver Jeep Grand Cherokee parked at her front gate.

What on earth was Austin Barlow doing here? Especially this early in the morning.

When she opened the front door, he was holding his big cowboy hat in his hands. "Sorry to bother you, Jill. I thought you usually got up earlier than this. You always were a morning person."

"It's okay. I was up."

He gave her robe a pointed glance.

"I was awake, anyway. What's up with you?"

He hesitated. "Thought I'd see if you wanted to come out for coffee. Maybe even breakfast down at the bakery. They've got some pretty good popovers."

"Breakfast?"

"Yeah, you know, as in coffee and food? Old friends talking over old times?"

She studied his expression for a moment. If she didn't know better, she'd think he was lonely. "I have some breakfast casserole sitting in the fridge. I was going to try it this morning and see if it'll work for an overnighter I'm going to with some friends."

"Is that the one with Doris, Peggy and Sherry?"

Jill blinked in surprise. "Where'd you hear about it?"

"Jed Marshall told me the other day before he stopped speaking to me."

"He isn't speaking to you?"

Austin shook his head. "You girls are planning the class reunion, right?"

"Yes."

"Well, whatever you do, try not to seat me with the Marshalls. I'm not exactly their favorite person lately."

"Why not? Did you and Jed get into some kind of argument?"

Austin hung his head and fingered the rim of his hat. "Guess you could say that. I heard tell you asked about an autopsy for Edith."

Jill frowned. "You're getting around a lot."

"I hang out at the old haunts. Nothing ever changes around here. Or, at least life and gossip don't change. Say, why don't you hop into some clothes, then hop into the truck? Tell you what, we can go down to the bed and breakfast. Bertie's at least speaking to me."

She sighed. "Would you like some of my breakfast casserole? It won't take long to bake, and my coffee will brew quickly." She stepped back and gestured for him to enter.

He hesitated for a moment, then smiled and stepped in. "That sounds good to me."

He glanced around the sitting room with apparent appreciation. "You always were good with color and decorating and such. I was going to talk to you Wednesday at Bertie's after the funeral, but you weren't there for long."

"It was a busy day. I still can't stop thinking about Edith."

"I know. Neither can I." He placed his hat on the bentwood hall tree at the foot of the stairs, and followed her into the kitchen-dining room. He glanced around the room. "You've done a lot with this place since your grandparents lived here."

"It needed some updating, and I enjoyed the remodel. Noelle helped me."

"Then I'm surprised she didn't hang my picture up somewhere on a wall for target practice." Austin's voice and expression failed to deliver the lighthearted tone he was no doubt aiming for. It had always hurt him that Noelle resented him. In fact, Austin had always had a need to be liked. He covered it well most of the time, but Jill had known him before he had the techniques perfected.

He wandered around the room, glancing out the bay window that overlooked the flower garden in the backyard.

"Why don't you have a seat?" Jill turned on the oven. Austin was making her nervous. Not that that was a new experience for her these days.

He nodded, but continued looking out the window. "You can see Edith's house from here if you look between the two oak trees in your neighbor's backyard."

Jill pulled a small baking dish of egg casserole from the refrigerator. "I used to watch for Edith's porch light to come on when I was a little girl, staying with my grandparents. I would always walk down to her house, and she would serve me milk and freshly baked oatmeal chocolate chip cookies."

"Did you go for the cookies and milk, or just to talk to her?"

Jill took some juice glasses from the cupboard, and some mugs for coffee. "I went for the hugs. I loved to sit on her front porch swing and chatter away about my day."

"I can't forget about how Ramsay shot her cat." Austin's voice suddenly held all the horror with which he had first discovered the news about his son. "She found the little thing right there on her front porch."

Unfortunately, Ramsay's past behavior had become public knowledge. Everyone remembered the day Ramsay had offered to take Cheyenne to pick up some things for the Hideaway festival two years ago. Instead, he'd taken her to an isolated creek and tried to drown her, in full view of Dane, Blaze and Austin, who were tipped off and coming to the rescue.

"I've never gotten over the shock, Jill." Austin's voice was rough with emotion.

"I know that." Though she had never heard him admit his feelings so openly.

"I needed to apologize again to Edith about her cat."

"You apologized to her about that. I remember, because she told me."

He looked at her. "I needed to do it again. Selfish reasons, but I needed to do it."

She nodded. She understood. Sometimes she felt as if she

could never apologize enough about the mistakes she had made in the past that had hurt others. If she'd had a child who had tried to kill someone, that guilt would scar her for life.

"You ready for coffee?" she asked, holding up the pot.

He pulled out a chair at the dining-room table and sank into it as if he had done a hard day's work. "Sounds great. Smells good, too."

She reached for the mugs she'd taken from the cabinet. "Austin, is everything okay?"

He sat frowning at the table for a moment, not answering.

"Is Ramsay doing any better?" she prodded.

The heaviness of grief—something she easily recognized—drew down his once-handsome features. "Ramsay's struggling, Jill, but he's…he's going to be okay. He needed a lot of counseling, and a lot of love. He's getting it."

She frowned at the catch in Austin's voice. Something else was on his mind.

Chapter Twenty-One

❧

The squeak of the old, wood-framed glass door of the barbershop put Rex in mind of the *Mayberry RFD* episodes he used to love watching on television. In fact, quite a few things in this town put him in mind of a simpler place and time, where neighbors sat out on their porches in the warm, late-summer evenings and waved at friends who cruised by, or walked or rode bicycles. Many more rode bicycles on these quiet streets than he'd seen in any other town.

Now he understood why Hideaway, Missouri, had so many visitors. Some locals predicted they would soon surpass Branson in visitors per capita, especially in the autumn when the craft show and antique sales were held. He wasn't sure he believed that. Hideaway was too compact to carry that kind of load.

Still, there was something…so quaint, yet so gentle about this place, where the antique stores abounded on the square, and more shops radiated from the central municipality. Old things brought back memories of times that seemed simpler, their sharp edges dulled by the passage of years.

People still did show interest—even if, at times, too much interest—in the welfare of their neighbors. It was simply the way of small towns, and yet this town had that little something extra that set it apart. The interest shown was often kind, not voyeuristic—not much, anyway.

Why was it that darkness often attempted to outpace the light? Hideaway was one of the most charming places he had ever visited, but from what Rex had learned this week, ugliness, deception and death had also haunted the local hollows.

Dane Gideon sat in the barber's chair, getting his gray-blond hair trimmed. When it was safe to move his head, he gave Rex a friendly nod.

"I hear you're whipping our clinic into shape, Dr. Fairfield."

The eyes of the other men in the shop, including Frank, the barber, and Cecil Martin, turned to him with interest.

"It's already in excellent shape. Cheyenne's done a good job."

"Too bad," Dane said. "She doesn't particularly like directing. She just wants to be a doctor. I don't suppose you'd consider settling around here and taking over the reins eventually? Then maybe I'd get my wife back for a few extra hours a week."

The other men chuckled. "Wish my wife would spend a little more time out of the house," one man said. "Then maybe she'd stop griping about all the hours I like to fish."

"It'll only get worse, Dane," Frank said. "You should've thought about that before you talked her into starting the clinic."

"Now, Frank," muttered Cecil, "What do you think she came to Hideaway for? Certainly not for the company."

The other men chuckled again, and Rex picked up on the forced tone of their laughter. He saw Dane watching Cecil with affection and concern.

Rex knew the clinic staff had been almost as concerned about the effect Edith's death would have on Cecil Martin as they were about the effect on Jill and Bertie.

As the men continued to joke with one another, discussing everything from the price of beef to the abundance of rain this summer, Rex felt a wave of longing to belong someplace again. He traveled so much, and felt so detached from his former life, he thought he'd learned to deal with his loneliness.

He'd discovered that, after all, he couldn't help a certain need for connection. He thought about his stepsons and felt the familiar ache of loss. Their father had abandoned them for another woman. Did they feel their stepfather had also abandoned them?

"Dane," one of the men said from behind his newspaper, "I heard you and Austin are good buddies now."

"Did Austin tell you that?" Cecil asked the man. "Since when did you ever believe anything he said?"

"Heard tell he paid the Gideons a call at the ranch, and

there seemed to be a lot of handshaking and backslapping going on." The newspaper man chuckled. "Never thought I'd see that man pay the boys' ranch a friendly call."

"That's what he did," Dane said.

"Our former mayor's acting awfully strange, if you ask me," the newspaper man said. "He spends a lot of time just sitting down by the dock, watching the boats go by and looking all hangdog. You want to tell me when that man's ever been droopy like that?"

"I guess if your son had tried to murder the town doctor, you'd be a little long-faced, too," Cecil said. He glanced at Rex. "Doc, a couple of folks have asked if you were seeing any patients while you were in town."

Rex felt the sudden attention of the others in the room. That seemed to be a popular subject this week. He shook his head. "That isn't my job anymore. I'm strictly here as a consultant for the hospital."

Cecil shrugged. "Too bad. There's lots of men in these parts who'd sure like to stay local for their doctoring, but they get a little squeamish with a woman." He glanced at Dane. "No offense intended to your wife, boss."

"No offense taken," Dane said. "As long as I don't tell her what you said."

"I don't suppose Austin told anybody anything about his plans, did he?" Frank asked, dragging the subject back to the former mayor.

"Seen him steppin' up onto Jill Cooper's front porch on my way here this mornin'," said the man behind the newspaper. "You knew they was sweethearts back a few years ago."

Rex felt more than a twinge of discomfort.

"That was high school, you old coot," Cecil said. "Ancient history."

The coot shrugged and the paper rustled. "Could be Austin's thinkin' of settlin' back down in these parts, maybe lookin' for somebody to settle with."

Rex looked up to find Dane's gaze resting on him as Frank removed the protective cape from his shoulders with a flourish.

"Cecil, you're next. Hop on up here. I've got a busy practice. You snooze, you lose."

Jill refilled Austin's mug as the aroma of baking breakfast casserole filled the kitchen-dining room.

"You've always been a good cook," he said, nodding his thanks for the coffee.

He still drank it black. Jill didn't know if he drank it that way because he believed a real man should take it straight, or if he really liked it that way. With Austin, it had always been hard to tell.

Insecure at heart—and a little boy whose father had been an abusive hypocrite of a churchgoer—Austin probably didn't know what he liked and what he didn't.

His formative years had been spent trying to placate his father and avoid beatings. His adult years, from what she could tell, had been spent attempting to please the rest of Hideaway so he could make a name for himself. She had a suspicion any name besides *Barlow* would have made him happy. Now he had new reason to be ashamed of the name.

"So, Austin, did you manage to sublet Grace Brennan's apartment?"

He nodded. "I sure did. I have that pretty little gal, Fawn, to thank for giving me the heads-up on that. Grace'll be on the road for at least a month, and she has her condo in Branson, so her mother, Kathryn, told me I could keep the place as long as I stayed in Hideaway."

"You plan to stay in town for a while, then?" Jill asked.

Some of his usual bravado slipped from his expression. He blinked, and she thought she saw apprehension there. "I have a feeling that isn't going to be up to me."

"What do you mean?"

He swallowed another gulp of coffee. "Didn't I hear that Rex Fairfield is a doctor? You know, the guy working with Cheyenne to bring the clinic up to standard?"

"He was." Obviously, Austin didn't want to talk about personal things.

"Was?" he asked.

"Rex doesn't practice medicine now. What do you mean, 'it won't be up to you'?"

"Once a doctor always a doctor, unless he's had his license revoked for some reason."

"He hasn't. Austin, are you in some kind of financial bind?"

He tried with obvious effort to let the old Austin slip back into place, grinning and leaning back. His movements were wooden and awkward. "Don't you worry about me. I've saved enough for a rainy day, and I'm not completely out of the real estate business. Work like that gets into a fella's blood." He set the cup down. "Need some help setting the table or something?"

She reached for plates. "No thanks. I can get it."

"Oh, that's right. You like to do things just a certain way, don't you?"

She winced. She knew he meant nothing by that. In fact, when they were dating, he hadn't been aware of her struggle with OCD. In those days, the problem hadn't yet been named, and most of her classmates hadn't even realized there was a problem.

If Jill were honest with herself, she wouldn't have been aware of it, either, if not for Noelle's astuteness, and for the family's attitude about the curse. Living with a condition like OCD from childhood made it much less obvious than suddenly developing the disorder as a young adult.

As for Austin, he'd been too consumed by his own home life at the time to take much notice of anyone else's difficulties.

He sipped at his coffee and stared out the bay window, more reflective than Jill had ever seen him.

She sat down across from him. "Austin, won't you at least tell me, of all people, what you've had on your mind since you arrived in town?"

His gaze played over her face. He raised a hand and covered hers with it on the table. "Do you ever think about the past and things you could have done differently if you hadn't been such a bumble-headed idiot who didn't know right from wrong?"

She withdrew her hand.

"No, I'm sorry." He sighed and shook his head. "I didn't mean *you* were the idiot. I'm talking about myself, here."

"What part of the past are you talking about?" she asked.

"You name it, I probably blew it. I tried to blame Blaze

for those things my son did. Ramsay burned down the barn at the boys' ranch, which nearly killed Blaze. Ramsay committed all kinds of vandalism. And I blamed the wrong person."

"So apologize to Blaze and get on with life. You don't have to do permanent penance."

Austin wasn't listening. "If I had only realized sooner what was happening. That incident with Edith's cat? He shot the cat because of a disagreement Edith and I had during a church business meeting one Wednesday night. If I had only realized…"

"Austin, how could you? You didn't know what was going on in Ramsay's mind. No one did."

He leaned forward. "Why did you break up with me when we were in high school?"

The sudden change of subject startled her. It also alerted her that he might be circling in on the real reason he'd come to visit. "You're talking about Chet Palmer's death now?"

He nodded. "So that *was* why you broke up. You suspected me, too."

Jill was trying to follow his line of thought. Hadn't she had her own suspicions these past few days about Edith's death? "I believed you and Junior and Jed were involved in that practical joke," she said.

"It was a deadly prank."

She noticed he still wasn't admitting to anything. "Someone just made a horrible miscalculation. I know you never would have done anything like that on purpose. What does Chet's death have to do with anything now?"

He held her gaze for a moment, then sighed and returned his attention to the lake. "The thing is, I never could figure out how it happened."

"You mean you *didn't* plant a stink bomb for Chet to find?"

For a moment, she didn't think he would answer. "A stink bomb is a totally different thing from a poison bomb."

"Selenium instead of sulfide," Jill said. "A mistake of ingredients."

"As dumb as I was in chemistry, even I knew that selenium would be deadly in that mix. In fact, the selenium was in a different place, entirely. It's been bothering me all these years." He spread his hands across the table.

"Why did you suddenly decide you had to say something about it?" Jill asked. "Why now?"

He sat staring at his own hands for a long moment, then looked up at her. "I have a good reason to be here, Jill, but it isn't something you need to worry yourself about. Just let it go, okay?"

She scowled at him. The old Austin was raising his hard head again. "Just like that? Forget about it?"

"I'm sorry I brought it up. It isn't fair to you. You have enough to worry about right now." He took a deep, appreciative breath. "Something sure smells good. Is that casserole ready?"

With great reluctance, she got up and got busy. She knew Austin well enough to know he would tell her no more until he was ready.

Chapter Twenty-Two

❧

Jill sat on the deck of the log cabin at Big Cedar, listening to the boats on the lake just beyond the stand of trees in front of her.

Doris Batson—tall, long-legged and still with a figure to die for even after giving birth to three children and divorcing two husbands—raised the lid on the barbecue grill. Smoke wafted out across the deck and rose upward. "Not long until dinner. Jill, didn't you bring the watermelon?"

"Melon balls," Jill said. "With a delicious sauce of balsamic reduction. Big difference." A watermelon made a big mess, you had to spit the seeds out, juice dripped everywhere and it drew ants.

Melon balls were easier to eat, and preparing them had

given her something to do for the afternoon—making sure every single ball was as perfect as she could get it—and eating the imperfect ones. There had been a lot of imperfect ones.

"I brought German chocolate cheesecake." Peggy Fenton, taller than Jill by half a foot, and heavier by at least fifty pounds, leaned back in her chair and rested her feet against the railing around the deck, notepad in lap.

"Salad, here," Sherry Randall said. "The best you've ever tasted."

"We need some icebreakers this year," Peggy said. "I swear, if Deb Rakoski doesn't come to this reunion I'm going to hog-tie her and drag her there myself. It isn't as if she lives in another state, and she could leave that design business of hers for one night."

"She's a woman in demand now, finally, after all those years of hard work," Sherry said. "Most popular designer in Branson."

"But she needs to remember her roots." Peggy, who had the singular ability to draw everyone into the conversation, couldn't understand it when not all their former classmates returned for the reunions. She could have been a top talk-show host. No one felt left out for long with Peggy.

"You're jealous," Sherry teased. "I'm so proud of her I could bust." Sherry Randall was still as disgustingly cheerful and optimistic as she had been in high school as captain of the cheerleading squad. "I have a great idea for an icebreaker. Let's have a contest to see who can remember the worst date anyone had in school."

"Sorry, no contest there," Doris said. "That would be me

with Fish Lips in eighth grade. Remember that dance? He kept trying to get me to slow dance with him. It was *not* a romantic experience. He not only had fish lips, he had fish breath."

"I got you beat," Peggy said. "Remember the community dance they held at the City Hall every year during the festival? I agreed to go out with Junior Short one year."

Doris gasped. "You didn't!"

"I felt sorry for him."

"Why didn't we know about that?" Sherry asked.

"None of you went to the dance that year, and I kept a low profile. It isn't something I'm proud of," Peggy said. "He picked me up in his old beater with booze on his breath."

"He was drunk when he picked you up?" Sherry asked. "And you still went out with him?"

"If my dad had smelled his breath, that date wouldn't have happened."

"So what did you do?" Doris asked.

"I went to the dance with him. He only wanted to slow dance, and when we did, he became Mr. Octopus."

"Could've told you that," Doris muttered.

"I finally slapped him. He got mad and hung out the rest of the dance with his best buddies in crime."

"Austin Barlow and Jed Marshall," Jill said.

Peggy nodded. "Those guys were inseparable."

"After that thing with Chet Palmer, I guess they couldn't find any other friends," Sherry murmured.

The deck grew silent for a few long beats as the meat sizzled on the barbecue.

Jet bomber. Jill couldn't forget Edith's gasping breaths that day, her hoarse, barely there words. Chet Palmer. Why was that incident suddenly topmost in everyone's mind lately?

"You think they really did that?" Doris asked, her voice hushed. "Nobody ever admitted to planting that poison bomb."

"Sure they wouldn't." Peggy nodded toward Jill. "You would be the expert on that."

Jill tried not to fidget. "How should I know?"

"You broke up with Austin after Chet's death," Doris said. "You must have believed he did it."

"Austin wouldn't endanger Chet's life on purpose," Jill said. "I just thought he was moronic enough to try to pull that practical joke, and got the wrong chemicals."

"So you do think he did it, then," Doris said.

"He never admitted to anything."

"Not that Austin Barlow would ever admit to doing something wrong," Sherry said. "Neither would Jed or Junior, after Chet died. I mean, if they'd admitted to that, they could have been in huge trouble. Maybe even juvenile hall."

"I think something was up with those three, though," Peggy said. "They sure didn't talk much after that. Jill, didn't Austin say anything to you about it?"

"Why would he? I wasn't exactly sympathetic to the cause at the time. I mean, Chet died because of that stupid stunt."

"Jill, did you actually see anything that would lead you to believe Austin and his buddies did the deed?"

"If I had, I would have reported it. You expect me to remember something clearly that happened half a lifetime ago?" Jill couldn't hold Peggy's stare.

"Of course we do," Peggy said. "You're the genius with a photographic memory. You were the class brain."

"I do not have a photographic memory, and I wasn't the class—"

"Spill, Jill," Doris said.

"I didn't know anything for sure then," Jill said with a sigh. "As I told you, Austin clammed up after Chet's death. I thought I sensed something between those three, but I was suspicious, anyway, so who really knows? Peggy, you didn't finish your story about your date with Junior Short."

Tension eased for a moment when Peggy gave her characteristic giggle. "The guy was so snockered before the dance was over, I tried to get a ride home with Raymond Mettlach and his date. Junior got mad and said he could get me home."

"My parents were there," Sherry said. "They never missed a dance. They'd have taken you."

"By then I was too embarrassed to ask," Peggy said. "I was an idiot, I know, but since I only lived at the edge of town I didn't think he could get us killed here in Hideaway. He decided halfway home to try to take me parking."

The women burst into laughter, startling a squirrel at the base of the nearest cedar tree.

"What did you do?" Jill asked.

"He climbed into the back seat, I stayed in the front seat and waited for the fireworks to begin."

"What fireworks?" Jill asked. "We never had fireworks at the festival."

Peggy rolled her eyes. "Verbal ones, Jill. Junior had parked right in front of the police chief's house. The guy's wife came out with a broom and started beating the ugly off his car. Junior peeled out, laying rubber and swerving all over the road."

This time, at the sound of their laughter, a flock of birds flew from the treetops and circled.

"Of course, he didn't get in trouble over it because his dad was buddies with the police chief," Peggy said. "But he got me home three minutes later. He didn't get a kiss good night, either."

"The jerk," Doris said.

"Still is," Peggy said.

"Oh, hey, wait a minute." Sherry grabbed a photo album from a huge bag of goodies she had brought to the party. "Sorry, Peggy, that was good, but I think I've got our winner. I forgot all about this until I was pulling pictures for the reunion and saw it." She slid a snapshot from its sleeve and tossed it onto the circular deck table. It spun to a stop in front of Jill.

The photo was of the four of them with their dates for the Junior-Senior Prom. Austin looked so much younger standing behind Jill, arm draped lazily over her shoulder, hair a brighter red than it was now.

Jill marveled at the smile she had given to the camera— one that amazingly reached her eyes. Maybe some of her memories were faulty. She couldn't remember being happy much of the time after Mom's death.

A few feet beyond the four of them and their dates stood Mary Larson, who became Mary Marshall when she married Jed.

Sherry tapped her long, polished nail against the image of

Mary, who was standing slightly behind Austin. Mary wore a long, white dress with a blue velvet wrap over her shoulders.

"What do you think she knows about the Chet tragedy?" Sherry asked. "Mary was always tight with Jed."

"Why should she know any more than I did?" Jill asked. "I was close to Austin."

Sherry continued to place other old pictures on the table. Most were of the four of them. Some were of Mary and Jed. It was startling to see Mary smiling.

"Unless I'm blind," Peggy said, "that sure wasn't who she was with that night. Who did she go with?"

Sherry reached once more into her photo album. "Don't you remember? She and Jed had a fight a couple of weeks before the dance."

"Oh, sure, we're going to remember that," Doris said. "Get serious, Sherry, I can barely remember my own telephone number these days."

"Mary broke up with Jed and went to the dance alone. She danced with practically every guy there, even Chet Palmer." Sherry spread more photos out, one atop the other. "I think she did that just to make Jed mad. Everyone knew Mary and Chet were always competing for top scores."

The table fell silent, and the women exchanged long glances.

Jill frowned. She did remember that. Mary had been so outgoing and cheerful that night. Almost too cheerful. As if she were drunk. Since Mary was a teetotaler, that had been a surprise.

Sherry tossed another snapshot onto the table. "Would you look at this? That daughter of Mary and Jed's could be

Mary's double. And do you remember this gorgeous sweater? Would you believe Mary made this herself for a Future Homemaker's project? She even made the buttons."

Another photo fell onto the growing stack, and Jill picked it up. "What's this?"

"This was taken later the night of the dance. Notice anything different?" Sherry asked dryly.

It was another photo of them, only this one was shot outside after that same dance. Mary once again was in the background, but she certainly wasn't posing for any picture. Her hair, which had been up in the first picture, had now fallen around her shoulders. Her dress was smudged with dirt, and her wrap was missing. She had her head turned from the photographer.

"What happened to her?" Sherry asked.

"Good question," Doris said. "If I remember correctly, Jed went to the dance that night."

"With whom?" Sherry asked.

"He went stag. Even though Mary and Jed weren't seeing one another, no one was willing to risk her anger by going with him," Doris said. "I would have gone with him myself, if he'd asked. That girl didn't scare me."

"You don't think he'd be angry enough to hurt her, do you?" Jill asked. "Jed was always crazy about Mary."

"I'd believe something like that of Junior Short, but not Jed," Sherry said. "Maybe Junior thought he was doing something to protect his friend's so-called honor."

"Or Austin?" Doris asked.

Again, there was a moment of silence.

"When a guy grows up in an atmosphere like the one Austin grew up in," Sherry said at last, "he starts to think violence is the best way to handle a situation."

"Well, I don't believe a simple dance or two with a class rival is going to rile anybody enough to get that rival killed the next year," Peggy said.

Doris sat studying the pictures for a moment longer. "I'm sure you're right. Must've been a tragic mistake. I say the boys simply wanted to play a prank on a jerk, and someone grabbed the wrong chemical. Those three boys weren't exactly geniuses in chem lab."

Jill caught Doris's gaze. "You really think that prank was just a mistake?"

Doris fixed her with a stern stare. "If you have reason to believe it was anything else, you'd better have proof."

"Anyway," Sherry said, "Mary wins the worst date contest. She came alone, maybe got into a fight with someone. I don't remember seeing her smile since that night."

Chapter Twenty-Three

❧

Rex sat alone in the executive suite of the Lakeside Bed and Breakfast with a completely charged cell phone and a number that had been on his mind since he arrived here last week. It was once his own telephone number, and Margret hadn't changed it since the divorce.

He spoke the voice tag into the handset. "Home."

The dialing was automatic. He drummed his fingers against the armrest of the chair as he sat staring out over the surface of the lake. This suite commanded an idyllic view of the cliffs across the lake, and he saw a canoe sliding through the water with Blaze Farmer and Fawn Morrison sitting face-to-face.

He smiled. Just yesterday afternoon at the clinic, Blaze had come in for a few hours after his last class, and during a lull between patients he'd started asking questions about Rex's love life.

Cheeky kid.

Then Karah Lee had shared some interesting news about the teenager's prowess when it came to matchmaking.

If Blaze thought he was going to jump-start a romance for Rex in this town, he was going to ruin his hard-earned reputation.

Rex refused to allow hope to get a foothold at this point. Jill had made it clear she wasn't interested.

Not that he had ever accepted discouragement at face value. Jill hadn't always been one to say exactly what was in her heart. In fact, he suspected she honestly didn't always know what was in her heart.

After the fourth ring, Rex was prepared to hang up. Then someone picked up.

He gave a silent lightning prayer that it wasn't Margret. If she answered, there'd be the interrogation and the litany of complaints about his influence on the boys because of his continued contact with them.

To his relief, Rex heard the shy, deep voice of Tyler, his oldest stepson.

"Hey, Ty. Hope I didn't catch you at a bad time."

"Dad?"

The sudden joy in that beloved voice made Rex's eyes sting with tears for a moment. How he missed his boys.

"Where are you?" Tyler asked. "Are you here in town?"

"Not even close, unfortunately." Not that Margret would agree to allowing him to see Tyler and Jason, even if he *were* in Kansas City, not since her most recent outburst at him. "I'm down in the Ozarks on a job. Ever heard of Hideaway, Missouri?"

"Sure. That's the place where the big condo project collapsed last year. What're you doing there?"

"Working to turn a clinic into a hospital. How's it going up there in the big city?"

Tyler groaned. "Worse all the time. Mom's impossible, she wouldn't even let me go on the float trip with the group from church, and she won't let me get a job so I can save for a car."

They'd had this conversation before. "You know it won't do any good for me to talk—"

"I don't want you to talk with her, I want out of here." There was suddenly more frustration—more anger—than Rex had ever heard in the boy's voice.

"Where would you go?"

There was a painfully long hesitation. "I could come… live with you."

Rex caught his breath. He had wondered if this situation wouldn't arise someday. For the sake of the boys, he'd hoped it wouldn't. Selfishly, however, he felt a little thrill at Tyler's words.

Time to tread with caution. Margret had enough to deal with. Having an ex-husband attempt to turn her own children against her might just drive her over the edge—she was close to it already.

"Tyler, you know how I feel about you guys." He'd made sure, before marrying Margret, that he would be able to love and accept her children as his own. And he'd done so with exceptional ease, simply because those boys were so easy to love. His bond with them had only grown stronger as they grew older. In spite of all the warnings he'd received from well-meaning friends, he'd found he enjoyed his boys even more as teenagers than as young children.

In spite of her shortcomings, Margret had done a good job with those boys, and Rex liked to think he had helped.

One of the lessons he'd learned from his breakup with Jill was not to smother the people he loved.

He'd also learned, however, that being a stepfather always meant there was a natural father. He would never have that tangible right as a parent to actually *be* a parent.

"Why didn't you adopt me when you and Mom were married?" Tyler asked, his voice crackling around the edges. It made him sound younger, less sure of himself.

"You know why, son." Rex knew it had been a rhetorical question. Tyler's and Jason's father would not allow an adoption, even though it meant he would have to continue paying child support. He'd never made an effort to keep routine visitation, and when the boys were little they had been disappointed time and again on holidays when they didn't hear from their father, who was a busy CEO of a thriving investment company in New York City.

"Son, this is a tough time in your life, but believe it or not, it's also pretty tough on your mom."

"That's her fault."

"But you know she needs you to be as supportive of her as you can."

"She'd have your support if she hadn't kicked you out," Tyler snapped. "Don't tell me about support. She thought Kirk was such a winner until he dumped her right after the divorce was final."

Rex winced. One thing he didn't need was the reminder that he had been so easy for Margret to replace. She'd had at least one affair while they had been married, and Rex suspected more. The reminder was like salt in an open wound.

But Tyler needed to talk about it, apparently, and Rex wanted to be there for him, if nothing else, just to listen.

"Tyler, we've talked about forgiveness."

"And we've talked about stupidity, Dad. She's gone through three boyfriends since Kirk, and none of them—"

There was an angry, feminine exclamation in the background, and Tyler fell silent. Seconds later, Margret's voice came over the line.

"Let me guess who this is. Rex Fairfield, I presume. Don't you have a life somewhere else now? I want you to stop trying to interfere in ours."

Doris skewered a thick steak and eased it onto Jill's plate. "Eat all of it, honey. You look like you could put a few pounds on those hips."

"You don't get to Hideaway much, do you?" Jill grumbled. "I just evicted those pounds this summer, and they aren't welcome back."

"So that means you aren't having any of my German chocolate cheesecake?" Peggy grinned and patted her belly. "More for me. You've been dieting?"

"Some."

"Just some?" Peggy asked, making an exaggerated gesture at Jill's newly slim figure. "What diet did you use?"

"I started out on a low-carb, low-fat diet and followed up with portion control and lots of exercise."

Sherry wrinkled her nose. "Exercise? What's that?"

"It isn't something you'd understand, honey." Doris closed the lid over the grill and turned off the switch. "You'd have to do something more energetic than applying nail polish. You didn't even do that in high school."

Sherry scowled at her oldest and best friend, then returned her attention to Jill, studying her face thoughtfully. "The hair is darling. You look younger—"

"Than the rest of us," Doris complained. "Which is disgusting."

"And perky," Jill said with sarcasm. "Don't forget the perky part."

"That's it," Peggy said. "You do. You look great."

Jill suppressed a laugh, then told them about Fawn. Fawn would score big points with these women.

"Wish we'd had someone like that around when we were in high school," Doris said.

"Oh, that reminds me." Peggy reached for a stack of napkins and passed them around the table. "Did any of you pick up your old records at the school? There was a notice in the paper about three weeks ago. They're destroying boxes of files twenty years and older."

"I got mine," Sherry said. "And I should have brought them with me for a good laugh. Those things were so bogus. No way the teachers could keep accurate records on all of us."

Doris gave Sherry a wink. "You mean the gym teacher actually gave you a grade?"

"I picked mine up." Peggy's voice, suddenly subdued, betrayed her tender heart. "Mrs. Potts was helping pass them out. Did you know, even after all this time, she remembered my name, my older brothers and sisters, and how many times I got sent to her office? When I walked in last month, she greeted me, went straight to the box with my file, and handed me the files for my sisters Mary Lou, Donna and Karen."

"They didn't destroy the rest of the files," Doris said.

Peggy passed out paper plates. "They said they would."

Doris leaned forward, voice lowered. "Those pages of records were living history, and I couldn't bear to see something like that destroyed."

"So where are they?" Peggy asked, suddenly stern.

"In a safe place," Doris assured her.

Jill made eye contact with Doris, and Doris gave her a slight nod.

"You *took* them?" Sherry exclaimed. "Those were private records."

"Oh, give me a break, every teenager who ever worked in the office had access to those files," Doris said.

Jill cleared her throat. "Have you…you know…looked through them?"

Doris gave her a level look. "Why would I want to?"

Jill could think of several reasons.

"You did, didn't you?" Sherry accused.

Doris shrugged, nonchalant.

"Since we're on the subject," Jill said, "could someone remind me who Miss Marilyn Sheave was?"

All eyes suddenly focused on her.

"You don't remember the school counselor?" Sherry asked.

"She was the counselor?" Jill asked. "I never had to see her for anything."

Sherry frowned. "So where would you have seen her name?"

"On a school record I shouldn't have."

Sherry sighed. "I'm partying with a bunch of lawbreakers."

"Any idea where Miss Sheave is now?" Jill asked.

Doris laughed. "You're kidding, right? She left after our junior year, married Mr. Moore, the art teacher, and moved out of state."

"You mean the Mr. Moore you had the crush on?" Sherry teased.

Doris made a face at her. "No telling where they are now, or even if they're still together."

"But you could find out," Jill said. "Right? You're the computer genius."

"Why do you want to know?" Sherry asked.

"Just curious."

For a moment, the only sound on the deck was the sizzle of fat dripping from the remaining steaks on the grill. A boat gunned its motor on the lake below them, beyond the screen of cedars.

"There wasn't anyone else like Mrs. Edith Potts," Doris said at last.

Chapter Twenty-Four

❧

Fawn watched Blaze as he stared into the water, focusing on the strokes of his paddle. He'd been so quiet lately, snapping at her for little things that would never have even caught his notice before. Like her driving. When he'd asked her at school yesterday if she'd come canoeing with him this afternoon, she'd nearly turned him down. But she had heard about Austin Barlow's visit to the ranch. Everyone was talking about the reconciliation between him and Dane Gideon.

The ranch was Blaze's home. Dane was like a father to Blaze, and Cheyenne like a mother. How must Blaze be feeling if the man who had made his life difficult ever since he'd arrived in Hideaway was now all buddy-buddy with the people closest to him?

"You know, Blaze, you don't have to take it out on me just because you're upset about Austin Barlow's return to town." Might as well get the subject out in the open.

"Who said I was upset? Just because you're talking about throwing your life away, does that give me a right to get upset? Besides, I stay out of Barlow's way."

"Hiding from him?"

"I don't choose to be around where he is. That doesn't mean I'm hiding."

"Aren't you the one who told me to forgive my mom for everything she did to me?" Fawn asked. "Even after she disowned me?"

"This is different."

"You haven't forgiven Austin."

"He hasn't asked me to."

She tapped his paddle with the tip of hers. "You told me not to wait until my mom apologized because it might never happen, and you said that forgiving is for my sake, not my mom's. Changing your mind about all that stuff now?"

Blaze watched her for a moment, then his dark eyes seemed to fill with his old, teasing humor. "Where'd you get the idea Austin was my mama?" he asked softly.

"If it works for mothers like mine, it works for everyone."

"I don't get the whole apology thing with him." Blaze suddenly plunged his paddle into the water and shoved them away from a boulder. "Most folks liked Austin. He wasn't a jerk to most folks in town, just Dane, the ranch boys and me, in particular."

"And now he and Dane are friends again?"

"They were never friends. Austin blamed one of the ranch kids for his wife's death. Folks felt sorry for him because his wife was killed, so they overlooked it when he took to flingin' accusations and meddlin' too much in city stuff."

"I thought he was the mayor."

"A meddlin' mayor. He's still meddlin'. Dane has a theory about that. He thinks Austin's trying to fix things now because he can't fix his own son. I guess you know why Ramsay went crazy."

"I never heard."

"His mom and dad had a fight, and Austin left angry. Ramsay tried to go with him—he was just a little kid then—and his mom wouldn't let him go. He shoved her, she slipped on something and fell, hit her head and it killed her. Ramsay never told anyone what he did, just let that ranch boy take the blame, until he told me, years later."

Fawn closed her eyes. How awful. That's something she might have done when she was younger, because she was always so angry with her mother...with everyone.

"While Ramsay tried to keep that secret all those years," Blaze said, "it affected his mind, and he finally convinced himself he was some kind of instrument of God."

"Why would he think that?"

"You know what people are always saying when someone dies or is sick. That it's God's will and all. So Ramsay figured he was just carrying out God's will."

"That's scary."

"So most folks around here just feel sorry for Austin."

"Not everybody," Fawn said. She'd heard a few mutterings about Ramsay's uncomfortable relationship with his father.

"Oh, sure, some people realized he could be a jerk, especially to Dane and the boys—"

"And extra 'specially to you."

"But his son's actions humiliated and devastated him."

"Wow, you really can talk like a mature male of the species when you want to," Fawn said. "Austin offered to help Bertie if she sells her business."

"I don't trust him."

"Jill seemed glad to see him," Fawn said, not sure why she felt like taunting Blaze all of a sudden. "She stood outside the bed and breakfast and talked to him when he first arrived last week. I heard, too, that he went by to see her at her house this morning."

"Jill and Austin went steady in high school."

"Really? Two old boyfriends in a week? Jill must be getting popular."

"What do you mean?"

"I overheard something else," Fawn said.

"I don't want to listen to what you learned from eavesdropping."

"That wasn't what I was doing. I was just sitting in my room, minding my own business, and I couldn't help hearing Karah Lee and Cheyenne talking in the kitchen about Dr. Rex."

"He's the one Cecil Martin hopes will join the clinic staff, so you'd better be nice to him."

"You think you're pretty smart, but I know something you don't know."

Blaze splashed her with the paddle. "You know a lot of things I don't never want to know."

"I know they'll kick you out of college for using double negatives."

"They haven't yet."

"And I know Simone in the bakery at the college wants you to ask her out."

He frowned. "Why didn't you tell me that before?"

"Because she just said so yesterday, when I was still mad at you. And I also know Dr. Rex was engaged to Jill Cooper about a thousand years ago."

The expression of shock on Blaze's face was beautiful to behold, as Karah Lee would put it. Finally, a good gut reaction.

"*Our* Jill Cooper? *Nurse* Jill Cooper?"

"Yeah, I know, doctor-nurse romance, it's a cliché and all that."

"But when?"

"Back when they were young."

"Whoa. You're right. A thousand years ago." He shook his head, still stunned. "Is it going to be a problem with them? Jill's been awfully quiet, but I thought it was because she was upset about Edith."

"He's divorced." As soon as Fawn said it, she knew she shouldn't have sounded quite so excited about that.

Blaze's eyes narrowed. "So?"

Fawn trailed her fingers in the water as she gazed back toward town. "Jill never got married."

"She isn't the marrying kind," Blaze said.

"Maybe she is, but she's just been pining for Rex all these years."

Blaze snorted. "She's never even been out on a date since I've known her."

"She went out with the deputy sheriff."

Another snort. "Tom? That wasn't a date, that was fishing. She knows all the best fishing holes."

"Anyway, that doesn't mean anything, Blaze Farmer. You've never been out on a date, either, but I see you watching Simone all the time."

His skin was too dark to show a blush well, but she could see she'd made a direct hit.

Chapter Twenty-Five

Jill watched her former schoolmates eat, unable to pick up her own fork as grief enveloped her once more.

What was she doing here with these three women? Yes, they had been her friends in school, but that had been a lifetime ago. Were they even the same people they had been then?

At a pointed look from Doris, Jill finally picked up her utensils and sliced a piece of grilled steak. Tough grilled steak. Why was she not surprised? This was Doris cooking the food. Why had they allowed this travesty?

She tasted it.

Some things didn't change. Doris never was much good in home-ec cooking classes. Who else could mess up a grilled steak?

Their basic personalities, which Jill knew were the main feature that drew people to each other, hadn't changed. Even she hadn't changed that much. She was still a worrier, and her friends still considered her to be overly fussy, judging by their response to the perfectly shaped, beautifully displayed seedless melon balls that decorated the center of the table, drizzled with balsamic reduction sauce that perfectly complemented the fruit. These women had no taste.

Though Doris still couldn't cook, she had always had an aptitude for computers. Now she utilized her skills with a company that paid her very well for her expertise.

Peggy was still a consummate diplomat in any crowd, always the peacemaker. She had always had more friends than she knew what to do with. She'd grown up on a farm, and she still lived on a farm of sorts—though now she and her husband owned a thousand acres populated with longhorn cattle. They were most likely happy, well-balanced longhorns.

Sherry still loved to portray herself as a social butterfly without a brain in her head, when, in fact, she was one of the best tax attorneys in Springfield—she'd always been a math whiz.

Jill took a generous serving of salad and melon balls, hoping Doris wouldn't be hurt when the plate-sized steak was pushed aside in favor of edible food.

At a look from Doris, however, Jill decided to double her efforts. Good friends endured a lot for good friends. Maybe a sharper steak knife—

She remembered, suddenly, that some people did change. She recalled what Sherry had said earlier about Mary.

"Doris, weren't you and Mary Larson good friends in high school?" she asked.

Doris poured a generous helping of the balsamic reduction on her steak. Jill bit her tongue to keep from protesting. That was meant for the melon balls.

"For a while," Doris said, "we lived on adjoining farms. She and I rode our bikes to the cemetery every Halloween and hid behind the tallest tombstones until trick-or-treaters drove past, then we'd jump out with pillow cases over our heads, screaming at the tops of our lungs. Those cars threw some gravel."

"You were so ornery!" Peggy said with a giggle.

"It was more fun than begging for free candy."

Sherry rolled her eyes. "These days you'd be sued for causing post-traumatic stress disorder."

"Blame Mary, it was her idea."

"So would you say she was, at one time, fun-loving?" Jill asked. "Friendly? Interesting to be around?"

Doris nodded somewhat distractedly as she wrestled with her steak. Next time they would have their dinner catered. This was ridiculous.

"That isn't how I remember her," Sherry said. "I think she flipped out when we were in eleventh grade. She got cranky with the teachers, nearly took my head off when I was nominated homecoming attendant after all Jed's efforts to convince his friends to vote for her."

"I just took for granted part of that was because she was overlooked as chem lab assistant in favor of Chet," Peggy said.

"No, because he wasn't assistant until our senior year," Doris said. "Remember?"

For a long moment, their movements slowed to a thoughtful stillness.

"You don't think *Mary* was the one who played that practical joke on Chet, do you?" Doris asked. "In retaliation?"

"I still think Jed and his buddies did it for her." Sherry said. "You know, the good-ole-boy hero complex was always alive and well in Hideaway."

"It doesn't matter, anyway," Peggy said. "Whatever happened is far in the past; it was a tragic accident, and nothing can be done about it now."

"And Mary is a bitter old woman at the age of forty-five," Sherry said.

"Which could be the result of guilt over an unfortunate accident," Doris suggested.

Jill attacked the steak once more. "I wouldn't say old, but she's aged, and she never smiles. She works part-time at my sister's new spa. Her daughter works there full-time."

"Noelle has a spa now?" Doris exclaimed. "Jill, I'm so proud of her. You sure had your hands full with that little girl when she was growing up. Sounds like you did a great job."

Peggy looked up from her knife-mangled steak. "I bet I know when it happened."

"When *what* happened?" Doris asked. "Noelle was always a wild—"

"Focus, Doris," Peggy said. "What were we talking about earlier? You know, the worst date photos? Sherry's right. Do you remember ever seeing Mary Larson smiling after that prom night?"

"Or ever hear her speak a kind word to anyone?" Sherry asked.

"I wonder if she ever picked up her school records?" Peggy asked.

"No," Jill said.

Again, all eyes focused on her.

"I have them. And some other students', too. Edith's nephew brought them to me the day of her funeral."

"Whose do you have?" Sherry asked hesitantly, as if she weren't sure she wanted to hear the answer.

"Austin's, Junior's, Jed's and Mary's, although hers seem incomplete."

Sherry dropped her fork. "Edith Potts gave you those records?"

"They were with some other things Edith wanted me to have. Jonathan was sure she wanted those particular things shared."

The years had not destroyed Jill's ability to read Sherry's expression. First, there was the incredulity that Edith Potts would ever break the rules. Then there was that same incredulity that Jill would.

"What's going on we don't know about?" Sherry asked.

"Oh, hush, Sherry," Doris said. "Edith left some of her personal effects to Jill for some reason. Jill, you should have brought them."

"There's nothing to learn from them."

"Well, no, probably not, but we could have done some hilarious things with those silly old files," Doris said. "For instance, did you read yours? When we were in sixth grade, school kids were given ratings from one to five on things like attractiveness, personal grooming and how well we played with others during recess. Did you know there was actually a repulsiveness rating? If school authorities did anything like that these days, parents would sue the whole school district."

"Whatever," Peggy said. "We need to have a look at those records, Jill."

"You can't do that," Sherry said. "They're confidential. No one has a right to read them."

"Nonsense." Doris rose from the table with her plate in her hand. "You have my permission to read anything you want in my files. Anyone want more steak?"

"We did a good job with Karah Lee and Taylor, didn't we?" Fawn asked Blaze.

"That doesn't mean we oughta start a matchmaking service."

Fawn dipped her paddle in the water and thrust it backward. "If I become a professional wedding planner, matchmaking would be good for business."

"Why don't you just focus on college for a few years?"

"Boring. So you're saying Austin Barlow and Jill Cooper dated in high school, huh?"

He groaned. "Don't go getting any ideas about that. She broke it off when he got involved in some prank that killed a kid."

She placed the paddle across the bow of the canoe and stared at Blaze. "He killed someone?"

"Nobody knows for sure what happened. Ol' Cecil told me about it. He was the Hideaway High science teacher when all that happened."

"Austin Barlow sure gets into messes, doesn't he? Did he do time or anything?"

"From what Cecil told me, the sheriff didn't do much investigating. Austin and the two guys who were suspected with him were all cleared."

"You mean a kid died, and nobody got blamed?" Fawn exclaimed.

"The sheriff was buddies with the parents of the kids. Cecil says that guy didn't have a right to wear a badge, but he was all Hideaway had at the time."

"There were three kids? Who were the other two?"

"Junior Short—you know him. His boy, Danny, is the biggest bully in Hideaway. He even beat me up once, right after I first came here."

"You're kidding! Didn't he know you were a bleeder?"

"Doubt he'd have cared. But I didn't tell anybody about that when I first came. Anyway, Danny Short didn't graduate high school, and I think it's because he's so mean nobody wanted him there. I hear he's already been busted for a meth lab over in Mountain Grove."

"Who was the other guy?"

"Jed Marshall. You know, the city clerk? Nice guy. Nothing like Junior or Austin."

Wow. "Sheena's dad?"

"That's right."

"She's neat. I've been hanging around the spa when she's working. She's teaching me some massage techniques."

"So now you're going to be a masseuse as well as a wedding planner and bed-and-breakfast owner? What can't you do, Fawn Morrison?"

Fawn wrinkled her nose at him. "So nobody was convicted, and no one knows who was to blame?"

"That's right. Nobody knows for sure."

"Maybe you're being too hard on Austin. For an old guy, he's not bad-looking, and he seems really nice. Maybe Jill would be—"

Blaze covered his ears. "Have mercy!"

Fawn chuckled and splashed him again. "Good, then you'll help me connect her with Dr. Rex."

"I'm not gonna help you with nothin'."

"Language, Blaze. Watch the language. I know you weren't brought up like that."

Chapter Twenty-Six

Rex sat with the phone to his ear, watching the sunset over the far shore of the lake. The trees at the top of the ridge formed a dark lace pattern against the mauve, purple and pink of the sky.

When had it become his job to be whipping boy for his ex-wife every time she broke up with a boyfriend? How long would this diatribe last?

And yet, he had to take it. If verbal abuse could pave the way for him to see his boys, then he'd take it gladly.

"Margret, of course I'm not gloating—"

"Did you know Tyler has decided he's going to leave home and live with you?" The anger was tinged with a characteristic tone of defeat. She'd been that way a lot lately, especially since her latest breakup. She must have really cared about the guy, because this split seemed to have hit her harder than the others—harder even than their divorce.

"The boys have always loved you, Margret. You'll always be their mother." She needed his prayers and compassion, not his arguments or reminders that the decision she'd made had changed not only her life, but his and the lives of the children.

"You must have heard I had to go back to work," she said.

"I hadn't heard."

"I'm surprised Tyler didn't tell you. He's reminded me at least twice a day that it's all my fault."

Yes, more than his own sense of loss, Rex hated seeing what his stepsons endured.

"Are you enjoying the work?" he asked.

"I'm a bank teller." She sounded resentful.

"You've always loved working with numbers." He could hear from the tone of her voice that she somehow blamed him for her situation. And yet, how could she? The divorce settlement had been more than generous in lieu of alimony. A few wise investments, along with the child support she was receiving for Tyler and Jason, should have kept her comfortable. But what was comfortable for her, and what was comfortable for others were an ice age apart.

She was obviously unhappy. At this point, however, the kids were taking the hardest hits. It was always more difficult to be a helpless victim with no control.

Not that Rex had any influence over her decisions, either.

"The boys don't listen to anything I tell them," she said. "All they do is complain, and if I hear one more time about how great you are, I'm going to—"

"I'm sorry," Rex said. "I don't put them up to it, but I'm sorry you have to hear it. If you want me to come back to Kansas City and have a talk with them—"

"What I want is for you to leave them alone. Give me a chance to be their mother without your interference. You call them and stir up their hopes that we're going to mend a destroyed marriage. It isn't going to happen, and they need to stop being disappointed."

"They need to know I love them. How do you think they're going to feel if the person to whom they have turned for a father figure suddenly abandons them?"

"And how would you feel if your own children told you that they wanted someone else to be their parent?" she shot back, voice cracking. For a moment, there was silence over the line.

"Maybe we should stick to how this is affecting them, Margret."

There was a long silence, and then she said, "I'm sorry, Rex. I know you feel that you don't have the rights of fatherhood you seem to think you deserve—"

"I didn't say that, I simply wanted time with—"

"I want you to stay away from Tyler and Jason."

"You want me to cut off my relationship with the boys?"

"You're a distraction. They treat you like an authority figure and me like a flunky. I don't want to deal with that any longer, Rex."

"I'd be glad to help you deal with them," he said. "A united front not only keeps the peace, but gives them a sense of stability."

"I don't want your help at all," she snapped. "Can't you

get that? What I need is for you to get a life of your own and stop nosing around in mine."

He gritted his teeth. "I'm not thinking about my own life right now, I'm thinking about Tyler and Jason. Maybe you should try that, yourself." *For once in your life.*

Unfortunately, his unspoken thought reached her with clarity. "So now you're the all-mature man who thinks he's God's answer to a teenager's prayer. Where were you when Tyler broke his arm in soccer practice? Or what about when Jason got beat up by Billy Watson in eighth grade?"

Now she was complaining because he'd missed soccer practice one day? And he specifically remembered rushing to the ER when Jason's nose was broken. But it wouldn't be wise to respond.

Margret had complained a lot about his long hours at the hospital, which was one reason he had taken steps to change that. Then, when he started this new business and their income dropped initially, she decided she didn't want him around that much, after all. Or perhaps the damage had already been done.

"Rex, I mean it. I don't want you to contact my children again. Is that understood?" she said quietly.

His gaze remained on the darkening sky as shock and anger filled him. *Stay cool. She'll get over it.*

"Rex?"

He didn't reply.

"This time I mean it. I want you to leave us alone."

In the background over the phone, there was a shout of outrage from Tyler, and then the call ended.

Rex resisted the powerful urge to redial and force the

issue further. He had no legal right to do so. Love was apparently not a firm enough foundation for him to stand on.

He wanted to pack an overnight case and drive to Kansas City tonight. Right now. He wanted to see those boys, and he couldn't help feeling they needed to see him.

Margret's initial defection, her infidelity, had been a shock more painful than anything he had ever experienced, and the divorce proceedings had been emotional torture, in spite of the lack of overt hostility. His and Margret's fiercest battle had been over the children. He had known he would lose before he even began, but losing those boys had been the cruelest blow.

Even after three years, he missed his stepsons with the pain of lingering grief, and the times Margret had allowed him to see them were determined by her mood or her situation in a relationship. If she needed someone to spend time with the boys so she could spend more time with her current boyfriend without feeling guilty, Rex suddenly became a popular addition to her sons' lives for a few months.

Then her relationship would end, and she'd want her boys to herself again. The boys were tired of it, and so was Rex, but he had no legal recourse. She was their mother. He was simply a man who obviously made poor relationship choices.

It would do no good to harbor regrets about past choices. It would also do no good to harbor resentment over others' choices—or their lifestyles.

But there was no way he could simply accept Margret's actions—not with the boys involved.

So what could he do?

* * *

Fawn crossed the dark street to the general store, relieved to see the lights still on. Cecil usually closed up before dark; he had trouble seeing his way home after the sun went down. But Bertie needed five dozen eggs for the breakfast bar tomorrow, and Fawn was in the mood for a short walk up the block…or another quick canoe trip across the river to the boys' ranch.

The ranch always had extra eggs, and now that she and Blaze were back on speaking terms, she enjoyed his company again.

Poor Blaze. No wonder he was in such a bad mood lately. Austin Barlow and his son had caused Blaze more trouble when he first arrived at the ranch than even his own mother had caused him when she'd blamed him unfairly for starting a fire. And now Austin was back in town, making nice with everybody except Blaze—the one he had hurt the most.

"I don't like that man," she muttered. "He's still a bigot."

As she neared the store, she saw that good ol' Cecil had the lights on and the door unlocked. This was unusual for Cecil.

How the old man would make it home in the dark, Fawn didn't know. He'd quit driving three years ago because his eyesight just wasn't what it used to be.

She'd probably have to walk him home. That would be okay with her, because he lived only five blocks away, at the edge of town. Cecil always told the best jokes—over and over again.

Still, he was funny. Or at least he had been until Edith's

death last week. It was probably really hard to be old, to see so many friends die, then be surrounded by a bunch of people who were too young to understand why you liked the old-time songs during church worship, or moved so slowly on the sidewalk, or no longer drove.

Fawn had tried to spend extra time with Cecil lately, in spite of her full schedule. She loved old people. They reminded her of her Great-Grandma June, who'd loved her more than anyone else.

Like Great-Grandma used to say, old people weren't any better than anyone else, they'd just had more opportunities to allow the years to sculpt them into works of art.

She'd said not all old people were works of art, because some were pieces of work. The way she said it didn't make it sound like a good thing.

Some were grumpy and some were whiney, and some older folks just didn't like teenagers. It was like they'd just never grown up, Great-Grandma used to say. They'd gone from being shallow and spoiled kids to shallow and spoiled adults, and age didn't soften the edges, but made them sharper.

Fawn agreed. But she figured she'd probably have a bad temper sometimes, too, if she had sore feet and couldn't get around, or if her hands hurt all the time from arthritis, or if she watched too many loved ones die. Maybe the deaths she'd seen lately were what it took for her to grow up. She hated that.

Bertie Meyer was one of the beautiful people, and Edith had been, too. Cecil was.

Some folks thought Fawn was weird because she would

rather spend time with the older people than with kids her own age—but not Blaze.

Blaze understood why she liked old people. He liked them, too. Especially Cecil.

She shoved open the door and stepped inside. "Cecil, you here?"

This general store wasn't exactly a supermarket, but it was bigger than it looked on the outside. Cecil told her that Dane Gideon had purchased two properties—an old restaurant and a hardware store that had gone out of business—then knocked out the wall between them.

Tourists loved the great selection of groceries and dry goods they found along these aisles, from paint and farm supplies to milk and bread—even some organic produce in the refrigerated section.

Dane Gideon knew how to meet the needs of Hideaway—and especially the needs of his good friend, Bertie Meyer. He kept the store supplied with everything she needed for her breakfast bar so she wouldn't have to go out of town for anything.

"Cecil? Hello? Got any eggs tonight? Bertie's got enough for waffles tomorrow, but you know how the church crowd loves omelets and fried eggs."

She scanned one aisle, then turned and searched down the next. She should probably get some onions and peppers. Karah Lee was trying to lose weight, and she could only restrain herself from chowing down on Bertie's black walnut waffles if there were omelets with plenty of grilled onions and peppers and Canadian bacon.

Without the low-carb choices, Karah Lee wouldn't fit

into her wedding dress come the day of the wedding. She was already pushing it, eating too many crullers for breakfast.

Cecil was nowhere to be found.

"Cecil? It's me. Fawn. What's up?"

He might be in the back. He was hard of hearing lately. Blaze said he needed his ears cleaned out. Fawn thought the poor old guy just got tired of listening sometimes.

She gave up looking for him and went to the dairy section. Good, there were plenty of eggs. While she was at it, she grabbed some vanilla bean and oat bran for a recipe she'd been working on in the kitchen when Bertie wasn't looking.

She grabbed the onions and peppers, took her armload of purchases to the counter and called for Cecil again. Still no answer.

She frowned. This wasn't like him. He never left the front of the store unattended.

Suddenly, the silence of this place bothered her. She'd never been here alone. She was seldom afraid of the dark—after all she'd seen and been through in her life, she knew it wasn't the dark she had to fear. Something about the hovering stillness bugged her, though.

There was always music playing from the speakers overhead, and Cecil usually whistled or hummed along with the music—mostly old country songs, which were his favorites. And typically there were other shoppers in the store. It was a busy place.

Tonight there was nothing.

Could Cecil have forgotten to turn off the lights and lock the front doors?

Fawn walked along the front of the store, checking each aisle, then went to the back and pushed open the swinging door that led to the storeroom and office.

She hesitated in the doorway. It was darker back here. Even more silent. Isolated.

She glanced at the wall beside her. Two of the switches were off. Cecil and his helpers often did this when they weren't stocking or using this area.

A quick flip of those switches lit the room, driving the shadows back, but not extinguishing the tension that suddenly made her stomach clench for no reason.

Then she saw a good reason. A large can of tomatoes was on its side on the floor next to the metal shelves. A can of soup and two cans of mushrooms had rolled beneath the shelf.

She held her breath. Her heart pounded. Something was wrong.

"Cecil?" Her voice came out in a croak.

Slowly, fearfully, she stepped toward the back of the storeroom.

In the center of the rear aisle, a ladder was wedged between the shelves, as if it had fallen. She could see more canned goods scattered over the linoleum floor.

In the shadows beneath the ladder, she saw the shape of a man, lying facedown.

"Cecil!"

She rushed to him, tripping and scrambling over canned goods, shoving the ladder so hard it clattered with a horrible racket.

She knelt at Cecil's side and touched his face. It was stiff and cold. Too cold.

Chapter Twenty-Seven

❧

Rex sat in the recliner with his laptop humming softly in front of him. Working on a Saturday night.

Okay, so he wasn't exactly working. Brooding was more like it. He was banished from his family, boys he had helped raise, and whom he had loved for twelve years.

Tonight he felt more lonely than he had felt in the three years since Margret asked him for the divorce. He also felt isolated, and he couldn't take the complete blame for that, though he did take more than his fair share.

He'd made sure that Tyler and Jason knew he still loved and missed them. It was difficult to express his regret about the divorce without appearing to place all the blame on their mother, but that balancing act had to be attempted. While the boys didn't need to hear verbal abuse heaped on their mother, they did need to know they were loved.

He stared out the open window over the dark street and up the slope of the hillside. From this suite, on the top floor of the main lodge of the Lakeside Bed and Breakfast, he could view the lake from the back deck, then walk through the kitchenette to the sitting room and view the town of Hideaway. Often in the evenings, instead of using the air-conditioning, he would open windows on both sides of the suite and enjoy the cross breeze as it floated through the spacious sitting room, kitchenette and bedroom.

From here, he could see Jill's sky-blue, two-story Victorian with the burgundy and navy trim, a few blocks from the town square. After learning from Blaze where Jill lived, he remembered that Jill's grandparents had lived in that house.

Tonight the sun had already set, but he still knew the exact location of the house.

Was it possible his loneliness was somehow intensified because of Jill's presence here?

A breeze drifted through the open window, billowing the curtains toward him. He pushed the panels aside, catching the scent of cedar mingled with the smells of the lake. Somewhere, someone was grilling outdoors. It was perfect weather for that.

Glancing toward Jill's house, he saw no lights, and wondered if she had gone out for the evening. From what he had observed and overheard, she didn't get out at night very often.

Knowing Jill as he had so long ago—as well as hearing

recent comments about her—he gathered she hadn't changed much in twenty-two years. She was very much a creature of habit.

Apparently, so was he, because he found himself glancing in the direction of her house most evenings as he sat reading or working on the hospital project. He had noticed, without trying to, the lights glowing from the front of her house early in the evening, and then almost precisely at ten-thirty every night the downstairs lights went off, and the upstairs lights came on for a few moments before the house went dark.

Tonight he saw no lights. Maybe, in spite of all accounts he'd heard this past week, she did actually have a social life.

He was considering this possibility when an unexpected flicker of light caught his attention. It wasn't downstairs, or upstairs where he assumed her bedroom was located, but in a dormer window of what was most likely the attic.

The brief beam of light puzzled him. It wasn't his business what she was doing in her attic, but this was a startling switch from her usual routine, especially since no other lights were on in the house.

He gave in to his urge and picked up his cell phone, punching the number he had memorized when he'd wanted to call and ask how she was doing, maybe even apologize again for what he'd said on their walk from the cemetery.

After looking up that number, however, he'd realized he was being selfish and had decided not to call. She didn't need more stress on top of her grieving.

Tonight, however, his defenses were down and his instincts were telling him something might be wrong.

Spontaneity wasn't like him. All his life, he'd been a planner, deciding ahead what actions he would take in what situations. It wasn't until his residency that he'd discovered how little could be planned ahead. Patients, being human, had a tendency to take a doctor off guard.

Even with that lesson, however, he knew he had remained a slight control freak. Maybe Jill wasn't the only one who struggled with compulsive tendencies.

As he held the phone and waited, her answering machine went through its spiel.

"Hello, Jill, this is Rex," he said after the beep. "I just called to talk and see if everything was all right." He gave his cell number. "I'll most likely see you at the clinic on Monday."

And then he hung up, feeling silly for worrying.

Still stinging from Margret's warning, now he felt doubly dejected. The light he had seen was no longer there, which meant Jill was elsewhere in the house. She obviously didn't want to talk on the phone, especially to him, it appeared.

He disconnected and folded his phone, placed it back into his pocket.

"Stop it," he muttered, disgusted by his own self-pity. He was alone because he chose to be. There were other people in this town besides Jill Cooper.

He could have gone fishing with Dane Gideon and Blaze Farmer this evening after dinner. Bertie Meyer could have used some company downstairs. Or he could have invited Ginger Carpenter, the clinic's part-time physician's assistant, to a Branson show.

Now, *there* was a fun lady. Ginger had a heart and sense of humor as big as her...uh...derriere. She had the copper hair, freckles and friendly brown eyes of a typical redhead.

But whenever he closed his eyes, his thoughts went to a dark-haired woman with a generous mouth, a serious, blue-eyed gaze and a need for control of her own life that surpassed his own.

If Rex had been in Jill's situation, he might have become bitter. Jill didn't know the meaning of the word, not even when it came to him.

Serving others seemed to be a joy in her life.

He was still thinking about their situation when a light from the general store down on the square attracted his attention. The store was usually closed by this time of night.

A slight figure appeared at the door, then stepped out on the sidewalk. He heard a faint cry.

Fawn Morrison.

"Help!" she cried, running out into the dark street. "Please, someone help!" Her voice suddenly carried well through the still, heavy evening air.

He shoved the computer aside and jumped to his feet as the scream came more loudly.

"Help! Somebody, help! It's Cecil! I think he's dead!"

Chapter Twenty-Eight

Jill sat in front of the fireplace in the cabin at Big Cedar, listening to her old friends catch up on the past and plan the final touches of the reunion.

"I still think Jill should bring those old school records," Doris said. "I could bring mine, and we could compare."

Sherry gave her a disapproving look.

Doris shrugged. "If nothing else, there will be a lot of people at the reunion who weren't notified about the destruction of the records. Besides, if Jill and I have them, confidentiality's already been broken."

Sherry cleared her throat. "Excuse me?"

"Well, I'm just saying—"

"You're just snooping, Doris, admit it," Sherry said.

"It isn't like a doctor-patient privilege," Peggy said.

Before they could drag Jill into the discussion, her cell phone chirped.

"Hey," Doris complained, "we were all supposed to turn off our cells."

Jill shrugged and checked the caller ID. It was Noelle. "Sorry, I have to take this."

She stepped out onto the deck, enduring glares and mutters of reproach. The thought of cutting herself off from contact with the outside world overnight had been appealing to her when Doris first suggested it, but somehow she hadn't been able to bring herself to take that drastic a step.

"Noelle? What's up?" She closed the French door behind her and stepped across to the wooden railing of the cabin's deck.

"There's been another…" Noelle's voice wobbled. "Oh, Jill, it's Mr. Cecil."

"What about him?" Mr. Cecil was the name they'd used for Cecil Martin when they were children.

"Fawn found him at the store tonight, dead."

Jill stared into the blackness of the cedar trees that surrounded the cabin, unwilling to hear those words. Not again. *Please, God, no.*

She sank into a deck chair. "How?" she could only whisper the word.

For a long moment, Noelle didn't reply.

"What is it?" Jill asked.

"The sheriff says he fell from his ladder and hit his head on the floor."

Jill heard the tightness in Noelle's voice. "And what do you think happened?"

"Why ask me? The sheriff has already—"

"Noelle, this is me you're talking to. We've been through this before. What do you suspect?"

"It isn't just a suspicion."

"Did you tell our sheriff not to jump to conclusions?"

"I suggested that it's too much of a coincidence for Cecil to die just a week after Edith's death."

Jill knew her sister would never tell the sheriff about her gift. Very few people knew of it, and even fewer accepted it as an authentic gift from God.

"What did he say?" Jill asked.

"Same old thing. He patted me on the shoulder and told me it was natural for me to feel that way, after all my family's been through, but that I needed to let it go. Not every death is a murder, even if it must seem that way to me."

"He just dismissed you."

"He was nice about it. Greg's not a jerk, you know that. But he has his feet firmly planted in solid facts."

"Has Nathan spoken with him about it? Maybe he can convince Greg to see—"

"Nathan's in conference in New York, and I'm not calling him. Jill, I'm dropping it. I'm not a private investigator, and I can't buck the system. I'm just going to leave it up to God."

"You're quitting."

"I'm using common sense. I can't fight it, and neither can you."

"You're thinking there might have been foul play, just like with Edith."

"I'm not saying anything anymore."

"Just tell me, okay? Is that what happened?"

Again, a long silence, punctuated by sniffling. Noelle was crying.

"You want me to come back to Hideaway tonight?" Jill asked. "You shouldn't be alone."

"I'm a big girl. I'm fine."

"I'll leave right away."

"No. Stay there. You can't do anything here, anyway. Greg won't listen to you any more than he would—"

"I'm not coming for Greg, I'm coming for you. I'll be there within the hour."

"Jill, no. I'm fine."

Jill disconnected. Time to pack and say good-night to her friends. She was back in "protective mother" mode, a role she'd assumed for many years—protecting her sister from danger. Last time the threat had lurked within their own family. Now if a killer suspected that Noelle was guessing Cecil's death was no accident, she could be in danger from someone besides family—and Nathan wasn't there to protect her.

For a moment, Jill debated calling her brother-in-law. She rejected the idea. Noelle would be livid with her if she did that.

Still, Noelle didn't need to be alone. Not tonight. And Jill didn't, either. She got up from the deck chair, pushed the French door open and stepped back inside the cabin. Noelle knew her well enough to be expecting her.

Rex sat in the overheated dining room of the Lakeside Bed and Breakfast late Saturday night, observing the aftermath of shock. Fawn was still shaking, holding on to Karah Lee, eyes reddened with tears, nose pinched and pink. Karah Lee and Bertie tried to calm her, but she wasn't calming easily. She sat curled up in a tight ball on the chair, legs drawn up beneath her.

The kid had loved Cecil, and to find him like that...not something she should have had to experience, especially after all the other emotional traumas she'd been subjected to in her young life.

Something else disturbed Rex. When he'd rushed into the store in response to Fawn's cries, he'd found Cecil lying facedown. And yet, the deadly injury had apparently been from a blow to the back of his head. It was possible one of the larger cans had hit his head after he had fallen.

Somehow, Rex didn't feel all the pieces of the puzzle fit neatly. Yet the sheriff wouldn't even consider this to be anything but an accident.

Like many people, when it came to the death of the elderly, Greg immediately blamed it on natural causes—or a simple accidental death.

Rex was still mulling over the situation when Austin Barlow came barging through the lobby into the dining room.

His face was paler than usual, his eyes darting anxiously from one face to the other. He was breathing hard. "So it's true?" he asked softly.

Bertie looked up at him. "You already heard?"

"Cecil?" His voice held a distinct tremor.

"Word sure spread fast." Bertie returned her attention to Fawn.

"A fella doesn't…doesn't miss much when he's staying upstairs on the town square."

"You saw what happened?" Rex asked.

Austin shook his head. "I was just walking back from the lake when the hearse pulled away. I met Frank on the sidewalk and he told me what he saw from his barbershop. What happened?"

"The sheriff says he fell from a ladder in the stockroom," Karah Lee said.

Austin winced and seemed to catch his breath. "He sure about that?"

Rex studied the man more carefully, remembering the incident Thursday on the sidewalk outside the clinic, when it seemed as if Cecil was trying to evade Austin.

"Why do you ask?" Rex waited until Austin met his gaze.

This time the staring match wasn't so much a contest of wills as it was a strange communication.

Once again, Austin was the one who looked away first. "This is Hideaway, Doctor. Folks who've lived here all their lives have learned not always to take everything at face value." He shook his head. "I just saw him earlier this evening."

"Where did you see him?" Rex asked.

"Where else? At the store, when I got some groceries."

"What time was that?"

Austin shrugged. "Guess about an hour or so before sundown. There was a crowd of tourists in the store, and he was busy, so I didn't hang around to talk."

"Did he seem okay?" Rex asked. "Not dizzy or anything? Maybe confused?"

"Not Cecil. He was just as sharp as he'd always been. He even talked me out of buying some apples because they looked mushy to him. Who found him?"

Karah Lee and Bertie looked at Fawn. Austin pulled out a chair at the table and reached over to touch Fawn's shoulder. "That must've been bad. You okay?"

She flinched from him, barely nodding, tears once again washing down her face as Karah Lee wrapped her in a hug.

Austin hesitated, as if unsure of whether or not to sit down, obviously aware he wasn't exactly welcome at the table.

Rex pushed his chair back, gesturing to Austin, then nodding toward the lobby. "Mind if we have a talk?"

After another confused glance at Fawn, the man followed Rex into the alcove off the main lobby.

"Why do I get the feeling something else is going on here?" Austin asked, voice soft.

"I'm wondering the same thing." Rex sank into an ornate Victorian chair.

Austin perched on the edge of the settee.

"You knew Cecil well when you lived here?" Rex asked.

"Pretty well. He's been in this town all his life, just like me."

"He was one of your teachers in school?"

"Yes. Were you the one who pronounced him dead?"

Rex nodded. "That's right."

"And you did that with the authority of a physician." It wasn't a question. "Which means you're still licensed to practice medicine."

"I'm licensed."

"So as a physician, did you notice anything…maybe that didn't seem just right?"

"Are you asking me if I think Cecil's death was an accident?"

Again, Austin caught and held Rex's gaze. "That's what I'm asking."

What, exactly, was Austin thinking? Rex avoided a straight answer. "I'm not the sheriff," he said instead. "I have no jurisdiction here."

Austin nodded again, then rubbed his face wearily, clearly getting Rex's meaning. "So you're not convinced, either. Greg's a good man, but he doesn't have a suspicious nature, and he's not rooted here."

"You suspect it was something else."

"I don't know what to think right now. I know I don't feel safe, but I'm not going to go pointing fingers. Not yet. I did that before, and the guilt will follow me the rest of my life."

Rex thought about Cecil's seeming urgency to avoid Austin late Thursday afternoon. Why would that be?

If Austin were a guilty party, wouldn't he behave just this way? Suspicious, trying to cast suspicion on someone else?

"So you're still licensed to practice medicine," Austin said again. "I've been wanting to get into the clinic to see you, and they keep telling me you aren't taking patients."

"That's right. I'm here only as a consultant."

"What would you say to a simple consultation with a patient, then?"

"What does this have to do with Cecil?"

"Nothing at all. But, as you said, we can't do much about Cecil at this point. So, doctor, a consultation?"

"I'm not on staff at the clinic, I'm not keeping patient files. Legally, I would need to have a file on any patient with whom I consulted."

Austin gave a frustrated sigh. "You know what? I've always felt sorry for doctors who couldn't escape their jobs. People come to them at all hours of the day or night with medical questions. They don't have a life to themselves."

"It's been awhile since I've had that problem."

"And I vowed to never do that to anyone, myself."

"Good for you."

"I'm about to break that vow."

For some reason, Rex wasn't surprised. That was the kind of thing a person usually said when they planned to become an exception to the rule. "Oh?"

"What would it hurt for someone like me, meeting you on the street, or right here in this dining room, to ask you a couple of questions that most docs could answer, but that us poor common saps don't know anything about?"

"I don't think there'd be anything wrong with that. Most folks like to talk about their work. As long as it's a casual, general question."

"Mr. Barlow."

Both men looked up to find Karah Lee standing in the opening to the alcove, arms crossed. She looked stern.

"Cheyenne Gideon and I will be perfectly willing to make an appointment for you at the clinic," she said.

"Well, you see, there's the catch," Austin said, spreading his hands apologetically. "I'm one of those uptight rednecks who don't like to burden the women with his private problems."

"We're doctors," Karah Lee said. "We treat patients, up-tight rednecks or otherwise. It's what Cheyenne and I have both chosen to do with our lives. I'm sure you don't realize it, but when you say something like that, it's a slap in the face to us."

"I'm sorry," Austin drawled, his Ozark accent more pronounced. "Sure didn't mean to imply you weren't good at what you do. I know for a fact Cheyenne's good, because I've seen her handiwork. I don't suppose anyone mentioned that I was the one who first invited Cheyenne to begin the clinic in an official capacity."

"I did hear you weren't too keen on the idea of a clinic," Karah Lee said.

"That was before I saw the error of my ways…and I have to admit, I've always had that hang-up about having a female doc." He turned to Rex. "Sure does seem like a waste to me, all that education, all those years of study and all the doctor shortages, and you not being in practice."

"You recruiting for us?" Karah Lee asked. "Because if you are, I have it on good authority that Cheyenne likes to choose her own staff. You'd better check with her before you issue any rash invitations."

The man closed his eyes and nodded. "Of course," he said quietly. "Fawn going to be okay?"

"I'll see to it," Karah Lee said. "Bertie's making her some hot chocolate right now. This will take her some recovery time."

"Yes." Austin looked around, as if he was missing something, and Rex noticed for the first time that he wasn't wearing his hat. "Well, I guess I'd best get out of the way so the recovery can begin."

"Why don't you call us Monday for an appointment?" Karah Lee suggested.

Looking drawn and tired, Austin nodded, got up, left.

Karah Lee glanced at Rex. "What's up with him?"

Rex watched through the glass door as Austin paused on the front porch, rubbed the back of his neck and glanced in the direction of the town square. He then stepped into the night.

"Good question."

Chapter Twenty-Nine

Jill didn't take the time to pull into her garage behind the house when she arrived home from Noelle's late Sunday afternoon. It felt strange, parking in front like a visitor, but it had been a strange and horrible week. She felt like rebelling against the habits that so often imprisoned her.

Though relieved that Nathan was back from his conference, she felt somewhat…cut adrift.

On the drive back to Hideaway from Noelle's, Jill had done some soul-searching and drawn a disconcerting conclusion that she wished she had discovered decades ago: all these years when she'd proclaimed that her sister needed her intrusive influence in her life, she hadn't admitted to herself or anyone else that she *needed* to be needed. She needed

Noelle as much as—or even more than—Noelle had needed her.

How many times had she intruded, over the years, when she should have kept her mouth shut?

She was brooding about that when she stepped onto the front porch and was startled to discover three more storage boxes stacked neatly beside the door.

They were larger than the ones Jonathan had brought her last week, and were shaped like the filing boxes in which the school stored old records. A sticky note stuck to the box on top was written in Doris Batson's exquisitely beautiful script.

Honey, we officially elected you keeper of the files until the reunion. Sherry pouted and declined to vote, but I don't think even she would be willing to see these bits of history—and ridiculousness—destroyed. I just happened to find a number for our former Miss Sheave, believe it or not, and she has her maiden name back. I never did think that silly old art teacher would make a good husband. I thought I'd let you do the honors with the phone call, since you're the one who was curious. Maybe you could invite her to our reunion. It never hurts to ask these things, you know.

She had jotted a telephone number at the end of the note.

With a quick glance around, Jill unlocked the front door and lugged the boxes inside. She hadn't asked for this responsibility. Why was Doris so bent on saving worthless old records? Especially private records that no one had any business reading.

And yet, there could be information in these files that she needed. In fact, if Jonathan had seen someone skulking around Edith's house the night he arrived, that skulker might have been in search of these school records.

But what was he looking for?

By the time Jill had stacked everything in the sitting room, she was trembling, and not from exertion. What if someone knew she had the records now? Anyone could have walked or driven past her house and recognized the file boxes.

She closed the front door, locked it and sank into a rocking chair.

With another wary look at the boxes, Jill picked up her telephone and punched the number Doris had given her for Miss Sheave. The area code wasn't in Missouri.

The call was answered on the second ring. Jill introduced herself.

"Jill Cooper?" came the reply. Miss Sheave had a pronounced Southern accent. "Why, yes, I remember you. Who wouldn't remember the student most likely to become the next mayor of Hideaway," she said with a chuckle.

"Oh, yes, I think that was a joke. Actually, Austin Barlow did that very thing."

There was a short silence. "Who?"

"He was a classmate of mine. Perhaps you didn't have any encounters with him."

"Actually, I used to pride myself on my memory of all the students. I soon discovered I didn't have perfect recall," she said with a self-deprecatory chuckle.

"I've been asked to invite you to our class reunion in two and a half weeks, at the Hideaway festival."

"Are they still having those events?" Miss Sheave exclaimed. "The one I attended was the most fun. I mean, talk about your hometown parties, that one was the best I've ever seen."

"So you might be interested in joining us?"

"I would if I didn't live all the way down here in Alabama now."

Okay, Jill had known she was out of state. Now she knew how far. "I had a question for you that you may not be able to answer."

"Well, you'll never know unless you ask."

"I had a classmate named Mary Larson, who, according to old school records, apparently saw you during our junior year. We have a situation here right now." She explained the deaths of Edith Potts and Cecil Martin.

"Oh, my goodness! How awful! Those two must have been, what, well into their eighties? But what would Mary Larson's visits to me have to do with that?"

Jill hesitated. She didn't want to explain everything. Not yet. "I'm just gathering information about some things that happened when we were in school, trying to come up with a connection. A student was killed in a practical joke gone bad the year after you left, and Edith and Cecil were the two adults most involved in that situation. I could be way off base here. I hope I am. But if I'm not, any information you could give me may be important."

There was a long, expressive silence, and Jill held her breath.

"It seems to me you're talking about more than an accident, Jill. Are you saying these deaths might have been…intentional?"

"That's right. Do you have any records that might help me connect these things?"

Another long silence, then a sigh. "Can you give me time to do some research?"

Something alerted Jill to a change in the woman's tone. She was holding something back.

But Jill had no choice. If she pressed Miss Sheave at this point, the woman might well shut down completely.

"Take all the time you want," Jill said. Sometimes the prospect of living and working in a large, impersonal city appealed to her. Then she wouldn't be so connected to half the town—and feel personally responsible for them.

Miss Sheave ended the conversation with a half-hearted promise to call Jill back when she found the information she needed. But Jill suspected the former counselor already had the information. If she'd prided herself on remembering the names of the kids who had never even stepped into her office for counseling, she would recall Mary.

Miss Sheave was holding something back.

Rex couldn't help it. He was worried about Jill. He'd been unable to sleep last night, and so, after attending church this morning, he'd returned to his suite and dozed off and on for several hours. He had resisted the urge to call Jill again, but hadn't resisted the frequent compulsion to glance up the hill toward her house.

Did she even know about Cecil? If she didn't, she needed to.

It wasn't until late afternoon that he saw her blue car in front of her house, and he frowned. Why was she parked in front?

He could stand the questions no longer; he called.

She answered on the first ring. "Rex? Is something wrong?"

Of course. Caller I.D. "Yes, I was pretty sure you'd been told about last night's tragedy, but I knew that if you hadn't—"

"I heard. I wasn't home when it happened, but Noelle reached me on my cell phone."

He frowned. "You weren't home?"

"No, in fact I haven't been home since late yesterday afternoon, so I'm trying to play catch-up with some…work." She sounded distracted.

Something didn't make sense. "You were gone last night?"

"Don't sound so surprised. I do have a semblance of a life. Sometimes. You know, friends and things. Somebody has to plan our class reunion."

He glanced out the window toward the house. "You weren't in your attic with the light on…or a flashlight or something…early Saturday evening?"

There was a long silence.

"Jill?"

"You saw a light in my attic?" Her voice had tightened with tension, immediately confirming Rex's worst fears.

"Yes, I did." As he spoke, he walked out of his suite and locked the door behind him. "It was just before I heard Fawn's cry for help at the general store. She'd just found Cecil in the back room."

"Then there's no way I could have been at my house." The

tension turned to fear. "I was at Big Cedar when Noelle called to tell me about him."

He went down the stairs, rushed across the lobby and out the front door. "It might have been a flicker of headlights hitting your window. Or maybe a reflection from your neighbor's television." He didn't believe that. He wanted to tell her to get out of her house, but that would be overreacting. Wouldn't it? She already sounded frightened.

"You've been watching my house?"

"Don't worry, I'm not stalking you," he said dryly as he reached the road and turned to race up the hill.

"I mean, you're sure it was my house where you saw the light?"

"The blue Victorian with navy and burgundy trim. I could have been mistaken about the light."

"But what if you weren't? Rex, I need to hang up and make a call."

"To the sheriff?"

"That would be a waste of time. I'm calling a locksmith."

As soon as she disconnected, Rex called the sheriff. He was disappointed with the response.

Heart pounding, Jill punched the number of her second cousin, Jimmy Dale, who lived down the road from Noelle and Nathan. She gave him the pertinent information and hung up. She expected to see him pulling up in front of her house in his panel truck in ten or fifteen minutes. He was the best locksmith in the four-state area. He also installed alarm systems, and if she knew Jimmy Dale, he'd have the whole house rigged with new locks, deadbolts and a top-of-the-line alarm system before the sun went down. He'd been pestering her to let him fit her out with that for years.

Why hadn't she listened?

She clamped down hard on the panic that threatened to overpower her. Someone had been here, but she could be pretty sure no one was here now. An invader didn't just enter someone's home and set up residence, he got in, got what he was looking for, and got out again before anyone noticed. So what was he looking for? And why was he in her attic?

Rex hadn't imagined that light in her window. She knew that, especially since someone had already been in this house recently.

The drapes, which had alerted her to an intruder last time, were hanging in place, undisturbed. She rushed to the back door. The strip of tape she had placed between the bottom of the door and the threshold was still intact.

She searched the downstairs rooms with her own style of compulsive thoroughness, then hesitated before starting up the stairs. Telling herself no one was here now, she was aware of every creaking floorboard, every swish of her clothing, and all other sounds. She heard nothing unusual.

Other sufferers of OCD could become so focused on a particular compulsion they failed to notice the rest of their surroundings. She, on the other hand, became so acutely aware of all the elements of her surroundings that it, indeed, became her obsession.

It was during times such as this that she questioned herself—how could a woman who belonged to God, who was a strong believer, continue to have such mental weakness? Why couldn't she overcome that with her faith?

A woman in her church had once assured Jill that when she reached spiritual maturity, she would, indeed, be able to cast off OCD.

So, according to that woman, I'm still spiritually immature.

Edith had been livid when Jill had told her about the conversation. "Jillian Diane Cooper, let me tell you something," she'd ranted. "You are beautiful in God's eyes just as you are this moment in time. How dare that woman, or anyone else, imply there's something lacking in you? Can she know God's mind? She has a thing or two to learn about grace and perfection. And you, my dear, have some things to learn about suffering."

Jill had been taught all her adult life that the state of suffering—which she had reached often in her life—was a discipline for a believer. But she was tired of that discipline. What had she done to deserve such overwhelming punishment?

Suddenly, a shadow moved against the white, gauzy curtains on the window of her front door, backlit by the sun. Jimmy Dale hadn't had a chance to get here from his place.

She sucked in her breath, prepared to scream, when the figure stepped forward, and she could see his face.

Rex.

Before he could ring the bell or knock, she had the door open. It seemed the most natural thing in the world to reach for him.

He caught her in his arms and drew her close. He was breathing hard, as if he had run the whole way. "Are you okay?"

She nodded, still shaking from reaction. He didn't let her

go. Instead, he held her more tightly. She didn't want to look into his face at the moment, for fear she might see the same thing she had seen in Greg's and Tom's faces the last time they were here.

And yet, the way he held her, the way he was breathing, the concern in his voice reassured her.

"I'm sorry," she whispered. "I panicked."

"You're not the only one. Jill, I know how you feel about the sheriff, but I called him and told him about seeing the lights."

She pulled away at last, feeling his reluctance to release her. When she looked into his eyes, all she saw was concern, tender concern.

No, there was something else….

She turned and led the way into the house, and he followed. "Is he on his way here?"

"No. I told him I was coming here, and he told me to call him again if I needed anything. Meanwhile, I'm to reassure you that you're safe and everything is okay."

"And his explanation for the light you saw?"

"A reflection of headlights from the road above the cliffs."

She decided not to let it bother her. It was enough that Rex believed her.

"Have you called the locksmith?" he asked.

"Yes, and he should be here very shortly."

"There has never been any sign of forced entry?"

"No, but that doesn't mean much," she said. "I never had the locks changed when I first moved in, and several keys could be floating around town. My grandparents had an open-house policy when they lived here, and it seems half the people in town had piano lessons from my grandmother at one time or another. For that matter, Noelle leaves her ring of keys in her desk drawer at the spa. Anyone who knows her habits could enter her office and lift a key from her ring, make a copy of it down at the general store, then return—"

"Do you have any idea who might have been here last night?"

"Don't I wish. Then I could pay a visit and ask a few questions."

"Does Hideaway have a lot of trouble with burglaries?"

"No, just too many deaths lately."

He reached out and took her hands in his. "Here's what we're going to do. First, we're going to wait until the locksmith gets here. Do you know this person?"

"My cousin Jimmy Dale."

"We're going to wait until Jimmy Dale gets here, and then the three of us are going to search the house."

"His brother, Bart, will probably come with him."

"Then the four of us will search the house together, basement to attic. Then when we get done with that, I'm staying here until those locks are changed, and—"

"He'll be putting deadbolts in, too, I'm sure. And an alarm system. Jimmy and Bart will probably be here until midnight or later, because even after the work is done, they'll sit around and talk forever."

Rex shook his head in wonder. "You really are related to half the town, aren't you?

"Yes, and when my other cousins Cecil and Melva hear about this, they'll be camped out here, as well."

"Then we might as well prepare for a party. I plan to stay on until the end."

Jimmy Dale and Bart Cooper arrived four minutes later. It was the beginning of a long night.

Chapter Thirty

On Tuesday morning, Jill finished her coffee, rinsed the mug and set it in the kitchen sink. The locks were changed, deadbolts in place, alarm system up and running. She'd already set it off twice yesterday—in the morning as soon as she got up and when she got home.

She was safe. So why didn't she feel safe? Several times Sunday night and twice last night she had awakened suddenly, sure she'd heard something in the house.

Rex had called her last night, and Noelle had dropped by just to make sure everything was okay.

At Noelle's urging, Jill had even picked up a jar of that wonderfully scented facial mask from the spa. She planned to give herself a facial today after Cecil's funeral.

Last night, she hadn't eaten dinner, and she woke with no appetite this morning. She needed either to get rid of some tension or increase her medication for a few weeks, which she preferred not to do unless absolutely necessary.

She was just about to step out her back door when she caught sight of the blinking light on her answering machine.

With a sense of wonder, she stepped over to it. In all the excitement, she hadn't checked for messages on Sunday or Monday. She had actually failed to make one of her habitual checks.

In spite of all the stress, Jill could not prevent a little swell of pride. During her worst times with her compulsions, she would never have left a message on the machine overnight. There had been a time when she checked for messages six times a day, sometimes more.

Now, although her medicine couldn't have returned to therapeutic range, and though she was under nearly as much stress as she had been last year, she had missed this message.

What small accomplishments it took to make a person happy.

She pressed Play and listened to the sound of Rex Fairfield's low, drawling voice drift through the room. He'd wanted to talk to her Saturday night. Had he called when he saw the light?

How had he come to be so important to her in such a short time?

Once again, she checked to make sure the house was secure, then set the alarm system, let herself out the back door, locked it behind her and set off on foot to the clinic.

* * *

Rex stared at the ledger sheets he had spread across the table in the clinic's conference room. He was stretching, mentally coming up for air, when someone knocked on the door. Blaze entered with a fresh cup of coffee and three chocolate iced crullers.

"Ah, the bakery run." Rex set down his automatic pencil and shoved aside his calculator. "You people do know how to spoil a guy. And his waistline."

"We aim to please." Blaze sank into the chair across the table and reached for one of the crullers with a grin. "Can't chance ruining your health, though, before we get the hospital complete, so I'll help. You really think we can do it by the festival?"

"I think so."

"You'll stay until it's done?"

"I have some other obligations in the next couple of weeks, some follow-ups on other projects, but, yes, that's in my job description. I plan to do anything it takes to help the present administration turn this place into a rural hospital." In fact, the idea of leaving Hideaway depressed him. "I thought you had classes on Tuesdays."

"Funeral this afternoon. I have bereavement leave." Blaze leaned back in his comfy swivel chair, eyeing Rex for a moment, then looking away as he sank his teeth into the cruller.

Blaze wasn't typical of other kids his age group. He attended College of the Ozarks, which had a work-study program, so not only did he have to work the same amount of hours per week as his class hours, he also worked at the clinic as much as he could. Rex heard he helped out at the bed and breakfast, as well, when he could.

"Weren't you a resident in internal medicine when you and Jill were engaged?" Blaze asked.

Rex suppressed a grin. Leave it to the Hideaway grapevine. "That's right. It's a specialty you might like. It's for workaholics."

Blaze shook his head. "Not for me. Give me a barn full of cows and goats and pigs."

"Vet school's harder than med school, I hear."

"Not if you love what you're doing." Blaze looked down at his half-eaten cruller, then at Rex. "Guess you didn't, huh? That why you got out of it?"

"I did love it, actually. I've always loved medicine. Treating patients can be the most rewarding occupation in the world."

"And so you changed professions…why?"

"I have the opportunity now to help even more patients with what I'm doing, and this way I have a chance to influence policy from the inception of the hospital, instead of being a puppet of politics."

Lately, he wasn't sure he believed that, himself. The real reason he'd begun this business was because he needed to work shorter hours to save his marriage and have a better quality family life. This was the best way he could do that and still make an impact in the medical field. And now where were his marriage and family?

Blaze finished off his cruller and washed it down with a final swallow of coffee. "You're not catching Jill at her best right now, you know."

Rex raised an eyebrow at the sudden change of subject. "What makes me think you brought an agenda in with the coffee and doughnuts?"

Blaze spread his hands. "Just thought you'd want to know. She doesn't usually misplace files and get grumpy with patients." He thought about that for a minute, then amended his comment. "Or at least, not that grumpy."

He was referring, Rex guessed, to an unfortunate incident earlier this morning when Jill had snapped at poor Richard Cook for being late for his appointment, then jumped him for complaining about his hemorrhoids.

"Jill's known Cook for a long time," Blaze said. "He lives at the boys' ranch and takes care of us. Bertie calls him a chondromaniac. She means hypochondriac. Anyway, Jill's still freaked about the deaths."

"You don't have to defend anyone, Blaze. I'm not here to do the hiring and firing." Or to hear about anyone's hemorrhoids.

"Anybody ever tell you about the drama with the Cooper family last year?"

"Jill told me."

"It hit her pretty hard. Just thought you'd want to know that," Blaze said. "Didn't want you getting the wrong impression about her."

"That isn't going to happen," Rex said. He'd jumped to the wrong conclusions once before about Jill, and held expectations that were unrealistic and unfair. That would not happen again.

Blaze patted icing from his lips with a napkin. "So you're saying she hasn't changed much since you two were engaged?"

"The basics are still there."

"She sure loved Edith."

"Yes."

"And Cecil."

"I know."

Another pause, then, "She's not convinced either of the deaths were from natural causes."

"No."

Blaze's thick, black eyebrows rose in surprise, an obvious invitation for further comment. "She talked to you about that?"

"Did she talk to you about it?"

Blaze shook his head. "I just hear it in her voice when she mentions them. I can see it in her eyes sometimes when she thinks no one is watching."

"How can you see something like that in a person's eyes?"

Again, that shake of the head, as if Blaze was trying to figure that out, himself. "I guess I can read people, but it isn't something I do consciously. I've heard her ask Cheyenne questions a time or two about Edith's heart, and this morning she was asking about Cecil."

"She was?"

"I know she's grieving, but there seems to be more involved than simple grief." Blaze hesitated, cleared his throat. "Sometimes she tends to get carried away."

"I know about the OCD, Blaze. I don't think that's what this is."

"You don't?"

"No. I have to agree with Jill that she has reason for suspicion. However, I'm not the law around here, and right now the law has other ideas. Are you sure you wouldn't consider pre-med? You have a way with people."

Blaze watched him for a long moment, as if digesting what he'd just said. But Rex had learned early on that Blaze wasn't always easy to read, and he apparently wasn't in the mood to divulge his thoughts at this moment. "Give me a squealing piglet over a squealing kidlet any day."

There was another knock at the open door. Jill stuck her head in. "Blaze, we need you in Two for X-rays on Mrs. Mann's ankle."

"I'm on it." Blaze wiped his hands once more, tossed his napkin in the trash, and nodded to Rex as he stepped past Jill. "Nice talking to you, Doc."

As Blaze swept past Jill, she glanced at Rex.

"Are you doing okay today?" he asked.

"I'm good. Thanks for checking on me last night."

"You know I would have been glad to come over."

She blinked. Jill had that wide-eyed blue gaze that had always entranced him. One look from her could imprint her image in his mind for the rest of the day.

But that was twenty-two years ago.

"Is everything okay with you?" she asked, her voice softer. "You've been…more thoughtful the past couple of days."

He should have told her it was because he was concerned about her, but he didn't. "I had an unfortunate telephone run-in with the mother of my stepchildren Saturday night. I'm presently banned from seeing them."

Now, why had he said that?

"Oh, I'm sorry." And she really did sound sorry. She also

sounded ragged around the edges, as if she hadn't slept well. "Why didn't you say something about that? Here I went on and on about my own problems, and you were—"

"I was more concerned about you at the time. I know what a shock these two deaths have been for you. I also worry about those lights in your attic, and—"

"I can handle it."

"I know that."

"Cecil's funeral is at one this afternoon," she reminded him, "but if you want to keep working—"

"No. I'll be attending the funeral."

She nodded. "I'm sorry to hear about your stepsons. I hope you get to see them again soon."

"I'm sure I will. My ex has done this before." He heard the weariness in his voice, saw the responding compassion in Jill's eyes, and twenty-two years fell away.

He was a young man again, remembering every reason he had loved her.

His first choice, all those years ago, had been the best. Definitely the best. Perhaps that was why he had waited for several years after his breakup with Jill to get married.

Someone called her name from the reception office.

"Coming," she called over her shoulder, then with another brief look at Rex, she left him alone again.

Blaze met Jill in the hallway, looking dazed. "Jill, you're not going to believe this."

"Try me." She picked up a clipboard and wrapped her stethoscope around her neck.

He leaned closer, voice softening. "It's Austin Barlow in One. He's asking for you."

"What's he doing here? He didn't have an appointment. In fact, if I remember correctly, he refused to see our lowly *women* doctors."

"Doesn't look as if that'll be as much of a problem this time," Blaze said.

"And that's because…?"

"He's half-blind."

"Stop with the word games. What are you talking about?"

Blaze crooked his finger at her and led her to the first exam room, where Austin Barlow sat on the exam bed, sweating profusely, eyes wide with obvious distress. In the chair against the wall, forest ranger Taylor Jackson sat watching the man with concern.

"We've got us an emergency," Blaze said.

"I didn't hear an alert," Jill said. "What happened?"

"I told you," Blaze said. "His vision's gone out of one eye."

"Jill?" Austin's voice trembled. He looked at her, then at Blaze, then at the wall in front of him.

She reached for his hand. "What's going on?"

"I was hoping someone here could tell me."

"Which eye is affected?"

"My right."

"When did you lose your vision?" she asked.

"About fifteen minutes ago."

"That was when he called me," Taylor told her.

"Has this happened before?" Jill asked.

Austin hesitated. "A couple of times, but it never lasted as long as this. It doesn't hurt. It feels like sunspots. You know, when you look too long at a light, and things blank out on you?"

"Did you contact a doctor about it before?"

He closed his eyes then. "No."

"Why not?"

Austin didn't reply.

"Hello?" she snapped. What was it about noncommunicative men? Especially when they needed help?

"It didn't last this long," he said. "I don't suppose Dr. Fairfield would happen to be here today."

"Still the macho good ol' boy, huh?" She injected gentleness into her voice. Any other time he would have smiled at that comment. Now she only saw fear.

"I guess a skunk doesn't always lose his stripes," he said. "Can't help myself."

"You should know by now he isn't seeing patients."

"Is Cheyenne here?" he asked more softly.

"I'll get her."

Chapter Thirty-One

Rex couldn't help himself. Sound carried well down the hallway, and he was curious when he heard about Austin Barlow.

He met Cheyenne in the hallway as she emerged from Austin's exam room. "This one has me intrigued," he said to her. "How about a consult on the case?"

"You heard?"

"I heard. Has he given the name of his family doctor?"

"He says he doesn't have one at the moment." Cheyenne looked worried. "He's blind in his right eye, Rex."

"Any pain?"

"None."

"Then we're thinking about a possible clot or vasculitis."

"I've already ordered a sed rate to look for an inflammatory cause, as well as the usual blood work. He'll be going for a CT scan in just a few minutes. The mobile scanner is here today, and we can get him in as an emergency."

"What does the eye exam show?" Rex asked. "Does it look like central retinal occlusion, or—"

"I didn't see any abnormalities on fundoscopic exam."

"What about intraocular pressure?"

"Normal," Cheyenne said. "For both eyes."

He was impressed by her thoroughness, but by now it didn't surprise him.

"I have a call in to an ophthalmologist," Cheyenne said. "I think we can get Austin right in—"

"That won't be necessary," came a deep male voice from the entrance to the exam room. Austin stepped into the threshold, his large frame filling the doorway.

"What are you doing out here?" Cheyenne said. "We need to get you into the CT—"

Austin covered his left eye with his hand, and with his right eye, held Cheyenne's gaze. "It's over. Just like before." He dropped his hand and nodded to Rex. "Hi, doc. Looks like we've got us a false alarm."

"Not so fast," Cheyenne said. "We don't know what caused this blind spell. We can't stop trying to figure it out just because—"

"That's what I'm going to do." Austin nodded to her, then to Jill, who had just joined them in the hallway. With a quick glance back into the exam room, he thanked Taylor Jackson for bringing him in. Then he pivoted and walked out of the clinic.

Cheyenne looked at Taylor as he stepped out of the exam room. "Can't you do something?"

The tall red-haired man shook his head soberly. "Sorry. You know we can't legally hold him. He isn't suicidal, isn't homicidal."

"What if he tries to drive? He could lose his vision and run off the road, run into oncoming traffic. He could be dangerous to himself and others."

"I can't stop him just on the off chance he's going to lose his sight, Cheyenne."

Cheyenne looked at Rex. "He would be more likely to listen to you."

"No," Jill said. "He would be more likely to listen to me."

Cheyenne's dark eyes filled with relief. "That's my supernurse. Do whatever it takes to talk some sense into him."

"I'll go with her," Rex suggested.

"Nope," Jill said, rushing down the hallway after Austin. "I work alone."

Rex looked at Cheyenne. She shrugged.

The clinic director was a woman who, Rex had observed, seldom got rattled under pressure and took a hectic day at the clinic in stride. She stood in the hallway staring after Jill, who caught up with Austin as he reached the open entryway to the waiting room.

Jill was probably right. Austin was more likely to listen to her than anyone else.

Jill caught up with Austin before he reached the front door. She noticed the slump of his broad shoulders. "Austin Barlow, you really haven't changed at all, have you?"

His footsteps faltered slightly, then he turned right onto the sidewalk without acknowledging her.

"You're still stubborn and too proud to accept help from anyone." She fell into step beside him. "You shouldn't drive, you know."

"Who said I was going to?" His deep voice matched the slump of his shoulders. He sounded tired…defeated.

She took his arm, catching a scintillating whiff of yeasty-sweet aroma from the bakery ahead. "Let me buy you a Napoleon and a cup of coffee."

When he finally looked at her, she had the impression her face wasn't registering with him. "I told you I'm not going to drive," he said. "Tell Cheyenne I'm not her personal responsibility, and I'm not yours."

Jill gestured toward the front door of the bakery. "You still love Napoleons, don't you?"

He gave her a wry grimace. "Tastes change. Now I like cinnamon scones."

"And you like your coffee black. Come on." She glanced through the shop window. "There's no one in there except Steve, and he's busy frying more doughnuts with his new, cholesterol-free oil, thanks to Noelle."

Austin shook his head. "So that's what's wrong with them."

"Hey, watch it. Those doughnuts taste great."

"No, they don't."

"My sister is saving lives here."

"But she's disappointing taste buds right and left."

Jill was relieved when Austin relented and held the bakery door open for her. She had counted on his inability to turn her down. Austin Barlow was many things—ornery, manipulative, prideful and maybe worse—but he had an ingrained sense of chivalry that stemmed from his need for admiration.

When they had ordered and received their breakfast, complete with caffeinated coffee—Steve didn't make decaf until later in the day—they sat at the table by the window. Jill made sure they were out of earshot from Steve, and from the doorway should someone else come in.

"I don't want a CT," Austin said. "Or any other test Cheyenne wants to run on me. I'm not an experiment."

"Then why did you come to the office?"

"I panicked. I was weak. I'll try not to let it happen again."

"That's ridiculous. It isn't weak to seek help for a treatable problem."

"You don't know what kind of problem it is," Austin snapped. "And you don't have to play guard dog. I'm not an idiot. I realize this blindness could return at any time. Now can we drop the subject?"

"Why won't you do something about it?"

He glanced out the window toward the boat dock and the lake. "What if nothing can be done?"

"Something can always be done."

"Not in my family." He picked up his fork and cut a corner of his scone, then set the fork down and picked up his coffee cup.

"I know your father died young." Not to be callous about it, but in her opinion, that had been an act of mercy for Austin's family. Austin's father had been an abusive monster, drawing blood on Austin's back from the beatings he had given the small boy more than once when Austin and Jill were in grade school. When Austin was older, the stripes of abuse had been less obvious, and before he turned twenty, his father had died.

"And my great-grandfather and an uncle," Austin said. "They had a terminal illness called histiocytosis X that didn't show symptoms until it was already too late to stop the progression. My father's symptoms began with blindness."

"And you've just decided that's what's wrong with you?"

He leaned forward, giving her a straight look. "What are the odds, Jill? Be honest with yourself and with me."

"I'd say you shouldn't jump to conclusions. You're taking a grave risk with your life, here, Austin, and your son needs you."

He frowned at her. "Say that again?"

"We're talking about your life and Ramsay's."

"*Grave risk.* That's what Edith said about Chet. I heard her say that she and Cecil had taken a grave risk by not pursuing the incident further, and possibly allowing a killer to go free to kill again."

Jill digested that in silence for a moment, chilled by the words. But one thing at a time. "Right now, we're talking about *your* life, Austin. You're playing a deadly game with your life."

"I'm not. I'm making a very educated guess. My father died within three months of his blindness, and no treatment worked. Not only was he sick from the treatment, but his lungs collapsed from the illness. It was an awful death."

"It was a long time ago," Jill said. "Medical science has progressed since then."

"You don't think I've researched all I can about this condition? In all these years, the treatment hasn't changed that much, and it just caused my father more suffering. Nothing could be done about it."

"So you're convinced you've got the same disease."

"You have any other suggestions?" Austin growled the question.

"Come on, you can't just suffer through this and expect us not to try to help you."

He didn't look at her, but continued to stare out the window. "The only hope I have is that it could go into remission of its own accord."

"But you haven't even had it checked out, won't allow Cheyenne to run tests."

"If I allow those tests to be run on me, the results will be exactly the same as my father's, my great-grandfather's, my uncle's. And then there will be all kinds of pressure put on me to take the treatment for it, which I don't plan to do. You know the routine, and so do I. Doctors have to do what they have to do. And I'm doing what I have to."

"Don't you dare tell me you came back home just to die."

Austin met her gaze, and she felt the impact of it. In those eyes, she saw a world of regret.

"I came back home to set things right if I could, Jill."

"Austin, you're talking about Chet's death?"

He closed his eyes, looking sick and weary. "And Edith's and Cecil's."

"You were in Hideaway the very day Edith died."

His eyes slowly opened. "I could have set something in motion before I ever came here."

"How?"

"I called Edith before coming here."

"You *called* her? About what?"

"I needed to tell her the truth about my part in Chet Palmer's death."

Chapter Thirty-Two

Fawn woke late Tuesday morning to the cold gloom of a late autumn day, though it was still September. It seemed as if even the weather mourned Cecil Martin's death.

She tossed back the covers and went to stare out her bedroom window to the gray, fog-shrouded lake below. She wasn't going to school today, but she wasn't attending Cecil's funeral, either.

Blaze was mad about it and that hurt. But she'd made a promise to Cecil just last week.

Cecil had said, "Punkin', don't spend too much of your life brooding about the past and mourning death. Death's got to come, and when it does it's too late for anyone to do anything about it. When my time comes, I want you to promise me you won't mope around at some silly service, praying over this old empty shell. When we meet in Heaven, I want you to tell me what you did to celebrate life on the day of my funeral."

How she'd loved old Cecil. How she would miss him.

So she wasn't going to attend the funeral. The memory of finding him dead on the floor in the stockroom was enough to give her nightmares for a long time to come. She wanted to remember him as the smiling old buddy she'd come to love this past year.

Too many deaths. When would it end? She wasn't silly enough to think she was cursed—that God was making others pay for loving her—but it sure seemed to her that too many people around her had died.

Sometimes love hurt too much. Actually, most of the time it hurt. There hadn't been many people she could trust with her love. Great-Grandma June, when she was alive. Karah Lee. Taylor. Bertie.

Edith and Cecil.

She would not cry. She'd cried enough after she found Cecil on Saturday night, and she still burned with embarrassment over the lack of control she had shown.

She'd spent most of her life avoiding tears. They made a girl weak, and there'd been no room for weakness in her family. Any sign of it had made her an object of scorn, not only from her mother, but her stepfather.

She definitely couldn't show weakness to her stepfather. She hadn't even cried when her mother chose not to believe her about the rape.

So today she was doing exactly what Cecil had told her

to do. Listening to the singing pipes of the cottage while Karah Lee showered, Fawn opened her closet door and pulled out a dress—The Dress.

She could think of nothing that reflected life more fully than the upcoming wedding of her foster mother—the one woman in the world she wanted to call Mom—and Taylor Jackson. Both had endured pain in their pasts.

Karah Lee's parents had divorced when she'd graduated from high school, which had spooked her for marriage for far too many years.

Taylor was a forest ranger who still patrolled the Mark Twain National Forest that checkerboarded this section of the state, and also helped police the town and take call as a paramedic for medical emergencies. His tragedy involved the death of his teenaged son, and the subsequent failure of his marriage when his wife could no longer handle the grief.

That Karah Lee and Taylor—both sometimes prickly and awkward around the opposite sex—could forge a bond of love that completely involved their faith in God…well, it was a miracle. Definitely a reflection of the best life had to offer.

Fawn would celebrate by working on The Dress. And she would set aside her dreams of independence a little longer. Bertie was wise, and Blaze—much as Fawn hated to admit it—was smart. They both had given her good advice about her dreams for the bed and breakfast.

The one person who had helped her change her mind, however, was Jill. She'd said exactly what Fawn needed to hear. *You are loved.*

And in order to grow up, she was going to have to learn how to stick with relationships through the scary times. She was going to have to learn to trust.

Karah Lee loved her. Taylor loved her. Maybe, for just a year or two, she would give herself a chance to learn what it was like to be loved in a family. A real one.

She settled the material on her bed, then gazed once more out at the gray lake. She was just about to get up and reach for the tiny seed pearls that she would sew into the neckline of the eggshell silk, when she caught sight of someone on the community boat dock.

It was a tall man with dark hair and a mustache. Sheena's dad, Jed Marshall. He wore a denim jacket, and his hands were jammed into the pockets as he stared across the water toward the cliffs on the other shore.

Someone else stepped onto the dock, and Jed turned. It was another man—short, stocky, with dirty blond hair. Junior Short.

They spoke for a few moments. Jed shook his head and backed away. Junior reached forward and grabbed Jed by the sleeve.

Quick as a striking snake, Jed shoved the hand away and shoved Junior backward, toward the water.

For a few long seconds, the two men squared off like a couple of dogs circling for a fight.

There was a knock at her door, and Karah Lee poked her head inside. "Not going to school today?"

"Today's the funeral."

"But you're not going to the funeral." Karah Lee's gaze wandered with curiosity over the material on the bed.

"I'm doing what Cecil told me to do, Mom. Now get out of here. Isn't it bad luck or something for the bride to see her wedding dress being stitched?"

"Nope." But Karah Lee left anyway, wearing a grateful smile in spite of the pall of the day. She loved hearing Fawn call her Mom. She might also be a little excited about the wedding, even if she had threatened, on more than one occasion, to elope.

When Fawn glanced out the window again, all she saw was Jed Marshall, standing alone on the dock, head bowed, arms crossed over his chest.

What was going on?

The front door of the bakery opened and six elderly ladies from a tour bus entered, cameras slung around their necks, jackets and coats wrapped around their shoulders to protect them from the unexpected coolness of the day. Their laughter and chatter filled the small bakery.

"You're saying that Chet's death really was just a tragic accident?" Jill leaned closer to Austin.

"I'm saying it should never have happened."

"But you did have a part in it."

"I never meant for Chet to die."

"What do you know about it, then?" Jill asked.

"I already told you that the death bomb couldn't have been made with the ingredients we had accumulated for the prank."

"But the selenium could have mistakenly been placed in the sulfide container," Jill said. "Or someone could have grabbed the wrong container by mistake."

Austin glanced over his shoulder as the door opened once again, and more tourists from the bus entered. He scooted closer to the table. "I've had a lot of years to think about it, believe me. It's lived with me like another bad nightmare in my life."

"Who actually put the ingredients together?"

"Jed. He said he knew the recipe."

"You helped him?"

"Junior and I did."

"Could the sulfide have been replaced with selenium with you watching?"

"At the time, I didn't think so." Austin picked up his fork again and crumbled the scone onto his plate without taking a bite. "We checked and double-checked those ingredients."

"Whose idea was it to pull that prank?" Jill had lost all interest in her coffee. She hadn't wanted it to begin with.

"I can't remember who suggested it first. Chet was such a...such an unlikable person. Jed was outraged when Cecil chose Chet instead of Mary for his assistant."

"What was Mary's reaction?"

"She wasn't happy, I can tell you that, but that's no reason to kill somebody."

The noise in the small dining area had increased to the point that Jill had no fear of being overheard. "Could Jed have still been jealous because Mary had danced a couple of times with Chet the year before?"

Austin looked up at her. "Jed had a temper, but that would be just plain silly. She danced with lots of guys."

"What made you call Edith so long after the fact?"

"I had my school records mailed to me. Notations on my senior report brought it all back. Then I started having these symptoms." He pointed to his eyes. "Jill, I didn't want to die with that lie on my conscience."

"So if you had already called Edith and confessed, then why did you come to Hideaway?"

He picked up his coffee cup and inhaled the steam. "I found a message from her on my machine one evening. She wanted to know if it was possible someone else might have known about the plans we had for that prank. She sounded worried. At the same time, I got to thinking more and more about making things right with everyone I could, so I drove here."

"You drove."

He held his hands up. "Yes, I drove, and you saw me driving Saturday. After today, that won't happen again."

"So you just happened to show up the day Edith died."

"She'd called me just the day before. I needed to talk to her, anyway, and I wanted to do it in person, not over the telephone. I saw Edith's old car at the spa when I came into town that morning, and so I went in."

"Have you spoken to Jed and Junior about all this?"

Austin winced. "I tried to talk to Jed and Mary at Edith's funeral dinner. That was the wrong thing to do. First of all, Mary got mean in a hurry. Said if I exposed our actions now, it would ruin us all. She threatened that if I said anything, she would tell the sheriff that I intentionally poisoned Chet."

"What about Jed?"

"I think he was more shocked by his wife's response than

he was upset with me. That whole thing's been hanging over all our heads for nearly three decades. I think, in a way, it would be a relief to come clean."

"And Junior?"

Austin shook his head. "Mad as a bull. Wouldn't talk about it."

Jill recalled the discussion she'd had with the girls about Mary on Saturday evening. There was still something missing.

That button…that blue button. Edith would have saved that for some reason, but what could it have been?

And where had Jill seen that button before?

"Austin, before Edith died, she mentioned Chet Palmer. She also said something about records. I never figured out what she was trying to tell me."

"You think Edith might have said the wrong thing to the wrong person?" Austin asked.

"I don't know, but I have the feeling she might have thought she had."

"And Cecil?" he asked.

"I tried talking to him about it, but he wasn't willing to discuss it with me."

"Same here," Austin said.

"You should be careful, then. If you mention the wrong thing to the wrong person, you could be placing your own life in danger," Jill warned.

He shook his head. "My life doesn't seem worth much these days, Jill."

"Don't say that."

"I'll say what I want. But your life is valuable. You need to be careful. That's why I didn't want to drag you into this."

He stared down at his hands. "Guess I'm messing that up, too."

"This is all supposition, though. Nothing concrete. I've already tried to talk to Greg—"

"You stay out of this." Austin pushed his chair back and stood. "I'll have a little talk with Greg, and maybe give him a little more to think about. You'll be at the funeral?"

"Yes, then I have the afternoon off. Cheyenne's still worried about my stress level."

Austin sighed, and once again that shroud of heaviness seemed to descend on his shoulders. "I guess I'll see you at the funeral, then."

As he walked from the bakery, Jill watched him go. Time had been quite a proving ground for their graduating class. Her friends Doris, Sherry and Peggy had blossomed after graduation. But Austin, Junior, Jed and Mary all had issues that seemed to weigh their lives down.

Jill hadn't exactly had a chance to bloom, though most people would say she'd made a good life for herself. She was surrounded by family and friends, she had a job she loved. Still, she'd always thought blooming was connected to romance.

She thought about Rex as she cleared the table and placed the mugs on a tray. All this time, she'd believed their chance had come and gone long ago.

But was it truly gone?

Chapter Thirty-Three

Rex straightened his tie, checked his teeth in the bathroom mirror. He was attending the funeral of a man he barely knew, and yet he felt the need to be there, to mourn with the community. How quickly he had bonded to these people.

He should probably be back at the clinic, researching the sparse amount of information on Austin Barlow. But Austin was very unforthcoming when he wanted to be. That chart didn't give up squat. It was worthless. It was almost as if the man was being intentionally vague.

Why did Rex get the impression that Jill Cooper would know more about this particular case than anyone else?

That was easy. It was because she had returned to the

clinic with a haunted look in her eyes. When asked what she'd found out from Austin, she'd told Cheyenne that Austin would have to reveal that himself.

She definitely knew something.

Rex was reaching for the handle of the door to his suite when there was a knock. It was probably Bertie or Fawn, reminding him that the funeral would begin in thirty minutes. Of course, since it was being held in the Methodist Church, just down the road from the bed and breakfast, he had plenty of time to get there.

But when he opened the door, it wasn't Fawn or Bertie or even Karah Lee before him. A scruffy-looking, blond-haired sixteen-year-old with honey-brown eyes and an acne problem stood there, looking awkward and nervous.

"Tyler!"

"Hi, Dad."

Rex grabbed his stepson in a joyous bear hug, noting the stuffed backpack slung over the bony shoulders. "What are you doing here? Did your mother and Jason come with you?" He released the boy and glanced down the stairwell. Had Margret had a change of heart, after all?

"They didn't come," Tyler said. "And before you say anything, Mom won't know I'm gone until she gets home from work today, then the feathers are gonna fly."

The joy suddenly dissipated, to be replaced with dread. "Oh, son, you didn't."

"Sure did."

"How did you get here? I wish you'd called me before you left home. I'd have told you not to do it."

Those vulnerable eyes widened with impending hurt.

"Ty, I always want to see you, and you know it, but re-belling against your mother like this is the wrong way to go about making a protest."

"How else should I have done it? She doesn't listen to anything I say."

Oh, Lord, give me the words I need. "Something besides this, because it's got the potential to hurt everyone concerned."

"You mean because Mom's going to be so mad she'll ground me forever?"

Rex sighed and led the boy inside. Sometimes his oldest stepson had his head so far into the clouds he couldn't see what was happening on the ground. "Tyler, you're sixteen. You'll be considered a runaway." And if he thought his mother was unreasonable now, he hadn't seen anything yet.

Tyler peeled his backpack from his shoulders and tossed it onto the sofa in the sitting room. "Nice place, Dad. I can sleep on a sofa."

In spite of himself, Rex chuckled. "It's so good to see you." He caught the kid in another hug, then set him back and gave him a stern look. "You're not going to play your mother and me against each other."

Tyler gave him a blink of bewilderment. "But that's not—"

"It's exactly what you're doing, and it's got to stop right now. I know you don't intend to cause trouble for anyone—"

"Yes, I do. I want her to see what she's doing to us. You're our dad, and she doesn't have any right to cut us off like that. This whole thing is all her fault."

"That isn't true. It takes two people to ruin a marriage."

"Not just a marriage, a family. We were a family. Jason and I still feel you are our family."

"As do I. That's never changed, and it never will, son. I love you both very much. And that's why I can't help panicking just a little over what you feel you're trying to do here."

"Aren't you even curious about how I got here this time of morning without Mom knowing?"

Rex had to admit the question had crossed his mind. "Let me guess. You left early this morning for football practice before she woke up, and then…then what? Did you catch a bus?"

"Nope. My friend Brian is auditioning for a guest spot on the *Star Notes* show this morning. His parents brought him down here, and I faked a permission slip to come with him."

"That's lying, Tyler. You know better than that."

Tyler hung his head as he sank into the soft cushions of the sofa. "I'm sorry. I don't like to lie, but I couldn't think of another way to see you. Mom said—"

"I know what she said. But the thing is, if you had treated her with respect, allowed her some authority, she would have been much more likely to be lenient with visiting hours for us."

"You're saying I should have faked it so I maybe would get what I wanted?"

"No, I'm saying that if you'd been obedient to a higher authority, then you might well have regained our visiting hours without upsetting your mother. What you're doing will not make for peaceful family relations."

"Don't you even want to know what I told Mom in the note I left her on the kitchen table?"

"You left her a note?"

"Of course. Can't let her think I just disappeared. Then she'd be worried."

"You don't think she'll be worried about this, Tyler?"

"No, she won't be worried, because I told her I'd be with you. She'll be mad, and feel threatened and jealous, but not worried."

With a sigh, Rex sank onto the sofa beside his stepson. "Look, I have a funeral to attend in a few moments, but meanwhile, why don't you call your mother, tell her where you are, and tell her you will be back home tonight with—"

"No! How can you ask me to sell out like that? She'll just start screaming at me to come home, and she won't listen to a word I say. Dad, she needs to see what she's doing to Jason and me."

"Does Jason know you're here?"

"Yes. He wanted to come with me, but since he's only thirteen I'd have been in even worse trouble. Mom would have blamed me for influencing my brother, especially since she wouldn't be able to blame you for it."

That was where Tyler was wrong. She would find a way. She always did.

"If you don't call her, I will," Rex said. "And then I want you to call your friend and tell him to wait for you at the theater, because I'm taking you to Branson, and you're going back home today."

Tyler gave Rex a mutinous scowl. "They aren't going

home today. They're being lodged at a condo at the Branson Landing. I can't believe you're taking Mom's side after all she's done to you."

"I'm not taking sides, I'm doing what's right. Now, are you going to call her, or am I?"

Tyler continued to glare at him for a few more seconds, then crossed his arms. "If you don't want me here, I'll just leave. I've saved some money—"

"Stop that."

There was another knock at the door, and Rex glanced at his watch. If he was going to attend the funeral, he would have to leave now. But he couldn't, not ,with Tyler in this condition.

He opened the door to find Fawn standing there in denim cut-offs and a T-shirt.

"Hi, Rex. Bertie and Karah Lee want to know if you want to walk to the church with them." She glanced past his shoulder and her eyes widened at Tyler. "Hi."

"Fawn Morrison, meet my son, Tyler Stanphill."

Her face scrunched. "Stanphill?"

Tyler was suddenly standing at Rex's side. "*Nice* to meet you, Fawn. That's a great name. Rex is legally my stepdad, but to me he's the real dad and my blood father just sends the child-support checks."

Rex slanted his son a look. All charm and grace now that a pretty young woman had shown up. "You're not going to the funeral?" he asked Fawn.

"Cecil told me not to." At their confused looks, she shrugged. "Before he died. So, Rex, what should I tell Bertie and Karah Lee?"

Again, Rex glanced at Tyler. "Tell them something has come up, and my plans have changed."

"No, Dad," Tyler said, not taking his eyes off Fawn. "You go ahead. I'm not going anywhere. I'll just wait here, and we can talk about everything when you get back."

Rex shot him a warning look.

"I'll call Mom," Tyler said. "But I'm not going home. You did your job. You told me to call her and go home, so you're off the hook."

"That isn't going to make things better."

Tyler grinned at him, and Rex realized, for the first time, that the kid was as tall as Rex himself. "It can't get any worse than it's already been, can it?"

"Runaway, huh?" Fawn said.

Tyler grimaced. "I prefer to think of it as exploring my options."

"How old are you?"

Tyler glanced at Rex, his face taking on a slightly rosy hue. "Sixteen."

"You're a runaway," she said.

"Not if I'm with my dad."

"You are if your legal guardian didn't want you to come and see your dad. Trust me, I know. I was a runaway last year."

"You were sixteen last year? So that means you're seventeen now?"

"Eighteen. I just had a birthday. You're just lucky you had a place to come, and you'd better hope your mom doesn't call the police on your dad."

Tyler glanced at Rex, and the rosy hue deepened.

Rex found himself wondering if there was any possible way he could get Tyler back to KC and destroy that note so Margret wouldn't know he'd been gone and everything would blow over.

"Go on to the funeral, Dad," Tyler said. "Don't worry, I'll still be here when you get back."

Rex hesitated. He had the opportunity to spend some much-needed, precious time with this kid he loved so much.

However, it appeared there would still be time after the funeral, and there was someone else Rex needed to talk with. Besides, Tyler didn't seem to mind Fawn's company.

Chapter Thirty-Four

Jill stood in the cemetery at the edge of the crowd that had gathered for Cecil's interment. The funeral had been so well-attended that the ushers had brought extra chairs from the funeral home. Cecil had been much-loved and admired by his many students over the years.

She scanned the crowd around the tent. Was there a killer present? Had that killer entered her house? Too many things were happening for everything to be coincidences.

After the final prayer, the crowd dispersed slowly.

Jill experienced a sense of déjà vu; the ceremony for Cecil was almost an identical replay of the rituals the town had observed for Edith. She turned to find Rex standing a few feet away from her. She nodded to him.

"If you're going back to the clinic, I'll walk you," he said.

"Thanks, but Blaze and Cheyenne think I'm going to shatter under the pressure," Jill said dryly. "I have the rest of the day off."

"Then I'll walk you to wherever you're going."

"Why?"

He raised a brow at her. "Can't a man take a pretty woman for a walk without having to explain his motives?"

She gave him a suspicious look. This was a new approach for him. "Don't you have work at the clinic?"

"It can wait. Cheyenne and her staff have made this the easiest job I've ever had."

"Thank you."

"Besides, I have others to attend to before I get back to work today. I have a teenager in my suite who needs some parental attention."

"A teenager?"

His sudden grin melted her. She had always loved that grin, which involved his whole face, unselfconscious and filled with warmth.

"My oldest stepson, Tyler," Rex said. "He's sixteen. He showed up on my doorstep just before the funeral today."

"You weren't expecting him?"

"Nope, and there's going to be a huge blowup when his mother finds out."

"You don't sound too concerned."

"I've learned that worry doesn't do anyone any good." He turned, and they circled a tombstone and walked across the grass in silence for a moment.

She glanced at his profile. The years had refined and

mellowed him. Laugh lines around his eyes made him look much more approachable than he had seemed when she'd first met him. Now his face better reflected his heart.

He held the white wooden gate open for her. "I can't believe I'm saying this, but I'm touched that he would go to that much trouble. It's silly and selfish of me."

"How is that?"

"I should be concerned about his act of rebellion. Instead I'm afraid I'm enjoying it a little too much, especially after Margret banned me from seeing them. I had begun to feel I was truly losing those boys."

Jill glanced up at him. "Was that why you tried to call me Saturday night?"

He looked at her, holding her gaze. "That, and I was lonely."

"I know where you could get a cute puppy."

Rex shook his head, chuckled, rolled his eyes at her. "You're not the most romantic woman in the world."

"Sorry, but you should already know that."

"Why is that?"

Her steps slowed. "You can't be serious. We tried that romance once, remember? I think we clash too much."

"Maybe *romance* is the wrong word, then. How about *dating?* You know, as in a good friendship in which two people spend time together and actually talk and get to know one another. In our case, get reacquainted."

"I'm suspicious of dating," she said. "It increases everyone's expectations. If you date even a few weeks, people start hearing wedding bells, and then what do you do when you break it off? That just makes you look and feel like a loser. Why bother? We've been there, done that, moved on."

"Better to have a broken dating relationship than a broken marriage."

"Couldn't tell it by me," Jill said as they strolled toward the town square. "The first thing I see in someone's eyes when I mention I've never been married? They wonder what's wrong with me. Like being single is a disease."

"I get the same kind of response when people find out I'm divorced," Rex said. "They wonder what I did to mess up my marriage."

"So I guess that means we're just a couple of romance rejects," Jill said.

He frowned, then stopped and turned to her. Before she realized what was happening, he gently placed his hands on her shoulders and kissed her. Right there in daylight and everything.

She didn't have time to respond before he stepped back.

"I don't think we're romance rejects at all," he said softly.

She didn't reply. She couldn't. Her blood seemed to be singing through her body, in perfect rhythm to her heartbeat.

When he took her by the arm and led her forward, she automatically fell into step with him once again. But now even the touch of his hand felt like a tender caress, almost as powerful as the kiss.

"Don't you ever get lonely?" he asked.

Lonely. Hmm. The truth? Right now she couldn't even think straight. What was lonely? "Probably not as much as you do," she said at last.

He waited for her to explain.

She wasn't sure she could. But she wasn't ready for him

to know how much his kiss had affected her. How long had it been? Wow. It seemed like just yesterday…and yet it seemed as if the last time they'd kissed had been in another lifetime.

"Isn't it some kind of well-researched fact that most women—who are much more overtly social than most men—have no trouble filling their lonely hours with friendships?" she asked.

"Friendship is a wonderful thing to have. We were friends once," he said. "I've always missed that. Probably more than anything else."

She looked up at him, her lips still vibrating from the kiss. Actually, her whole body seemed to be vibrating, and her mind was having considerable difficulty focusing.

"Have you?" he asked.

She nodded. "I've realized lately that I have. A lot."

He sighed and shook his head. "So why were we so foolish as to break up the engagement?"

"Excuse *me,* but you sat right there in the hospital cafeteria and told me you didn't think things were working out between us."

"And you shoved your engagement ring into my hand so quickly I didn't have a chance to explain what I meant by that statement. I certainly wasn't expecting a breakup."

"You didn't even try to explain," she said.

"You caught me off guard, and of course our tempers were flaring all over the place that afternoon."

"Oh, I get it. You weren't going to beg me to take the ring back. That would have hurt your pride." Why was she suddenly enjoying this? Maybe because she was realizing that they really *had* a good relationship once. She was capable of it.

"Especially after what I'd just said to you. I kept thinking I would be able to talk to you about it, that since we did truly love one another, we would eventually work it out. But then, you refused even to talk to me after that."

She turned and faced him with her hands on her hips. "Rex Fairfield, don't you dare try to convince me I'm the one who actually broke our engagement."

"I won't."

"But you just said—"

"I'm simply saying we weren't exactly skillful communicators back then. There was a problem I believe we could have dealt with it much better had we behaved with maturity instead of blind emotion. If we were to have that same fight today, I believe the results would have been drastically different."

"How's that?"

Again, his gaze drifted to her mouth. He leaned toward her, but before he could kiss her again, she stepped back. "Hold it. You're saying people should rely on physical touch instead of words to work out their problems?"

He followed her. "No, I'm saying the results would have been different. We would have talked about our feelings instead of sulking like a couple of spoiled children. And then—" He reached for her shoulders and drew her forward.

His mouth covered hers—lips touched in such a perfect, sweet pairing. Her eyes closed, and her heart kept beating, though her breathing seemed to encounter a barrier.

His arms drew her closer, until she leaned against him,

and she couldn't tell if it was because she had suddenly grown so weak she needed him to hold her up or if she couldn't bear not to have that nearness.

When he drew back this time, she felt as if she'd suddenly lost a lifeline.

"Ever hear the old saw about those who don't learn from their mistakes?" he asked, still looking at her mouth as if…as if he wanted more. "They're doomed to repeat them."

"Well, I haven't repeated that mistake," she said.

"Haven't you? You should be happily settled with a family. Instead, you're still living your life for everyone but yourself."

"Look, I know I've always—"

"You don't have to explain yourself, Jill. I've spent enough time in Hideaway to discover some old puzzle pieces I wish I'd found a long time ago. I've learned more in this past week than I ever knew before."

"Like what?"

"Like what you've had to deal with, the pain you must feel when people misunderstand you. The fact that you don't always get the respect from others that you so very much deserve."

"You're listening to the gossip about me." She suddenly felt chilled.

"Relax. It wasn't told as gossip, but simply as a way to help me understand why you've been grumpy lately."

She glared. All those wonderful, sweet, languorous feelings suddenly vanished. "Grumpy!"

Fawn had stitched the final row of seed pearls onto the front of Karah Lee's wedding dress when she saw Rex's stepson, Tyler, walking along the shoreline of the lake, skipping rocks across the surface of the water. Or trying to.

Would he be offended if she showed him how to do it? "Hi," she called through the open window.

He turned and looked up at her, and she saw a familiar grin. He had a smile like his stepfather's—it took over his whole face. "Hi."

"Sorry, I've used up most of the flat rocks along this part of the shoreline. There are some good ones farther along, past the church."

He glanced where she pointed, then his gaze drifted toward the crowd dispersing from the cemetery at the far end of the churchyard.

Fawn tenderly placed the dress on its padded satin hanger and hung it in her closet. When she joined Tyler at the water's edge a moment later, he was still staring toward the road.

She glanced in the same direction, then smiled when she saw Jill and Rex walking side by side. "Aha. Just what I was hoping for." They appeared to be arguing at the moment. Jill loved to argue.

"Who's she?" Tyler asked.

"The love of your stepfather's life, even if neither of them knows it yet."

Tyler watched them, eyes narrowing.

"What's wrong with you?" Fawn asked.

"They've got a thing going?"

"No."

"Then what are you talking about?"

"They were engaged a lot of years ago. Long before you and I were even born."

"You mean they've kept in touch all this time?"

"Nope, they've just discovered each other again. What's wrong with you? You think he should still have a thing about your mother?"

He scowled. "He's not crazy. No man in his right mind would have a thing for my mother."

"Ouch. I hope you don't say things like that to her. If I'd said that to my mother, she'd have knocked my teeth out."

That earned his complete attention. "Your mother hits you?"

"When I lived with her. I live with my foster mother now." She found a flat stone and picked it up, curled her right forefinger around it, crouched toward the water, and flung the stone across the surface. It skipped fifteen—sixteen—seventeen times.

"Your stepdad's friend's name is Jill Cooper," she said as she searched for another stone. "You want to know what I think your stepdad's doing here in Hideaway? I think he's looking for something he and Jill lost a lifetime ago."

She skipped the next stone far out into the lake, then turned to enjoy Tyler's admiration. Instead, he was watching the couple up on the hill. Jill had her hands on her hips, glaring at Rex, who was grinning at her.

"Maybe that's why he doesn't want me here," Tyler said.

"That's silly. He's always talking about his stepsons. He obviously wants to do the right thing, and he wants you to do it, too."

"He doesn't know what it's like at home."

"He was married to your mother for how many years? And you think he doesn't know?" Fawn snorted.

He ignored the jibe. "I'm not going back to Kansas City. If he doesn't want me here, I can get a job in Branson at one of the shows."

"What do you think Rex would say about it?"

"He doesn't want to cause trouble. He's afraid any blow-up with my mother will only traumatize my brother and me."

"Well, if you have as good a relationship with Rex as it seems, I think he'd love it if you lived with him. Look at me and my foster mom Karah Lee. She's getting married in just a couple of weeks, and her fiancé doesn't act like I'm going to be in the way. Jill likes kids, too. She tries to mother the whole community."

"But Rex moves from hospital to hospital now that he and my mom are divorced."

"My foster mother overheard him saying he missed treating patients. Folks around here are already grumbling because there's no male doctor at the clinic. Lots of the older men still won't go to a woman for treatment. If Rex were to settle here, he'd have a stable home for you and your brother. Maybe you could both move in with him."

Tyler's attention once more focused up the hill toward Rex, his blue eyes filled with speculation.

Chapter Thirty-Five

Rex knew he shouldn't have laughed while Jill was still in fight mode, but he couldn't help himself. She hadn't been this outspoken twenty-two years ago. Maybe if she had, they would have been able to talk things out.

"You did what you had to do," he said gently, taking her arm.

Though she continued to glare at him, she allowed him to guide her farther from the cemetery. "Don't patronize me."

"I'm not. I can see a lot of things now that I couldn't then. I was too caught up in my own busy schedule and too arrogant to believe you had good reasons to spend so little time with me when I did have time off. I'd like to think we aren't the same people we were then, and that's a good thing."

"But some things haven't changed," she said.

"In reference to what?" he asked.

"I'll never be…normal."

Rex turned to look at her, and his heart went tender. "Do you know what normal is?"

She rolled her eyes. "You know what I mean."

"Explain it to me."

She strolled a few more steps, her newly shaped, dark brows drawn together in contemplation. "Normal is someone who doesn't have a compulsion or an obsession that makes people look at them strangely."

"Oh, so I should be more interested in someone who suffers from depression or bipolar disorder, is that what you're trying to tell me? Or perhaps someone with a psychosis, who hears voices that aren't there?"

"Now you're being silly."

"No, I'm not," he said. "I recently read that some ridiculously high percentage of the population is affected by some kind of emotional or mental illness. Fifty or sixty percent. My ex-wife, for instance, can't remain in a monogamous relationship. You'd be amazed by the number of women I've met who struggle with depression. Men, too, for that matter, but I've met more men who have unmanageable aggressive tendencies."

"And yet, the majority of people in this country are capable of having a good relationship with someone of the opposite sex," she said.

"You're sure about that? My experience has been the opposite. That could be because my own marriage was so much less than perfect that I tend to pick up on marital misery without much difficulty."

"Okay, I get your point."

"You sure?" Rex asked. "Because I could go on. I don't think there's a lot of normal out there, and I'm not sure I'd like what normal is supposed to be.

"Sorry. I didn't mean to set you off on a tangent."

"Of course you did. You wanted to divert the attention from yourself. You wanted to dismiss yourself from the human race. You think you should be some castoff just because your mind doesn't always function the way the rest of the world thinks. But you know what? I don't really care about the rest of the world. I like the way you are. I always have."

Her steps slowed, and he could almost hear the alarm sounding in her head. Time to back off.

Jill glanced toward the lake as they passed by the bed and breakfast. "Who's that with Fawn down at the shore?"

He glanced in that direction and smiled. "That's Tyler, my stepson."

"Smart kid. He's already found the prettiest girl in Hideaway to hang out with. Shouldn't you go spend some time with him before he has to go back home?"

"Why don't you come with me?"

"Because you need to spend some quality time with him alone."

"He's probably smelled the food in the dining room by now," Rex said. "He's bound to enjoy Bertie's black walnut waffles and maple syrup. She said she was going to open back up after the funeral. It'll probably be another community dinner day like we had after Edith's funeral. I overheard the church ladies sharing casserole recipes."

"Why don't you go enjoy a plate with him?" Jill suggested.

"Why are you trying so hard to get rid of me? You said yourself that you don't have to be at work today. You won't join us?"

"That boy needs your undivided attention right now."

"He needs to go home to his mother."

"Maybe he doesn't."

"You don't know the situation."

"He may have his reasons for coming here. Respect them. And find out what they are."

"Has it occurred to you that our roles seem to be reversed?" he asked. "This time it's me who has family obligations interrupting our time together."

"Notice that I'm being mature and encouraging you to spend time with your family—not that this is the same thing at all."

"I'm walking you home."

"No, you're not."

"We're sure someone was in your home Sunday without your permission, and maybe more than once. I think I should go with you."

"There's no one there now. Remember, I'm living in the equivalent of Fort Knox. Anyone steps foot in my house without my permission, alarms will ring all over town. Half of Hideaway will probably show up to see the excitement. You aren't responsible for me and your stepson needs you."

"It won't take long for—"

She turned and pressed her fingers against his chest. "I have a date with a jar of the most deliciously scented honey almond cream from my sister's spa that I picked up from Sheena just yesterday, and I'm due this break. Now go. I'll talk to you later."

Frustrated, Rex watched Jill walk away. Their conversation hadn't gone as well as he'd expected. Although, in many ways, it had gone better than he had hoped.

In spite of his strong compulsion to walk her home, he knew she was right. Tyler needed him now. Margret would, too, when she received Tyler's note, although her need would be more for someone to blame than for another adult with whom she could commiserate.

Had Jill felt this way when they'd been engaged? Like a rope in a tug-of-war?

Tyler was no longer down at the lakeside with Fawn. Instead, when Rex reached his suite, the boy was talking on the telephone in low tones.

"I'm sorry, Mom. I didn't mean to make you cry, but you can't keep us away from Dad.... To us, he's Dad."

Tyler turned and saw Rex standing in the doorway. The kid shrugged and held out his hand in a gesture of helplessness.

Rex reached for the phone, but Tyler shook his head. "I'm sorry, Mom, but I can't take it anymore. Until you can start treating me like a sixteen-year-old and not an eleven-year-old, and until you can agree to regular visiting hours for Jason and me with Dad, I'll be with Dad. If you want to take it to court, bring it on. I'll be glad to tell a roomful of people what you've been like to live with these past three years."

Rex's jaw dropped.

Tyler snickered and held the phone out to him. Rex took the receiver and braced himself. But what he heard wasn't a screaming Margret, it was a dial tone.

"Gotcha, Dad."

Rex gave him a mock glare as he hung up the phone. "You sure did."

"That was just a practice run."

"Maybe you should change your tactics a little. Remember, legally, you're a runaway."

"So maybe the police will take me away and put me in a boys' ranch like the one across the lake?"

"There's no telling what they'll do with an incorrigible kid like you." But Rex was only half-serious. Tyler had never been incorrigible. He had a sweet nature, avoided conflict as much as possible and had a strong sense of justice. That's what he was acting on now.

"It's what I'm going to tell her, though," the kid said. "A sixteen-year-old is allowed to choose in court who he wants to live with."

"That's when his natural parents are involved."

"I don't think she'll be willing to drag this through the court system," Tyler said. "She'll lighten up when she realizes how serious I am about seeing my dad."

Again, Rex was deeply touched. He was also torn between doing the right thing by making sure Tyler didn't get away with this, and celebrating the fact that this fantastic kid was willing to fight to see his old stepdad.

"Tyler, I never wanted to make you a pawn between your mother and me."

"That's not what's happening. I'm just telling it to her like it is. Fawn said something about food downstairs. I'm starved."

"Then let's go eat. We can discuss your mother afterward."

Chapter Thirty-Six

Fawn found Blaze at the clinic on the computer barely thirty minutes after she'd seen everyone leaving the cemetery.

He glanced up at her, then back at the computer monitor. "I can't believe you didn't go to the funeral."

"I told you—"

"I know, I know, Cecil told you not to go. But he didn't know he was going to die Saturday. How do you think he'd have felt if he'd known you not only used his funeral as an excuse to skip school, but to hang around flirting with strange teenagers down by the lake instead of honoring an old man's memory? He'd be crushed."

She grinned at him. "He'd understand. You saw me with Tyler?"

"Who's he?"

"The strange teenager is Rex's stepson."

The information didn't seem to improve Blaze's mood.

"You're jealous," she said.

"I disapprove. There's a difference."

"Sure there is." She glanced at the files beside the computer. "Got any filing for me to do? Papers to push? Things like that?"

"Plenty. We're set to reopen in an hour, and everything's behind schedule here."

She took the stack of files he handed her. Since she had done office work at the clinic several times in the past when they needed help, she was cleared to handle patient files. She left him to his work and carried the stack into the filing room.

She had them alphabetically sorted when she heard the irritating squeak of the front door opening—no one had oiled those hinges yet. It drove the doctors crazy, but Jill liked the fact that it served to announce new arrivals when they were shorthanded.

"Blaze Farmer."

Her movements stilled as she tried to identify that deep voice.

There was a long pause, then, "Yeah?" There was no missing the thread of caution in that one-word reply.

She nearly dropped the folder in her hand. Austin Barlow.

"Cheyenne told me you would be here," Austin said.

"You came to see *me?*" Blaze asked, the thread tightening.

There was a heavy sigh. "It's something I should've done days ago."

"But why—"

"No, make that two years ago. Fact is, if I'd behaved the way a man should behave, I'd never have done what I did to you."

Blaze's chair squeaked. Fawn heard quiet footsteps in the office as Blaze walked to the reception window. "I'm listening."

Fawn cringed. Here she was eavesdropping again, and Blaze knew it. She couldn't leave without calling attention to herself and interrupting something that sounded pretty important.

And she really didn't want to miss it.

"I guess you heard I went out to the ranch to talk to Dane and Cheyenne last week," Austin said. "I did Dane wrong for a lot of years. I almost wish I could say that I was taking it out on him because I couldn't face the fact that my own son was doing the things I blamed on the ranch kids. But I can't say that. I never even picked up on the fact that Ramsay was responsible for the vandalism, the death of Edith's cat and even the barn fire that nearly killed you."

"I never picked up on it, either, until it was almost too late," Blaze said. "I thought Ramsay and I were friends."

"I wish you truly had been friends. Maybe you'd have been a good influence on my son."

"And then again, maybe not."

Fawn could hear the gentle, teasing note in Blaze's voice, and something inside her relaxed. With Blaze, she could already tell, all was forgiven.

"Or, it could be," Blaze continued, obviously carried by a thought, "that I'd be a good influence on Ramsay's father, if the stubborn ol' cuss would let me."

There was a tense silence, then, "Jill been talking to you?"

"Didn't have to. I was here when Taylor brought you in, remember? You need help. Cheyenne can see to it you get that help. Just listen to her."

"It isn't that easy."

"It is, you know," Blaze said. "You grew up in Hideaway and you still don't know that your problem is everyone's problem? But folks can't help a guy if he's too proud to share his load with them."

Another silence.

"They've already shared too much of that load. If I'd not forbidden Ramsay to see you, if I'd encouraged your friendship instead of hurling accusations at you, maybe my son wouldn't have done the things he did, and maybe this town wouldn't have suffered like it has."

A long, heavy silence fell. All Fawn heard was the buzz of the wall clock and the hum of the fluorescent lights.

"But you know," Blaze said finally, his voice so soft she had to strain to hear him, "I think you're wrong. I'm no shrink, but sometimes I can read people almost as well as I can read animals. What happened to Ramsay happened when his mama died. I don't think anything you could've done afterward would've changed that."

There was another silence, then Fawn heard a loud sniff.

Austin was *crying*.

Blaze continued to talk to him in soothing tones, the way he might talk to a sick animal, but Fawn heard very little. She did hear Austin clearly agree to submit to tests.

Blaze Farmer was a miracle worker.

* * *

Jill managed to button-punch her way into the house without setting off any alarms. She stepped into her sitting room with a feeling of accomplishment. She couldn't erase the grin from her face.

Rex had put it there. Rex and his kisses.

She covered her face with her hands as the grin widened. She could feel her face flushing even as she thought about it again.

She stepped into the bathroom and looked at herself in the mirror, half expecting to see a major change. But she didn't. She was still Jill Cooper, with her morning makeup no longer in evidence. She still had noticeable strands of white in her dark hair—though the cut did, indeed, seem to lift her features.

Younger and perkier. Hmm.

With a chuckle, she reached for the jar of face cream she had lusted after since last night. Sheena had told her to apply a thick layer of it over her skin whenever she felt stressed.

Well, she should've been using it for the past week and a half, but now would work. She was supposed to lie down while the mask was in place, but she had too much to do.

In the first place, she hadn't heard from Miss Sheave, and she wanted to follow up on that call. She also wanted to go through those boxes of school records Doris had brought. There had been no time on Sunday to check them out, and last night, after work, she'd paged through them but was dissatisfied with the result—which was zilch.

Now would be a good time to revisit some of those records and see what might turn up.

The bluebird button still had her puzzled. She opened the medicine cabinet and took it out to look at it again. How was it connected to Chet's death? Could Edith or Cecil have found this button near the body? Obviously, Edith was convinced of a connection or she wouldn't have placed it in the envelope with the files of the boys. She stuck the button in her pocket.

The telephone rang just as she was smoothing the cream from her face to her neck and feeling the nice tingle. Chuckling at her green reflection in the mirror, she went to answer. It was Rex.

"I was wondering if I could convince you to come down and join Tyler and me in the dining room of the bed and breakfast. I think Tyler would like to meet you."

"Sounds to me like you're trying to avoid a one-on-one discussion with him," she said. "I'm not interfering in that."

"We've already had that. He's curious about you."

"I'm sorry, Rex, but now isn't a good time. I just finished applying this cream on my face."

"Well, then, later tonight?"

She smiled, loving it. "Sounds interesting."

"Okay, look, if you see the sheriff's car cruising past your house a few extra times tonight, don't worry. I called and asked Tom to keep a closer watch on you for a while."

The smile died. "You did *what?*"

"I told you, I don't like the thought of you alone in that house right now."

Great. "Greg and Tom already think I'm a neurotic female, and now they're going to think I put you up to this."

"Does it really matter what they think? I would just feel

more comfortable if there's extra security for the next few days, until we find out who's been so interested in your house. Or in you."

"Easy for you to say. You don't have to live in this town."

He didn't say anything.

"Okay, look. I'm getting a little bit of a headache, and here I am trying to relax. Why don't we talk about this later?" she suggested. "Meanwhile, try to spend some quality time with Tyler."

"Yes, boss. Will do."

"And Rex?"

"Yes?"

"Thanks."

"For what?"

"For caring enough to humiliate me."

"You're welcome."

When he hung up, she disconnected, then looked once more at the bluebird button. Where had she seen this before?

Rex closed his cell phone and stuck it back into his belt holster. Well, that had gone wonderfully.

"Is she joining us, Dad?" Tyler asked, standing at the door, looking like a starved waif.

"She will later. Right now we get to spend some quality time together."

"Oh, wonderful. That means I get to sit and listen to you lecture me about how to treat my mother like she's some queen or something, and take all the trash she tries to dish me and—"

"I won't lecture. Promise. We've both been under a lot of stress lately. Maybe we should just take a break from it and relax for a couple of hours."

"You mean it?"

"Yes." He meant it. Except he couldn't seem to shake a feeling of…heaviness. It would be an overstatement to call this feeling one of impending doom. Still, he couldn't let it go.

Jill pulled out her old high-school album, junior year. Despite the soft classical music she had just put on the player, and the soothing feel and smell of the mask, her headache threatened to get worse. She'd waited too long to take steps to stop the tension headache. She was surprised she hadn't had one before now.

Opening to the page where Austin had scribbled his macho version of "I love you" around the perimeter of her picture, she felt a wave of sadness. Poor Austin. With his dysfunctional family history, did he ever really have a chance at a normal life?

Come to think of it, did she? Neither of their lives had been normal. Certainly not happy. But in spite of her struggles, she was, for the most part, glad about the choices she'd made. She knew Austin was still struggling. She needed to tell him that he could make up his mind to make the right choices from now on. The first thing he needed to do was take steps to fight his illness so he could be there for his son. Giving up was not the answer.

Austin's condition could very well go into remission, even if he did have histiocytosis X.

She turned the page and saw photos of her friends, so many familiar faces. Mary Larson, in their junior year, wore a bright smile for perhaps the last time in her life.

And then Jill saw something that startled her. The button. It was attached to the blue sweater that Mary had made for an FHA project at school. She had worn it all the time in their junior year, and through most of their senior year.

Jill remembered her friends complaining because Mary liked to wear that sweater so often.

The button…it matched. Jill pulled the bluebird button from her pocket. It matched perfectly.

So what did this tell her?

Why would Edith have placed this button in the envelope, unless she saw a connection?

Time to make that second call to Alabama.

Chapter Thirty-Seven

Rex made a second trip to the food buffet. He was thoroughly enjoying Tyler's company, and dreading what he knew he had to do. Tyler had to return home before Margret called out the National Guard.

But there were other things on Rex's mind that superseded even Margret for the moment. He couldn't get his mind off Jill. He had such a powerful need to be where she was right now…as if something wasn't quite right. And yet his subconscious wasn't communicating with his conscious thought process at the moment.

What was bothering him?

* * *

Jill's head pounded as she waited for the phone to connect. Finally Miss Sheave answered, and Jill identified herself.

"I know this sounds crazy, Miss Sheave, but—"

"Honey, we're both adults now. Why don't you call me Marilyn?"

"Yes. Of course, Marilyn."

"I've been thinking about what you told me the other day. I'm bound by a code of confidentiality, and even though it's been nearly three decades, I don't feel right about—"

"What if I just tell you what I know?" Jill asked.

"And what would that be?"

Now she had to guess. "Something traumatic happened to Mary Larson during her junior year."

There was a hesitation. "Go on."

"It did something to her. She was never the same since. I told you about the death we had at the school my senior year."

"You didn't tell me much about it," Marilyn said, still hesitant.

"We had some boys in our class who liked to play practical jokes. They thought they were setting up a stink bomb in the chemistry lab supply closet for the lab assistant, but it turned deadly. Sulfur was replaced with selenium, which asphyxiated the assistant when he opened the door one morning."

Marilyn made no comment.

"Mary was a very good chemistry student, and she had hoped for the position of assistant. Cecil Martin chose Chet Palmer, instead."

There was an audible gasp over the line.

"I'm becoming more and more convinced, because of recent incidents, that Chet's death was a murder," Jill said. "I'm not saying for sure Mary had anything to do with it. It could be someone else committed the deed to avenge whatever happened to Mary. Her boyfriend—who is now her husband—was one of the pranksters."

There was a deep sigh at the other end. "You wouldn't be...your question wouldn't be in regard to the rape, would it?"

It took some effort for Jill to conceal the shock in her voice. "The rape."

"You guessed Mary was raped the night of the junior-senior prom, and you need me to verify it."

"That isn't exactly a logical conclusion for someone to draw," Jill said softly.

"Rumor. Word of mouth. I know how kids talk. Of course, it seldom reaches the teachers, but it's nearly impossible to keep something like that quiet among the student body, especially one as small and tightly knit as Hideaway's. Girls tell their girlfriends, and such as that."

"Mary Larson practically stopped talking to everyone after that dance."

"Yes."

"Rape would, of course, do that to someone."

"That's right," Marilyn said.

"So Chet Palmer was a rapist." Jill didn't put it in the form of a question.

There was a soft sigh. "You're probably wondering why I didn't tell the authorities about it."

"I'm not sure it would have made much difference, judging by the way the sheriff handled Chet's death a year later."

"Jill, at the time I wasn't even sure it was Chet, and in fact, at first, I didn't even know she had been raped. Edith Potts first sent Mary to talk to me because the girl was showing signs of severe depression."

"And then Mary told you?"

"Two sessions later, she admitted she had been raped."

"Did she say by whom?"

"She never did. All I knew about Chet was what I saw the night of that prom, when I was chaperone. Mary came rushing into the gymnasium from outside, where she wasn't even supposed to be. She had smudges of mud on her dress, her hair was a mess and she was crying. At the time, I thought she'd fallen or something. I don't even know why I remembered, later, that I had seen Chet follow her outside probably thirty minutes before that."

"You never reported the rape."

"Mary begged me not to. She said her father would blame her."

"He probably would have."

"Face it, Jill, twenty-eight years ago, public opinion was usually against the woman in cases like that. Were you a friend of hers?"

"Not really." *And why wasn't I? Why didn't I notice that something was bothering Mary that whole year?* "Marilyn, can you tell me if you think she might have been angry enough with Chet that she could have killed him the next year?"

There was a long pause, and while Jill waited, she

winced with each pounding of her head. This thing wasn't getting better.

"Mary internalized everything. In time, it's possible something might have given way in her mind. Looking back now, I'd have handled the situation much differently, but then I was young and eager to please the student body. I thought I knew what was best for 'my' kids."

"You're saying it's possible she did it."

A soft sigh. The answer was slow in coming. "It's possible."

"Thank you, Marilyn. That's what I needed to know."

After ending the call, with her head aching so badly it was making her sick, Jill dialed Rex's cell phone. The picture that had begun to form in her mind was an ugly one, indeed, but she was convinced now that neither Austin, Junior nor Jed had intended Chet's death.

Mary Larson, on the other hand, might very well have snapped when her rapist received the position as lab assistant.

Maybe she had simply overheard the boys planning the prank and had impulsively given in to a darker motivation. She'd always been close to Jed, of course, and privy to anything he would be planning.

If Mary had used those three poor dupes to do her dirty work, had Jed ever discovered how he'd been manipulated? Had he even suspected? Jed Marshall had always been like a besotted puppy when it came to Mary.

But why would Mary have killed Edith and Cecil? Especially if Marilyn Sheave had told no one about the rape. There would be no connection without that knowledge.

Once again, Jill considered the button. Handmade by Mary, herself, and distinctively different from any other button, it could very well have been found in a suspicious place. The most likely people to have found that button would have been Cecil or Edith.

Before Jill could continue her line of thought, Rex answered his cell phone. Jill could hear the sound of clattering dishes and chattering people in the background.

"Did you change your mind?" he asked.

"No. Look, Rex, can you find out where Mary Marshall was on Saturday night? I've just uncovered some information that's vital enough that Greg may need to know about it."

"Mary was in town last weekend. I just overheard someone asking Jed if they'd liked the new dinner menu in the dining room Saturday evening. What have you uncovered?"

She leaned her head back against the firm cushion of her recliner. "I think it's possible Mary killed Chet Palmer."

There was a quick intake of breath, but Rex recovered quickly. "Why Mary?"

"Rape. I'm just guessing here, but I gathered from some things Austin said that Edith was highly suspicious. I'm also guessing that Mary lost a button at the scene of the crime, and Edith has kept it all these years."

"Why haven't you called Greg yet?"

"He's not going to settle for this flimsy bit of evidence in a case as old as this. There's got to be more."

"Are you thinking Mary might have had something to do with Edith's and Cecil's deaths?" His voice was softer, and the clatter grew distant, as if he'd left his table to talk in a more private place.

"Mary had just left the spa before Edith died. If Edith had figured out the truth with this button and the other information in the manila envelope I found in her things, then she might have said something to Mary. Or to someone else."

"Someone like who?"

"Cecil, maybe? Or Jed? If Mary told Jed about the rape, he might have intentionally switched the ingredients for that bomb. But that doesn't explain the button. I still think it was Mary, or that she was in on it. Cecil was at the spa talking to Edith that morning. Maybe Mary overheard."

"So *how* did Edith die?" Rex asked.

"I don't know. Look, Rex, I'm not feeling very well right now. This whole thing has probably brought on a tension headache."

"Why don't Tyler and I come to check on you?"

"No, I just need to get this stuff off my face, take a pain-killer and lie down for a few minutes."

"Jill, why are you suddenly feeling so bad?"

"I told you," she snapped as nausea washed over her. "Tension headache."

"But don't you think—"

"Later, Rex." She disconnected.

Rex stood on the front porch and folded his cell phone, frustrated with Jill and with himself. She was being obstinate—a very familiar trait. And he was being dense. They were overlooking something here.

How had Edith died? Her symptoms had all pointed to heart…or most of them. But there was something—

"Dad?"

He turned to see Tyler stepping through the door.

"Something wrong?" Tyler asked.

Rex shook his head. But Edith…something about her had seemed different that Saturday, after the failed code that had played out in Noelle's spa. He even remembered thinking that she didn't appear dead. A dead body lost color. For some reason…

Tyler crossed the porch, watching him closely. "Something's up. Something big, I can tell. What is it, Dad? What's wrong?"

Jill had a headache, and she was feeling worse. She had that cream on her face. He couldn't take the chance that he was jumping to too many conclusions.

"Jill may be in trouble," he told Tyler. "Do you remember I pointed out the sheriff to you in the dining room a few minutes ago?"

"Sure. He's got his uniform on and everything. Hard to miss something like that."

"I need you to go get him, and tell him to meet me at Jill's place."

Tyler's eyes widened with excitement. "I'm on it, Dad," he said as he pivoted and charged back inside.

Jill stumbled into the bathroom and grabbed a towel, then opened the medicine cabinet. As much as she'd initially loved the scent of this cream, it nauseated her now.

As she wiped at it, she reached into the cabinet for some aspirin. She took two tablets, and gagged as she tried to swallow.

By the time she returned to her recliner, she was short of breath. Her chest felt tight.

Something was very wrong.

She reached for the phone on the table beside the chair, accidentally knocking it to the floor. When she scrambled to get it, dizziness and darkness pressed in on her. She fought it back.

Couldn't breathe well…couldn't see…what was happening here?

By the time she had the phone in her hands, she couldn't distinguish the numbers on the button pad, couldn't even think who she wanted to call.

"God, help me." Her voice sounded feeble to her own ears.

The phone slid from her hands and thumped onto the floor.

The room closed in on her. Finally, the darkness won.

Chapter Thirty-Eight

Rex punched Cheyenne's private number at the clinic on his cell phone as he jumped from the porch and ran to his car, jerking the keys from the pocket of his slacks. The car would save only a few seconds, but every second might count.

Cheyenne answered almost immediately. "Rex? What's wrong?"

"I don't have time to explain, so listen. We have a cyanide antidote kit at the clinic, don't we?"

"Yes. We keep it because there's a fumigation company in town that uses cyanide, so we—"

"Get it and get to Jill's house now."

"What's going on?"

"I think someone's trying to kill her the same way they killed Edith, possibly poisoning her through the skin. Come prepared. Have Blaze call an airlift." He disconnected and punched Jill's number.

Cyanide was a classic poison that affected the skin color after death. It had the telltale aroma of bitter almonds, but if it was mixed in a lotion or cream that was already scented with honey and almond, the aroma wouldn't be noticeable.

Jill didn't answer her phone.

"Lord, please let me be wrong," he muttered as he tossed the phone on the seat beside him and gunned the motor up the street to Jill's house. "And if I'm right, please don't let me be too late."

Jill knew how to battle the darkness. She'd done it since she was a child, and she could do it now.

She remembered Edith expounding on suffering, how it was a blessing in disguise. Suffering made one stronger. Suffering could bring about growth if one allowed it to draw one into God's healing light.

Jesus, be my healing light. Jesus, take me out of this darkness. Jesus…help me…

Rex slammed his tire tool through the window of the front door of Jill's house, setting off every alarm. He unlocked the door, burst inside and found Jill on the floor, her body still writhing in the final throes of a grand mal seizure.

Then she went still. Too still. She gasped once, twice, then her whole body went limp. She stopped breathing.

Rex dropped to her side and felt for a carotid pulse. There was none.

"No. Jill, no! Stay with me!"

As he tipped her head back for rescue breathing, Cheyenne and Blaze came running into the room with the antidote kit.

Dear Lord, don't let it be too late.

Fawn scraped a serving spoon against an empty casserole dish. She was finally catching up with the kitchen crew as they supplied the buffet table with fresh dishes.

What she really wanted to do was find out why there'd been such a sudden exit of people about forty-five minutes ago—first Rex, then the sheriff, Tyler, Tom.

Not that it was any of her business, of course. A helicopter had landed maybe fifteen minutes after Rex left.

That was nothing unusual. Cheyenne and Karah Lee called for airlift at least a couple of times a week for emergencies. Here in the boonies, a helicopter could arrive in a third of the time that a ground ambulance could. Of course, half the dining room had emptied to watch the show.

Fawn kept working, curious, but sure the crowd would come back in with news.

The crowd didn't come back, and as time went on, more diners left, until only a few remained, making quiet conversation amid the clatter of plates and glasses being collected by the kitchen crew.

It wasn't until the sheriff and his deputy returned—this time with their hats on, looking grim—that Fawn realized something more than a simple airlift was taking place.

The two officers walked straight up to the Marshalls, who sat finishing their dessert in seclusion in the far end of the dining room. Sheena had come into the dining room about thirty minutes earlier, and had joined her parents at their table.

Over the noise of cleanup and the chatter of the kitchen workers, Fawn couldn't hear what was being said, and so she did the unforgivable. Blaze would kill her. But Blaze wasn't here. Neither was Karah Lee.

Fawn picked up a basket of corn muffins and carried them through the dining room, going to the few occupied tables with the offering, then edging closer to the Marshalls. If Bertie caught her…

Mary's voice suddenly rose in a crescendo, eyes wide with shock. "That's ridiculous! Have you lost your minds?"

Jed's voice joined his wife's in outrage. "This is crazy," he growled. "Murder? Edith Potts died of a heart attack. Everyone knows that. And Cecil got clumsy and fell."

"We've had another attempted murder tonight," Greg said. "Mary, if you'll come outside with us, we can talk about—"

"No!" Sheena shoved her chair back and stood, stepping between her mother and the sheriff. "How can you even think my mother—"

"Sheena, stay out of this," Mary snapped.

"Now, everyone just settle down," Jed ordered. "There's been a mistake, that's obvious. I don't know what's going on here—"

"That's what we're trying to find out," Greg said.

"Well, coming in here and trying to terrorize my wife and daughter isn't a good way to—"

"I'm not trying to terrorize anyone, I'm simply doing my—"

"Stop it," Mary said. "Just stop it, both of you."

The cleanup crew and the remaining diners had fallen silent. Fawn had no trouble hearing now.

"They can't do this, Mom," Sheena said. "You've been through enough."

Mary's blue eyes filled with confusion as she looked up at her daughter. "What are you talking about?"

Sheena held an entreating hand out to her mother. "After what that kid did to you, he deserved…" She looked at Greg and Tom. "He deserved what he got."

Mary stared at Sheena for a few tense seconds, and Fawn saw some spark of alarm in the woman's eyes. "Sheena," she said softly, "we'll talk about this later."

Mother and daughter locked gazes.

Jed looked at his wife, puzzled. "Mary? What's she talking about?"

"Don't listen to her, Jed. She doesn't know—"

"What kid is she talking about?" His voice had gone soft.

Mary held his gaze. She held her hands out to him. "It was an accident. We always knew it was an accident."

Husband and wife faced one another.

Fawn didn't understand everything that was happening. In fact, she understood very little. But even she was observant enough to know when she saw a family dynamic shifting, falling into darkness, shattering apart like cracked eggshells.

"Mary Marshall," Greg said with a sigh, "you're under arrest for the murders of Edith Potts and Cecil Martin, and for the attempted murder of Jill Cooper. Murder if things don't go well for her tonight."

Fawn grabbed the tabletop beside her as the floor seemed to shift beneath her. Jill? No!

"Jill Cooper!" Mary exclaimed. "What happened to Jill?"

"She tested positive for cyanide poisoning just a few moments ago, just as Edith Potts's blood did once they knew what to test for," Tom said, earning himself a look of reproof from his superior. Tom never could keep his mouth shut. "Sounds like you might've had motive," he said to Mary, sounding almost apologetic. "And you're the one who mixes the herbs and stuff at the spa for those face creams. Noelle already told us that. The cyanide was in the face cream at Jill's house."

"No!" Sheena cried. "My mother didn't have anything to do with Edith's death, or with Cecil's. If you want to talk to me—"

Mary caught her breath, eyes widening with apprehension. "Young lady, shut your mouth and sit back down. None of this is your concern. You don't have any idea what you're talking about."

"But Mom, I do." Sheena's voice trembled. She leaned toward her mother. "I heard Edith Potts talking to Cecil. Don't you understand? I heard about the…the…what that guy did to you in school. I know why—" She shot a glance at Greg, and pressed her lips shut.

Mary leaned back in her chair and rolled her eyes, as if to show how silly she thought they were all being. But Fawn could see Mary's hands shaking, the tips of her fingers white where she gripped the edge of the table. "You're all being ridiculous. Of course I didn't kill Edith or Cecil, and I certainly never even knew about Jill."

"Mary," Jed said. "What's going on here?"

Mary reached for her husband's hand. "It'll be okay. They can't convict me for something I didn't do. You'll see." She rose to her feet at last. Pressing past Sheena, Mary nodded to Greg and Tom, and the two officers escorted the woman from the dining room.

Ashen-faced, Jed started to follow, but Sheena caught his arm. "Dad?" Her eyes filled with tears. "Daddy."

He turned back to her, frowning.

"I heard Edith and Cecil talking about a button Edith found in the chemistry supply closet." Her voice trembled, and the trembling seemed to spread throughout her body. "I *heard* them. It was a button Mom made."

"The chemistry…" Jed's eyes closed, as if in great pain.

"Dad, that kid raped Mom," she whispered. "He deserved what he got, but they were talking about opening up that old case, which might even have sent Mom to prison."

"So what are you saying?" His voice, always so gentle with his daughter, suddenly grew hard. "That your mother might have had something to do with Edith—"

"No, Dad." She swallowed hard. "She didn't."

He didn't reply. He simply waited, and his already ashen face turned nearly as white as the serving dish Fawn held.

Tears spilled down Sheena's cheeks. "I couldn't let it happen," she whispered. "I couldn't let Edith expose her."

Jed took an unsteady step backward, as if to avoid what his daughter was saying.

"And Jill was asking too many questions. She knew. I couldn't let her hurt Mom, either. I got the key to her house from Noelle's key chain, and looked for anything she might have to incriminate Mom. I didn't find anything. She must have known someone was looking for it."

Jed's face seemed to crumple. "So you…you stopped her, too?"

"I had to. Can't you see? Edith had lived a long life, and she was ready to go, you know? So was Cecil. Mom…Mom didn't deserve to go through all that. I'm sorry, Daddy. I didn't want to do it."

Suddenly, Fawn realized she was looking at someone quite different from her friend, Sheena Marshall. This young woman was willing to…what…kill? To protect her mother?

"I dated Bill Coggins, remember?" Sheena continued. "I told you about it. He worked for that bug extermination company. They use cyanide for—"

"Sheena, stop." Jed suddenly looked at Fawn.

She recoiled from the horror in his expression. She backed away from father and daughter, knowing she would never eavesdrop again.

"I'm sorry, Daddy," Sheena said. "When Mom left that day, I mixed that cyanide in one of the jars of facial cream and put it on Edith's face. It was so awful. I nearly lost it when she died, and I had to help revive her, when I knew she wasn't going to—"

Jed groaned and stumbled backward into a chair. He crossed his arms on the table, then rested his face against his arms. Great, heaving sobs shook him, his anguish filled the dining room.

Sheena turned a helpless gaze to Fawn, then closed her eyes and took a deep breath. "I've got to talk to Greg."

The darkness had never been so thick. So close. It invaded her lungs, her whole body. Her mind. Her spirit. She tasted it, bitter and cold against her tongue and throat. Cruel against her eyelids.

There was even a sound to this darkness, like the echo of a slow heartbeat.

Always before, she had fought against this darkness herself, even though she told others she was depending on God to get her through.

This time, she had no choice. She had no power. The fight was gone. In her heart, she prayed for the Light.

"Jill."

At first, that sound barely rose above the heavy rhythm of the darkness.

"Jill, can you hear me? I'm right here with you. I'm not leaving."

The heaviness lifted only slightly as she felt a different kind of pressure on her hand. She tried to move her fingers. The pressure changed, intensified.

"Jill, it's me. It's Rex."

Again, she tried to move her fingers, but she couldn't tell…it was still so dark.

Fawn wiped the final table, hours after the law had left with not only Mary, but Sheena. Jed had sat at this table for so long, head down, shoulders shaking, that Austin Barlow, of all people, had finally sat down beside him, put a hand on his arm and talked.

That, too, was hours ago. Finally, Jed had left, his face red from crying. Austin had gone with him.

"Girl, get off your feet right now, and that's an order!"

Fawn jerked around to find Blaze standing behind her, arms crossed, looking stern.

"I can't. I've got to keep working." If she sat down and started thinking again, she would cry, and she refused to cry.

"Bertie says you've not taken a break for hours. You keep that up and you'll have fallen arches and a stooped back before you're thirty."

"I'm not going to make it a habit."

Blaze took her by the arm, took the rag from her hands, and gently pushed her toward a chair. "Sit down. We need to talk."

Fawn obeyed as Blaze set two cups of hot chocolate on the table she had just cleaned and took a seat himself.

"Have you heard anything about Jill?" she asked.

"Sounds like she came through it. Not sure how much damage it might've done, but Rex is there with her. So's the whole Cooper clan and half the town, jamming up the waiting room, from what Cheyenne told me last she called."

"Sheena tried to kill…" Fawn choked on the words.

Blaze shook his head. It wasn't a denial, it was his typical I-can't-believe-this-is-happening head shake.

"How could she do that?" she whispered.

"Guess you know we'll have to say some prayers for that family."

"The Coopers, right?" she said.

"Mary and Sheena."

"But to murder—"

"All the more reason to pray for them. Mary and Sheena are blinded. Unless they see the light, they'll be facing a whole lot more than a prison cell here on earth."

"I don't think I can pray for someone who killed my friends."

"Gonna have to learn, then. Got to forgive them, simply because you've been forgiven for all the things you've ever done." He leaned toward her. "And we both know what a heap of trouble you were."

"I never killed anybody."

"Did you ever hate anybody?"

Fawn stared into her hot chocolate.

"Hating's just like killing someone in your heart," Blaze said. "Let me tell you something. Edith and Cecil are already dancing through their heavenly mansions, laughing and singing and happier than they ever were here on earth. You think they hold a grudge against Sheena?"

Fawn already knew the answer to that, because she knew Edith and Cecil. She shook her head.

"Well then, you think they'd want their good friend Fawn to hide resentment in her heart the way Mary did for so many years, until it made her a bitter woman, old before her time?"

Fawn sighed. "No, Blaze. Just give me some time, okay?"

"Okay, fine, but I'm going to nag you the way you nagged me about forgiving Austin."

She glared at him, but she knew he was right. If she wasn't so angry with Sheena right now, her heart would be breaking for that family.

Time, though. It was going to take some time.

Light conquered the darkness at last, and the heaviness eased from Jill's eyelids enough for her to raise them.

The echo of a heartbeat actually turned out to be the respirator, and the cold, bitter heaviness on her tongue and throat was a breathing tube.

Afraid to turn her head, she glanced to the side as far as she could. Rex stood staring out the window into the hospital corridor.

The connection was still there. He turned to look at her, then when he saw her watching him, he rushed to her side and took her free hand. How wonderful to feel that touch again.

"Hi, sweetheart. You're at Cox South in Springfield. For a while there, I thought we'd lost you."

She blinked twice, knowing he could read her mind. *I'm still alive.*

"Yes, you're alive and well." His gentle smile made her feel more alive yet. "I'll tell you all about what happened later. You're battling the effects of cyanide poisoning."

She blinked in surprise. Poison?

He bent down and pressed his lips to her forehead. "You're safe now," he murmured, barely louder than the noisy respirator. "Those lab tests you ran on Edith helped us clear up a lot of questions, once we knew to look for cyanide. The normal tests wouldn't pick that up, but when we knew what to look for, we found it."

Jill closed her eyes. Edith died from cyanide poisoning? Oh, Edith.

"Everything's going to be okay," Rex assured her. "I'm not leaving your side."

Epilogue

The statuesque bride stood facing the handsome groom beneath the shade of the rose arbor. Tears of joy sparkled on the bride's cheeks, and Fawn had never seen so much love in a man's eyes.

The dress fitted perfectly, of course. Bertie had helped Fawn with it at the last minute, when it became obvious that the bride had, after all Fawn's nagging, gained a few pounds. She still looked beautiful.

Thanks to Karah Lee's adamant refusal to have bridesmaids or groomsmen, it hadn't been necessary to worry about any other dresses. She'd just wanted a simple, heartfelt exchange of vows in the presence of close friends and family.

Of course, practically the whole town of Hideaway considered themselves close friends. Taylor didn't have much family. Karah Lee's sister and brother-in-law sat on the other side of Blaze. Her brother and uncles, aunts and cousins filled several rows.

The couple had written their own ring ceremony, and Karah Lee had agonized over it for the past week. The words were beautiful.

Fawn refused to cry. She couldn't take a chance on messing up her perfect makeup. She hated waterproof mascara, so even though she'd used it on Karah Lee this morning, she hadn't used it herself. Why bother? She seldom cried.

So why did she suddenly have trouble seeing?

Blaze, sitting to her right, cleared his throat. She glanced at him to find him grinning at her. He winked.

She felt a nudge to her left, and looked down to find Bertie holding an old-fashioned, lacy cloth handkerchief out for her.

Mortified, she took it and dabbed at her eyes. If Blaze laughed, she'd smash wedding cake in his face. Later.

As the preacher spoke to the bride and groom about loving and honoring and all that stuff, Blaze cleared his throat again. Fawn looked up to find him nodding across the aisle, where Rex and Jill, the latest matchmaking triumph, sat a few rows back.

Rex was watching Jill with an expression of such adoration, Fawn couldn't help smiling. Of course, Jill sat watching the service, totally unaware of Rex's attention.

Or was she?

To Rex's other side sat his two stepsons, whom he would

now have with him two weekends out of every month. Nobody knew how long that would last, but since Rex had recently signed a contract to become the new administrator for Hideaway Hospital, the community had gone out of its way to make the boys feel welcome here.

Noelle and Nathan sat at the end of that row, and Fawn felt a stab of pain. Neither Mary nor Sheena worked at Noelle's spa now.

Later, there would be time to grieve about that tragedy. Today, they would celebrate.

Behind Rex and Jill sat Austin Barlow, looking healthier than he had since Fawn met him. Tests showed that the big dummy didn't even have that histo-X disease after all, but some other hard-to-pronounce problem that had apparently gone into remission once Cheyenne found the proper medication for it. Polyarteritis nodosa. Why couldn't these people come up with simple names for their dumb diseases?

Anyway, Austin would probably be around Hideaway for a while. Blaze was okay with that now.

When the minister turned to introduce the bride and groom to the congregation as Taylor and Karah Lee Jackson, Fawn applauded with tears streaming down her face. Who cared about makeup?

Jill stood in the far corner of the multipurpose room in the new community building, observing practically the whole town of Hideaway. This morning, pig races. This afternoon, a wedding.

Taylor and Karah Lee posed for pictures in front of a cake

that was big enough to serve the whole community and half of Branson.

An arm came around Jill's shoulders, and she turned to smile at Rex.

His beard was neatly trimmed, he wore a three-piece suit. He looked almost as happy as she felt. "How about a walk around the grounds while they work on the cake? I have a feeling it's going to be a few minutes before the line forms."

She went.

"Jill, it hasn't even been three weeks, and I already feel as if we're reading each others' minds again," he said as they stopped beneath that same rose arbor of wedding vows. "Think you can tell me what's on mine?"

"That it'll be awkward for us to keep seeing each other now that you're going to be the new hospital's administrator, and I'm just a lowly nurse?"

He chuckled and took her hand. "You know better."

"That the pig races should at least be held *after* the wedding, to cut down on the smell?"

"Not even that."

"Then I'm out of guesses."

He turned to her then, and took both her hands in his. The laughter in his eyes faded, and he grew serious. "I'm thinking that some things do change, and all the changes I see in you are good ones."

"I still have you fooled, then."

"Be quiet, I'm not finished."

"Sorry."

"I'm also thinking that those qualities in you that haven't changed are the qualities I've spent half my life longing for."

Jill felt herself blushing. What was it about this man that could make a forty-five-year-old woman blush like a teenager again?

He took her in his arms, looking down into her face. "I've found a way to stay here, Jill, and I don't plan to leave. You can have all the time you need to decide, but I already know what I want. It's what I've always wanted. This time, I won't be chased off so easily."

He cupped her face in his hands and kissed her.

The darkness was gone. She had nothing more to fight. This day, this man, this abundant joy, had all been well worth the wait.

DISCUSSION QUESTIONS

1. When Jill and Rex meet again after so many years apart, it seems as if they were always meant to be together. Do you believe that there should be one soul mate for every person, or do you think God can make a soul mate out of any mate? What has been your own experience?

2. Before Edith Potts died, if she had known who wanted to kill her, what do you think she might have done differently?

3. Had you been in Edith's position many years ago, when she thought she knew the killer, what would you have done? Are there any examples from the Bible?

4. Jill has struggled most of her life with the knowledge that her obsessive-compulsive disorder made her different from others, but how much different do you really think she was? Do you know people who struggle with emotional problems? How can you help them feel more comfortable in your presence?

5. Mary Marshall's life is ruined as a result of her actions many years ago. What could she have done to prevent this, both in the past and in her present life?

6. Cecil Martin doesn't want Fawn to grieve his death or to attend his funeral. How do you think he would have planned his funeral, had he known he was going to die?

7. Jill's sister, Noelle, continues to struggle with the special gift of knowledge she has been given from God. How would you handle this gift if it were yours? Do you think others would consider you to be strange?

8. Rex's oldest stepson leaves home because his mother won't allow him to see Rex. How would you deal with this situation, if you were in the stepson's shoes? In Rex's? In the mother's?

9. Rex tells Jill he wants to pick up where they left off in their relationship. After all these years, do you think that's possible? Can you think of an example?

10. Edith's nephew, Jonathan, leaves several boxes of private records on Jill's doorstep. Should she have destroyed them without looking at them? What would you have done?

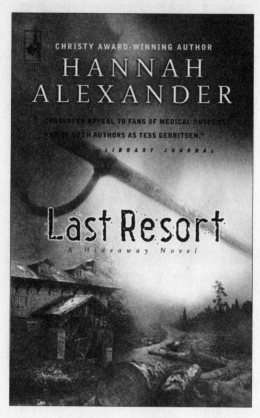

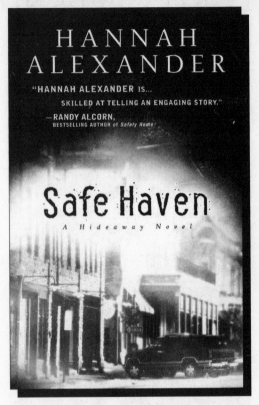

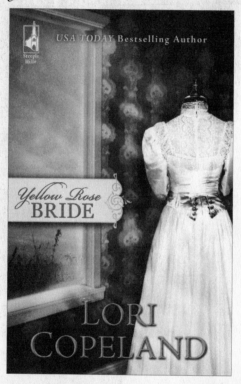

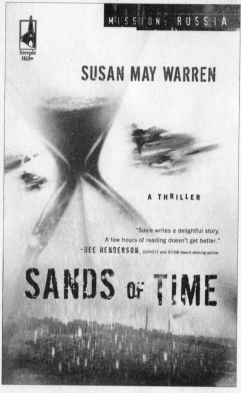